1/15

GREGORY'S GAME

GREGORY'S GAME

A Naomi Blake Novel

Jane A. Adams

severn
House

This first world edition published 2014
in Great Britain and the USA by
SEVERN HOUSE PUBLISHERS LTD of
19 Cedar Road, Sutton, Surrey, England, SM2 5DA.

British Library Cataloguing in Publication Data

Adams, Jane, 1960- author.
  Gregory's game. – (A Naomi Blake mystery; 9)
  1. Blake, Naomi (Fictitious character)–Fiction.
  2. Murder–Investigation–Fiction. 3. Kidnapping–
  Fiction. 4. Ex-police officers–Fiction. 5. Blind women–
  Fiction. 6. Detective and mystery stories.
  I. Title II. Series
  823.9'2-dc23

ISBN-13: 978-0-7278-8366-7 (cased)

All Severn House titles are printed on acid-free paper.

Severn House Publishers support the Forest Stewardship Council™ [FSC™],
the leading international forest certification organisation. All our titles that
are printed on FSC certified paper carry the FSC logo.

Typeset by Palimpsest Book Production Ltd.,
Falkirk, Stirlingshire, Scotland.
Printed and bound in Great Britain by
TJ International, Padstow, Cornwall.

PROLOGUE

They had been waiting for him when he came home from work on the Tuesday evening; grabbed him as soon as he came in through the front door. He was aware of two people; thought there might have been a third. He was also aware, sure as he was of his own name, that he was going to die.

He'd told them he didn't know the answers to their questions. That he hadn't been involved – hadn't even been there. Didn't recognize the names they threw at him, the accusations. At first they'd refused to believe him. Later, when they'd realized he was telling the truth (and how could he not? The pain . . . the pain was just too much to bear), he realized that they didn't really care.

No, even after they had realized he was telling the truth and he had finished begging for his life, knowing it wouldn't do a damn bit of good, they didn't let him alone.

In truth, he was already too lost in the agony to know what they were asking him, but he would have told them anything by then, had he known it. Anything. And maybe he did.

Had he understood – had he been able to take anything in – he would have been glad that the pair were so inept. That they couldn't keep him alive. That their expertise was in inflicting pain, not in keeping their subject conscious and breathing. The end came relatively fast; unconsciousness and then death.

They left him hanging there, blood pooling on the kitchen floor. No one had seen them arrive and no one saw them leave. The quiet road, the silent house, all seemed unchanged and as civilized and suburban as it had ever done.

It would be three long days before anyone found him.

ONE

'So, think of it as a business deal. A partnership if you like.'

'Junior or senior?' Gregory had asked, his tone jocular, as though he thought the whole proposition absurd.

'Equal,' Nathan said. 'I could use your skills.'

Gregory shook his head. 'I think, if you're planning for the future, you need another kind of skill set, and younger blood. I'm retiring, remember?'

'So you keep saying.' Nathan paused and regarded the older man thoughtfully. 'Do you think you can?' he asked and Gregory could hear that he was genuinely curious.

'I don't know, but I think I'd like to give it a try. What about Annie? What does she think about this?'

'Annie is busy being a domestic goddess with that husband of hers.' Nathan smiled and softened any harshness in his words. 'I expect she'll do the odd freelance job for me, but no more wet work; we agreed that. And nothing that takes her away from home for more than a few days.'

Gregory was dubious. 'You think she'll keep to that?'

'I do. You and I were born the way we are. Annie, well, life just dictated to her and I'm glad she's in a position to dictate back now. I want her to be happy.'

Looking at the younger man, Gregory realized that he had no more idea of what happy domesticity would be like than did Gregory himself. No more notion of how to live what might be termed a normal life. 'I need time to think,' he said.

'Take it. The offer will stay on the table for a while. Get back to me in, say, a month, and tell me what you think.'

And that was how they had left it: Gregory determined to retire and Nathan wise enough to know that now he'd laid his cards on the table there was nothing more he could do. Gregory was not someone you could persuade.

That had been, Gregory recalled, ten days before and he'd actually given Nathan's offer very little conscious thought, knowing that by the end of the month something or other would have emerged; some thought, some event, some circumstance that would make the decision obvious. Then, three nights ago, Gregory had dreamed a very vivid dream, one of those strange visions in which known reality had been overlaid by something more. The dream had stayed with him on waking; both the dream and the conscious sense that what it told him was important – if only he could figure out what that was.

In his dream he was lying on a ridge, half buried in an undergrowth of bushes and long grass, looking down into a valley. Tall trees filled with the sound of birds, surged upward around him and below, in the narrow valley, was a house, a track, a walled compound.

Vaguely, he recognized that this was not one single place, but an amalgam of several he had encountered in his career. Below him, in the valley, there was little movement, but he was aware of people in the house and others approaching the compound. He could hear the sound of a car engine approaching along the track, the change in pitch as the driver changed gear. There's a steep hill, Gregory thought, dreaming, a sharp bend and a sudden steep rise, then you can see the compound wall when you crest the rise.

He shifted fractionally, so he could keep the compound in view and see the car as it came into sight. The sun was hot and the earth dry, even beneath the trees, the scent of pine and wild thyme making him think of Corsica, but it could have been one of many places . . . or none.

Seeing the car come into view, Gregory lifted a pair of binoculars and peered down, hoping to get a glimpse of the driver as he got out. From where he lay, he could not make out if there was a passenger. Gregory rarely dreamed, but one thing he had discovered way back when he'd been just a boy was the faculty he had to *recognize* that he was dreaming – to stand almost outside of his own dream. As a child he'd thought this was the natural way of things and it had come as a surprise to realize that others found this kind of lucid dreaming impossible; that most people didn't even recognize a dream when they encountered it.

Another thing Gregory had discovered very early in life was that his dreams, when they came, usually told him something. Not in any prophetic or mysterious way; more that they represented unravelled or unravelling problems. Resolutions. Answers.

Gregory paid attention to his dream. He was conscious of the soft grass and scent of thyme and hard ground beneath him. Of a bird, some kind of raptor, high up in the very clear, very blue sky. Of the old car's engine sound, of the way it skidded sideways on the rough and rutted track, the mud baked in high summer heat.

Who is in the house? Gregory asked himself. Who is it in the car? Had they come with a message, a threat, or both?

The car entered the compound. There were no guards on the gate and no one came out to greet them. Yet there was, Gregory thought, a feeling of watchfulness as though no physical guard was required. Those inside the house knew what was coming, and who, and why.

And why? Gregory asked himself. Why are they here and why am I?

Two men got out of the ancient vehicle. One, the passenger, was tall and slender. Lanky, Gregory thought. The passenger stretched himself as though relieved to be out of the cramped vehicle, as though he'd been travelling for some considerable time. The driver was a smaller, darker man with a chunky body that might once have been fit and muscular. From the way he moved, Gregory guessed that the man still thought of himself in younger, fitter terms. He said something to his companion and they both headed for the house.

Unarmed, Gregory thought. At least, as far as he could see.

At the periphery of his vision, he saw a raptor stoop and he took a moment to watch its dive before it disappeared behind the ridge and was lost to him.

He turned his attention fully to the house, annoyed, in that part of his mind that stepped outside of his dream, that he had allowed his attention to waver, even for those few seconds. It was an impulse he would never have indulged in the real world.

He watched as the men disappeared into the house; waited for some sign either that they had been welcomed by those inside or that they were hostile. But there was only silence; just the sounds of the birds and the wind in the trees and nothing more.

Gregory relaxed. Sometimes, he told his dreaming self, a dream is simply a dream. A confluence of random memories, haphazardly amalgamated by the sleeping mind.

Wake up, he told himself. It's morning and there's nothing useful to be gained by staying here. And then it happened. A single gunshot. It came from somewhere below him. Somewhere inside the house. One shot, then nothing.

Slowly, in his dream, Gregory rose to his feet. Keeping in the shadow of the trees, he descended the hill and waited at the perimeter of the compound for some sign, some reaction, but there was nothing. Birds continued to sing and the soft breeze brought with it the scent of wild thyme.

Slowly, Gregory moved to the gate and cautiously entered the compound. His almost-waking brain told him it was a bad move; that he was most likely walking into a trap. His dreaming self reminded the nagging thoughts that he was asleep, safe in his bed; there was no danger.

Gregory walked into the house, past the old car and through the open door. His feet sounded far too loud on the tiled floor of the hall. Spanish tiles, he thought, glazed in red and blue. The house was cool, the walls lime-washed in a light blue. Four doors led from the hall; two were closed. Through one he could glimpse the kitchen and it occurred to him that the layout of the house was not what he might have expected. Somehow, a more open-plan space would have felt in keeping with the exterior, with the Spanish tiles, with . . . with what? With his memory of this place? This place or something very like it.

He moved towards one of the closed doors. A hall cupboard filled with brooms and buckets and general cleaning stuff. The second door led to an empty bedroom. So that left the other open door.

Gregory realized that he was listening intently and also that there was nothing to listen *to*. Even the birdsong was absent now, shut out when he entered the house. The scents were now of disinfectant, coffee, and something spicy that had been cooking not long before. He moved towards the open door and stepped inside. The room was square and large. The far wall had open glass doors that led out on to a shaded patio. Four men lay upon the tiled floor. The two he had seen getting out of the car and two more. One black, one Asian. The black man lay closest to the door. Gregory bent down. The body was still warm and there was no sign of rigor – though, he reminded himself, the ambient temperature would skew anything he could tell from a quick examination.

The second man was the passenger from the car; he lay facing the window.

The shorter man, the driver, was close beside him, facing into the room. The fourth man, small and slightly built – and, Gregory now decided, probably Japanese – was sprawled, half propped against a chair. A gun lay on the floor, close to his left hand.

One shot, Gregory thought. I heard just the one shot and yet all four men are dead and the gunshot wounds are all too obvious. Four men shot with one gun; fine. Four men shot with the same bullet? That took a little more believing.

Even had the two men been dead before their visitors arrived, that still left two yet to die.

It was possible he had been mistaken, of course. No. Gregory dismissed the thought almost as soon as it arrived.

Waking, Gregory held the dream in his mind, examining and analysing it, trying not to add anything to the detail of what he had seen. He knew just how easy it was to manipulate memories and especially the memories of your own dreams.

He could still not make any sense of it – but he knew he would. It was only a matter of time. That and leaving it alone.

The one question he had was: did this dream have anything to do with Nathan's proposal and, if so, was the message positive or not?

Leave it alone, he thought for a second time. Go and do something else.

The big problem for Gregory was what he should do. He began to wonder if Nathan was right; that retirement was not an option for the likes of Gregory. He'd spent his life *doing*; idleness did not come naturally.

Gregory tried to pinpoint the moment when his life had changed, when the idea of actually changing pace had started to coalesce, but the only response his brain made was to remind him of two things. A blind woman, a dog and two children standing on a Welsh beach; and a young man who could draw with a skill Gregory knew was rare.

Maybe, Gregory thought, the answer lay with them, though he didn't see how. Working on the basis that doing something was better than idleness, Gregory decided that at least this was a starting point, though he was far from sure of the welcome he would receive when he sought them out.

TWO

In the end Naomi and Alec's decision had been an easy one. After all of the anxiety and stress of trying to find a new place, they had moved back into an old one. A flat that had once belonged to Naomi had come up for rent, and with a little negotiation, rent had become purchase. A couple of weeks with the decorators in, Naomi and Alec camping out in friend Harry's spare room, and that was it.

Home.

Naomi knew that perhaps she should feel strange, maybe even a little disappointed about this. The flat, small and easily managed, with a single bedroom and a galley kitchen that only just accommodated two people, had been her first proper home. A single-person home. After marrying Alec she had moved to his much larger house and she had loved it for a while. The space, the garden, the stately isolation of it, set so well back from the quiet road. But that was then. It felt like a lifetime ago, not just the few months it had been since circumstances had forced them to leave. Now Alec's house had been sold and they were back where they had started in a way, but far from feeling disappointed, Naomi found she was actually quite profoundly relieved.

This place was familiar, comforting, small and stress-free – and Naomi felt that in their present circumstances, that was just as well.

Alec was recovering from the car crash of a few weeks before, albeit slowly. Twice a day they walked with Napoleon,

Naomi's big black guide dog, down to the promenade, released him from his working harness and allowed him to run on the beach. Usually, Alec sat on the sea wall or on a wooden bench close to the concrete steps that led down on to the strand. Naomi allowed the big dog to guide her down towards the water. She'd remove the harness and then spend twenty minutes or so throwing whatever toy he had chosen to bring that day – frisbee, ball, stick. She would stand and throw, relishing the cold sea breeze on her skin, the sound of the waves breaking close to her feet, and Napoleon would fetch until the time came for him to return to duty. Harness on, he would guide her back to Alec.

Back at home Naomi and Alec would cook, watch TV, relax and not talk. At least, not talk about anything that mattered. The rest of it was fine, but Naomi was starting to find the not-talking part something of a bind.

'He's depressed,' Harry said when she finally spoke of her anxiety. 'Get him to see a doctor.'

'It's a hard enough job persuading him to keep his hospital appointments. I don't think I'm going to be able to add the GP to the list.'

'Is there no one at the hospital you can talk to?'

She shook her head. Whenever she accompanied him to appointments he went into the consulting room alone, leaving Naomi and Napoleon parked outside in the corridor.

'He seems to be pushing me away,' she told Harry.

Her old friend hugged her. 'He'll get over it,' Harry said. 'Alec loves you. I think he's just still in shock. He nearly died.'

'Harry, it's been weeks. Months, actually. Soon it's going to be too damned cold for him to just sit and wait on that blasted bench. What then? Will he even stop going out with us altogether? Harry, I think I'm losing him.'

Time was, she knew, when Harry would almost have rejoiced in that. Naomi knew how her oldest friend had always felt about her, but she also knew, when he hugged her again and told her that everything would be OK and Alec would soon be himself again, that Harry was utterly sincere.

THREE

Mrs Meehan had lived at number six Church Lane for forty years. She had seen residents of number five come and go, marry, have children, move on. She'd been quite sorry to see the last owner leave with his wife and little girl. They had been quiet neighbours. She had sometimes heard the mother and daughter playing in the garden, but the toddler chuckles and motherly cajoling had been pleasant enough and the size of their two gardens was enough to make it a distant sound anyway. Chiefly, she had been bothered that when they left they had told Mrs Meehan that they planned to rent the place out.

Tenants, Mrs Meehan had thought. That could mean just anyone. You heard such dreadful things about people who rented.

The man who moved in had been single. No sign of a family. He had come to say hello and introduce himself and had told her that he would be out all day, working. Mrs Meehan, satisfied by his respectability, had settled back into her quiet routine once more. She had even gone so far as to take in the odd parcel that came for him. The postman always left a card and Mr Palmer was always prompt in collecting and grateful in manner. It was odd, therefore, that he'd not been round to collect this one. Odder still as, going round to knock on his door, she spotted his car parked by the side of the house.

The second time she went round, she'd been a little concerned. The car was still there, and she couldn't recall the house lights being on the previous evening. By her third visit, she was thoroughly concerned and decided she should do more than just knock on her neighbour's door.

Number five Church Lane was an ample cottage, front door set not quite in the middle, windows to both sides allowing a view into two comfortable and substantial rooms. Mrs Meehan let the front gate clang loudly and then hammered with the cast-iron knocker on the wooden door. 'Yoohoo. Mr Palmer, I've got a parcel for you. It's Mrs Meehan from next door.'

Tutting quietly to herself, she went to peer in through the left-hand window. Nothing. No one. Same when she looked through the right-hand glass. Finally, she opened the letter box and looked down the length of the hall, getting ready to call his name once more.

Mrs Meehan opened her mouth, but what emerged was not a neighbourly greeting. Freda Meehan began to scream. She screamed until she was breathless; screamed until she had regained the safety of her own house and locked the door. Screamed as the phone operator tried to ascertain what was wrong. Freda Meehan felt she'd never be able to stop screaming.

'He hanged himself,' she managed finally. 'Must have done. I saw his feet, just dangling there, and blood on the floor. Blood all over the floor.'

FOUR

Gregory knew that Patrick had seen him even though the boy had barely looked his way. Gregory perched on a low wall outside the university, enjoying the autumn sunshine and watching the stream of students emerge through the heavy glass doors.

Patrick was with a group of others, also obviously art students, portfolios slung across their backs and assorted boxes and bags of materials clutched in their hands.

Patrick was, Gregory noted, the most conservatively dressed of them all. Jeans, dark sweater, black jacket. Pale face and heavy dark curls falling forward on to his forehead, the Umbrian quality broken only by red Converse trainers and a brightly coloured scarf slung loosely around his neck.

He'd have gloves in his pocket, Gregory thought. Still only late October but autumn was already developing a winter bite and Patrick's hands were always cold.

Gregory watched as he chatted to his friends, the young crowd thinning and then dispersing until Patrick and his little group were the last ones standing outside the entrance. Eventually, they too departed. Hugging, waving, Patrick watched for a moment as they went, then turned and walked over to where Gregory sat.

'Hi,' he said. 'Fancy a coffee?'

Gregory smiled. 'Sounds good to me.' The casual welcome amused and pleased him. Few people greeted Gregory casually; actually, very few viewed his presence with any kind of enthusiasm, even those who had at various times employed him. At best, most people viewed him as a necessary evil; at worst they disregarded the 'necessary' part.

Patrick led the way to a cafe in the next street. It was above a bookshop and had a row of small tables flanked by comfortable chairs beside the window. Gregory ordered while the boy nabbed a table and propped his portfolio against the wall. Gregory watched him thoughtfully. Patrick was eighteen but still looked younger – except when you looked into his eyes. Patrick's eyes reminded Gregory of another dark-haired young man, the difference being that Nathan was dangerous. Gregory didn't imagine anyone could accuse Patrick of that.

'So,' he said, setting the coffee down. 'How's it going? The university thing?'

Patrick grimaced. 'OK, I guess. It isn't what I expected, I suppose.'

'Oh? So what's different?'

Patrick leaned back in his seat and regarded the older man thoughtfully for a moment as though re-familiarizing himself with Gregory's features. He noticed the boy's hand move, twitching as though he imagined a pencil held there and marks being made on an invisible page. Patrick drew obsessively. Harry, his father, reckoned it was the way he made sense of the world and Gregory was inclined to agree.

'Different?' he prompted and Patrick laughed self-consciously.

'I suppose I had this daft idea that it would all be painting, or drawing or making or something. You know, it being an art degree.'

'And isn't it?'

Patrick shook his head. 'No, not really. I mean, I know it's only been a couple of weeks but so far it's all been about analysing our process and mapping our route to uni using sticky tape and toilet paper.'

Gregory laughed. 'I can see how that might be annoying,' he said. 'But it might be a good thing. Make you think about things in a new way?'

Patrick's eyes narrowed as he tried to figure out if Gregory was serious. He shook his head. 'I guess,' he said. 'But what if you know why you paint? If you know why you make drawings? If you figured that out a long time ago?' He shook his head again. 'It's like, if someone wanted you to analyse your process, what would you tell them?'

Gregory considered. 'I'd probably tell them they really didn't want to know,' he said. 'Either that or show them how to field strip an AK 47.'

Patrick laughed, then swallowed about half of his coffee. 'The cookies are good here. You want one?' He got up and crossed to the counter, feeling in his jacket pocket for change.

He really isn't happy, Gregory thought. And maybe he was right. Some people were just meant to get on with doing what it was they were born to do. For some, their path was clear, always had been. It had been for Gregory.

Patrick returned with plates and cookies. Gregory eyed the confection. It was studded with chocolate and little flecks of green that closer inspection revealed to be pistachio nuts. 'I don't know if I eat cookies,' he said. 'I think I might be a biscuit sort of guy'

'Try it and see.'

Obediently, Gregory picked up the brown disc and broke it into pieces. It was good, he conceded, though a little too sweet for his taste. He was very aware of Patrick watching him, a smile tweaking at the boy's lips.

'Think you'll stick it out?' Gregory asked. 'University, I mean.'

Patrick shrugged. 'I promised Dad I'd give it until Christmas. He says I'm bound to find it strange and a lot of people drop out in the first term. I'm making friends and so on, so I suppose that's something. Dad doesn't want me to close any doors till I've given things a fair chance.'

'Your dad is a sensible man,' Gregory said.

Patrick nodded. 'I know. So,' he went on, 'what are you really here for? I mean it is good to see you, but I'm guessing you must have another reason.'

Gregory stirred what was left of his coffee and ate another piece of chocolate cookie. Patrick watched. Now he was here, Gregory wasn't really sure he actually did have a valid reason. It had been impulse as much as anything – another first for Gregory. He was not reckoned to be a man given to whim. He decided that the truth was the best approach.

'I'm not sure why I came,' he said. 'I genuinely wanted to know how you were all getting along. I wondered how Alec was doing. I wondered, I don't know . . . I wondered if you were all OK.'

Patrick nodded as if that was all completely understandable.

'You know,' Gregory went on suddenly, 'at risk of sounding foolish and, believe me, I hate to sound foolish, but it's like all of you are the last links in a very long chain. I broke most of the chain, and what I didn't break is mostly either dead, retired of strategically disappeared. Or people I'm not sure I want to get involved with right now. So I guess you and your dad and Alec and Naomi, you're like the only people I know that aren't in any of those categories. So I wanted to know if you were all OK. Considering.'

'Wow,' Patrick said. 'I think that's the most I've ever heard you say.' He laughed. 'You want more coffee?'

'Maybe in a minute.'

'You want to see if the conversation is going to go on long enough to last for another cup,' Patrick said. 'Hey, look, I hate awkward silences too. I'm no good at – what's it called – small talk, either.'

'Does anyone call it that any more? Small talk?'

'My dad does.'

Gregory chuckled. 'I suppose Harry would,' he said. 'So?'

'So I think we risk another coffee. Actually, if you don't mind, I could do with some advice. Or, rather, I think Naomi could. So . . .'

'I'm not sure I'm that good on advice.'

'Trust me.' Patrick handed his cup to Gregory. 'I think you'll do just fine.'

Gregory obediently went and bought more coffee. He had surprised himself with what he had said to Patrick and surprised himself even more that it was true. He felt cast adrift, purposeless and never in his life had Gregory encountered such a feeling. Life had been structured, organized. He received his orders and he followed them. Later, when he had left the army and become another kind of soldier, he had been given an assignment and followed it through to its conclusion. True, that usually had a negative consequence for someone else, but Gregory had always been thorough, conscientious, excellent and now . . .

He took the coffee back to the table and sat down. Patrick had taken a sketch book from his bag and was drawing. Gregory resisted the temptation to ask what he was doing. Instead, he said, 'So, this advice you wanted. About Alec?'

Patrick's hand stopped moving. He sat forward and laid the sketchbook down on the windowsill. It was a view from the cafe window, Gregory noted, but changed, transformed into something new and strange. The reflections in the window across the street seemed to be moving forward, out of plane and the little carvings that decorated the mock Tudor mouldings had come alive, writhing with personality.

'I like that,' he said. 'What are you going to do with it?'

Patrick shrugged. 'I'm doing studies for a painting,' he said. 'It's at home; I work on it at weekends mostly.'

'Not an art school project?'

The expression on Patrick's face told him all he needed to know. 'You have to plough your own furrow, you know. Be who you are.'

'Is that what you did?'

From anyone else that might have been accusatory; from Patrick it seemed merely curious.

Gregory nodded. 'I suppose I used what talents I had,' he said.

'To kill people?'

'Kill some, protect others. Sometimes it was hard to tell.'

Patrick nodded thoughtfully. There was, Gregory noted, still no judgement in the boy's eyes. No, not boy, he corrected himself. Patrick was the same age Gregory had been when he did his first tour of duty. He hadn't thought of himself as a boy then and would have resented the idea coming from anyone else.

Patrick sipped his coffee and Gregory nibbled what was left of his cookie, struck by how surreal this whole conversation actually was. The truth was he barely knew Patrick. Their paths had crossed in the early summer when he and Gregory had both been drawn into the same game. At the time, Patrick and his father, Harry, had been set on protecting a friend. Gregory had been set on finding out who wanted him blamed for something he had not actually done – a rarity and novelty in Gregory's life. Their paths had crossed obliquely since but this was the first time they had actually had a proper, face-to-face conversation.

'I think Alec's depressed,' Patrick said. 'Naomi doesn't know what to do with him. He hardly speaks and he only goes out when she makes him. He won't talk to her and he won't talk to us and we're all really worried.' He looked expectantly at Gregory.

'I'm not an agony aunt,' Gregory said.

'No, but you're probably the only person I know, apart from Naomi, who's almost died. Naomi seems to have found a way to cope with it. Alec can't seem to.'

Gregory nodded slowly. 'For some people, surviving can be almost harder than not,' he said. 'Sorry, that's a stupid thing to say, but what I mean is, for some people it's survivor guilt. They make it when their friends don't.'

'But that's not Alec,' Patrick said. 'No one died. At least no one he knew. There was nothing he could stop. His aunt Molly was in the car with him and she's fine.'

He had a point, Gregory thought. 'Did you ever meet Molly Chambers?'

Patrick laughed. 'She's fun,' he said. 'She knew Salvador Dali and Picasso. She's got this photo album—'

'Fun? Not something many people say about Molly, I imagine.'

'I like her.' Patrick's fingers twitched. He seized the sketch book again and the pencil moved swiftly across the page. 'Have you ever been depressed?'

Gregory thought about it. Had he? 'No, I don't think so. I've been sad to lose friends. I've been angry. I don't think I ever did depressed. It's not a weakness, though,' he added quickly. 'I think it can happen to anyone and I don't think the reasons always make sense. I think, maybe, it isn't one of those things you can always find a reason for. I think sometimes it just happens; it creeps up on you and before you know it the world is dark and you can't see your path.'

The drawing ceased and Patrick looked at him again. He nodded slowly, as though Gregory had said something important. 'Maybe that's it,' he said. 'I think Alec has always known exactly what he's meant to be doing. I think maybe he just can't see that any more.'

'Some of us are defined by what we do,' Gregory said softly. 'For some of us, that *is* our identity.'

Patrick cocked his head to one side, considering. He nodded again, the pencil now twirling between his fingers, and Gregory realized that he could have been describing the young artist by what he'd just said. In his own way, Patrick was just as driven as Gregory – though, unless he chose to ram a pencil into someone's ear, he was unlikely to do the sort of damage Gregory had spent his life inflicting.

On some level, Gregory realized he ought to have a conscience about that; it ought to bother him. He'd more than once been described as a sociopath – or worse – and he acknowledged that was probably true; not that he had given it a lot of thought over the years. Not that he planned to give it a lot of thought now.

'Want to come home and eat with us?' Patrick asked unexpectedly. 'It's Friday, so I'm cooking. Dad gets home later on Fridays.'

'I'm not sure . . .'

'Look, Dad wouldn't mind. You look like you're at a loose end. You can help peel the spuds.'

Gregory smiled. 'Why not,' he agreed. 'If you're sure Harry won't mind?'

Patrick shrugged. 'He's more adaptable than people think,' he said. 'People look at my dad and they think "accountant", which he is, but he isn't someone like you said. Someone defined by their work. He's good at it and it pays the bills, but that's not Harry.'

They rose and Gregory picked up Patrick's portfolio while the artist struggled with his bag. It held far too much stuff, Gregory thought. Packed so full the straps wouldn't fasten.

'What on earth have you got in there?'

'Art stuff, mostly. Important stuff. You know, the things you wouldn't want to lose if your house went up in flames.'

Gregory laughed and then realized that on some level at least, Patrick was serious.

'And is that likely to happen?'

'No, I guess not.'

'You want to explain?'

They started down the stairs and Patrick seemed to be considering. 'No, I guess not,' he said again.

'You're strange, you know that?'

A few steps below him, Patrick glanced back over his shoulder and grinned. 'Other people have commented on that,' he said and continued on down the stairs. Watching him, Gregory noted an odd, new tension in the younger man's shoulders and wondered what line his comments had crossed. He felt a pang of regret. Found that it mattered to him that he might have said something upsetting and was again disturbed. There had been few people in Gregory's life whose feelings he had worried about and, he reminded himself, he barely knew Patrick and his father in any real sense. This was an acquaintance of coincidence, not of type or purpose or . . . whatever else people founded their friendships upon.

By the time they left the bookshop below the cafe, Patrick seemed to have relaxed again and seemed also to have come to a decision.

'Stuff happened,' he said. 'Stuff that made me realize how fragile things were. From aged about six or seven, I suppose, I used to keep a bag packed with all my most precious stuff inside. I mean, back then it was stones and string and action figures and my pencils and a sketch book, but I did it so long I've found it a hard thing to break. I always want to be ready, you know? Prepared? I stopped doing it for a while, but then . . .'

'Did you start again after what happened earlier this year?'

Patrick shook his head. 'No, before that. Dad and Naomi and I, we got caught up in a bank raid. It shook me up a lot, like I kept thinking what I could have had with me that might have helped. I mean, it would all have been taken away, probably; I'm not talking logic here. Then a friend of mine, well, he got himself involved in something bad and ended up killing someone and then he killed himself and I think I started again after that. To be honest, though, it's got a bit obsessive the last week or two. Even Dad's started to notice.'

'Since you started at uni?'

Reluctantly, Patrick nodded, then he laughed. 'Pathetic, isn't it? It's only a university course, it's not life or death, but I've not felt so . . . I don't know, out on a limb, not for a long time.'

'I'm parked in that street over there,' Gregory said, pointing. They crossed the road while Gregory thought about what Patrick had said. He realized, belatedly, that he should have denied the 'pathetic' comment immediately. He really did need to brush up his social skills.

'Not pathetic,' he said. 'But I think you need to do something about it, now, before you need one of those old lady shopping trolleys.'

He was relieved when Patrick laughed. 'I know,' he said. 'I'm just finding it hard to do something about it.'

Gregory opened his car and stowed Patrick's stuff on the back seat. 'Isn't admitting a problem supposed to be the first step to solving it?' he asked.

'Now you really do sound like an agony aunt. But yeah, you're probably right. Dad and me, we went to America in the summer. My mum and her new family live in Florida and we went over to spend time with them and then went to New York.'

'That sounds very civilized,' Gregory commented. 'Divorces, in my experience, have usually messy consequences.'

'Oh, theirs did for a while. Mum wanted me to live with them and I hated it. I hated my step dad, resented her and didn't want to share her with the kids he had already. I wanted to be with my dad and she thought I was better off with her.'

'But you managed to resolve the situation, obviously.'

'Eventually. They moved to Florida, I stayed with Dad and slowly we all started to get on better. He needed me; she didn't.'

'How old were you?'

'Ten, nearly eleven.'

'And how did you convince them?'

Patrick laughed. 'I think it was just easier for everyone to give in. She said I could stay for the summer holidays and we'd talk about it before the new school term. I think it was just obvious by then that we were all happier the way things were. I think she felt really bad about it for a while. You know, realizing that

I didn't want to be with her must have hurt, but I'm glad it turned out the way it did. We've all managed to sort things out and, like you say, be civilized about it.'

But it's all left you feeling very insecure, Gregory thought. He analysed that emotion too, turning it over in his mind and examining it from all angles, before finally deciding he had not experienced that one either.

FIVE

DI Fuller was relieved the weather had been cold and even more relieved that the central heating hadn't been turned on but even so the smell was pretty bad. The cottage was isolated and, had it not been for the neighbour, the body could still have been undiscovered.

Tess Fuller doubted the neighbour would forget what she'd seen in a hurry and was glad the half-closed door had kept her from the full horror. The first officer attending hadn't been so lucky. He was still next door with the neighbour and a local on-call GP was treating the pair of them for shock.

Fuller had been waiting by the front door until the CSI in charge told her it was OK to come in. Square plates, like stepping stones, described the designated pathway and Tess moved cautiously from one to the next until she stood directly in front of the hanging man.

'We know who he is?'

'We're assuming it's the tenant. A Mr Palmer. Dental will have to confirm it.'

Tess Fuller nodded. 'How long did it take him to die?' she asked, not really expecting an answer. She hoped it hadn't taken as long as it looked. She tried to keep her breathing shallow, but her heart was pounding, demanding a level of oxygen she was unwilling to provide. The truth was that whenever Tess Fuller – calm, capable Tess Fuller – saw a dead body, her first and often lasting response was to run, to get the hell away as far and as fast as she could.

'Anything you want to tell me?'

The lead CSI shook her head. 'What you see is what you get, I'm afraid. It's going to be a hell of a scene to process. When you're done looking, we'd like to start taking the body down.'

Tess Fuller nodded. 'Go ahead,' she said. She took one last look at the body. It was naked to the waist and was suspended from some kind of what she took to be an ornamental metal beam that spanned the kitchen space. That he had been strangled was obvious from the swollen face, the protruding tongue and eyes, puffed and blackened with suffused blood and three days of putrefaction. But what was strange was that the man's arms had also been bound to the beam, so that his arms were outspread, almost in the attitude of someone crucified. The image of the crucifixion was reinforced by the gaping wound in the man's side. There was no sign, that Tess could see, of the weapon that created the wound.

The torso was criss-crossed by cuts: some deep, some shallow, barely breaking the skin. But the odd thing was the length of the cuts, the length of the lateral lines. Could you cut that straight if the man was struggling? She looked more closely at the pinioned arms.

'What is that thing he's fastened up to?'

'It's a tie rod,' the CSI said. 'This is an old house; that and two others are keeping it from falling outward. If you look outside you'll see two great iron cross pieces on the wall.'

Tess nodded, understanding. 'And what's he held up with? It looks like . . . well, fishing line.'

'It could be. It's certainly a monofilament of some kind by the look of it.'

'And it's strong enough?'

'Some lines can have more than a hundred pounds breaking strain. And it's wrapped and wrapped, so yes, no problem with it being strong enough. Trouble is, it cuts in. It doesn't break, just . . . well, you can see. We think that's what caused the cuts on the body. He was wrapped in the stuff, it was tightened, something threaded through at the back here and then twisted to tighten.' She pointed at some marks on the man's back that Tess couldn't see. She made no effort to go round and look. Her imagination was already into overdrive.

She tried to focus on the questions she should ask and just

nodded, not trusting herself to speak now. Where the man had been tied to the beam the line had sliced deep into skin and muscle, disappearing into the cuts it had made, seeming almost to dissolve into him. She tried not to think about the other monofilament that would have wrapped the man's body, bitten and cut his chest and abdomen. She had seen nothing like it before; heard of nothing like it.

'The fishing line, or whatever it is, stopped at the bone,' the CSI said and, though she was doing her best to sound matter of fact, Tess could see that she was somehow awestruck by this. That it had gone beyond the usual level of horror.

Tess nodded again. She managed to ask, 'But round the neck . . . wouldn't it have . . .?'

'Decapitated him? Yeah, probably; it looks like they used a nylon climbing rope or something similar instead. Step round there a bit and you can see.'

Reluctantly, her brain still screaming out its flight response and her heart now hammering twice as hard, Tess moved to the next plate on the pathway.

'See?'

A yellow rope stretched down from the dead man's neck. It had been stretched taut and then tied off round the back of a chair. The chair was then wedged beneath the heavy table so that the tension was maintained.

'I'm speculating, you understand,' the CSI said. 'But he's not a big man; two people could have grabbed him and strung him up. I'm guessing they used the rope round the neck to haul him up, then tied him. They could have kept him alive for quite a while, releasing the tension, then . . . I guess the filament wrapped round the body was just additional incentive. I'm not sure, yet, if it was the rope or the stab wound in the side that finished him off. That's where all the blood came from, so logically he was still alive when the knife went in. Whoever stabbed him, they twisted it in the wound, just for good measure.'

'They tortured him. I get the picture.'

'Yeah. Wish I didn't.'

Tess nodded, knowing they'd both be waking in the night, unable to clear the image and what it insinuated from their minds.

'I'll get out of your way,' Tess Fuller said.

SIX

If Harry was shocked to find Gregory mashing potatoes in his kitchen, he hid it well, expressing only polite surprise as he shook hands.

'Kettle's on,' Patrick said. 'And there's a pot of tea already made, should still be drinkable.' He gave his dad a quick hug as he passed him, then grabbed the oven gloves and opened the door. 'Sausage, mash, peas and I even did onion gravy.'

'Sounds good to me,' Harry said, dropping his briefcase behind the door and flopping down into a chair. 'Boy, what a day.'

Gregory poured him a cup of tea and placed it on the table. 'I hope it's all right,' he said. 'Me stopping for supper?'

Harry waved a dismissive hand. 'Of course it is. You'll just have to give me a minute or two to resume normal operations, as it were.'

'You spent the afternoon with Atkins,' Patrick remembered.

'I did indeed.' He gulped at his tea and then seemed to find the energy to shrug off his coat.'

'Shall I stick that in the hall?' Gregory asked, aware that he was now blocking the door.

'Thank you,' Harry said. 'Stick my bag out there too, would you. Lord knows I've seen enough of it for one day.'

'This Atkins fellow. He's trouble, is he?'

'A man with too much money and too little perspective when it comes to his actual importance to the world.'

Gregory laughed. 'And you're what, his accountant?'

'Yes, he's a client. Fortunately he has a business manager that I usually deal with, but two or three times a year, Mr Atkins has to come and do what he calls a proper audit. Anyway, let's leave the job in the hall. It's Friday evening and I don't have to think about it for a day or two.'

Gregory watched as father and son exchanged a smile. Their closeness had been obvious from the first time Gregory had encountered them and he wondered about it. What was it like, being that close to someone? He'd never been close to his father and never been particularly interested in his mother though he recognized she had done her best with her rather diffident and uncommunicative son.

'Ready to eat?' Patrick asked and gestured to Gregory to take a seat. Gregory sat, suddenly a little uneasy. As he'd told Patrick earlier, he wasn't good at making conversation – though he found Patrick surprisingly easy to talk to.

Patrick served up the food.

'Dig in,' Harry said. 'No need to stand on ceremony. Thank you, Patrick, much appreciated.'

For several minutes they ate in near silence, all giving attention to the food. Gregory realized that he was hungry and, from the way Patrick seemed to be wolfing his meal, that he was too.

'So,' Harry said eventually. 'What brings you to Pinsent? You've come to see how Alec and Naomi are getting along, I expect.'

'Something like that,' Gregory agreed. 'As I told Patrick, it was a bit of an impulse. I suddenly find myself with time on my hands and I'm not too sure what to do with it, I suppose.'

Harry nodded. 'It's not easy to stop being a busy person,' he agreed, then got up. 'More tea for everyone? Good. Well, as Patrick has probably told you, I think Alec is still in shock perhaps. I think it might have been easier if he'd had a job to go back to. He's always been a busy person too and it's bad for that kind of personality to come to a full stop.'

Harry set the mugs on the table and sat down again. 'I think going back to work would have been the best thing for him. Routine and other people's expectations can be remarkably . . . soothing is the wrong word; comforting, I suppose, in an odd way.'

'It struck me, when I saw them both, that he was enjoying the break in routine,' Gregory said. 'But I figured he'd soon get bored. I think they both would. It's not good for people used to having roots to suddenly be adrift.'

'Do you have roots?' Patrick asked.

'A very few tenuous ones,' Gregory told him. 'I always assumed that the only time I'd be fully planted was the day they finally put me in the ground.'

*   *   *

Meal over, Patrick excused himself. He had work to do that he'd rather get out of the way so he could have a free weekend. Gregory helped Harry to clear the table and wash up. Harry had switched on the radio and the news informed them that the populated world was still doing nasty things to itself. The local bulletin spoke of a car crash on the coast road and ensuing delays and reports of a suspicious death a few miles down the road at Halsingham. Gregory recognized the name of the village, but could not place what bell it rang. Maybe, he thought, he'd just passed a sign for it recently.

'Shall we go through to the living room?' Harry asked. 'I could do with a drink and I'm not keen on drinking alone.'

'I should go,' Gregory said. 'I've imposed for long enough.'

'Do you have somewhere to be or are you just being polite?'

Gregory smiled. 'A drink would be nice.' He followed Harry through to the small sitting room. It was plainly furnished. A sofa, a chair, a television in the corner and . . .

'You're into hi-fis?'

'My one real indulgence, I'm afraid. I love my music. It's not a new system, but it does the job. Truth is, the speakers are a bit over the top for the room and I've never had the amp up past three, but—'

'A Pioneer A400, that's something of a classic,' Gregory said.

'I bought it a long time ago, but it's a fine piece of kit and I'd have to spend a lot to better it. If you open that cupboard door, you'll find the music. Pick something.'

'The music cupboard,' Gregory laughed. It was just that though, stacked full of CDs and vinyl. He selected a Pat Metheny album and handed it to Harry and for a little while the two of them sat, whisky in hand, music surrounding and enfolding them, like two old friends who don't need to make conversation. Then finally Gregory asked, 'So, what's your story, Harry?'

'My story? I don't think I have one.'

'Everyone has a story.'

'And do you relate yours very often?' Harry wondered.

'Fair point.' Gregory leaned back in his chair and sipped his whisky. 'Does it bother you? That I'm here?'

'Bother me? I don't know. Why?'

Gregory waited for Harry to answer his own question.

'You're a guest in my house. Patrick brought you home and I trust his judgement and he's always been welcome to bring people home with him. To bring friends home.'

'And am I a friend?'

Harry scrutinized his visitor. 'You want to know how I feel about you, knowing something of what you are,' he said. 'For some reason, my judgement is important to you. Why is that, Gregory? Why should you care?'

Gregory nodded. 'Fair point,' he said again. 'And one I don't have a clear answer to. I suppose I'm at a crossroads in my life, Harry. I suppose I see you and Patrick as somehow neutral observers, if that makes sense.'

Harry laughed. 'I don't think our small dealings with you make either of us qualified observers or qualified advisers,' he said. He set his glass down and folded his hands across his rather ample stomach.

'I'm predisposed to like you. I'm also predisposed not to want to know too much. Was it Orwell who said something about us sleeping soundly in our beds at night because rough men fight our battles for us?'

'*People sleep peaceably in their beds at night only because rough men stand ready to do violence on their behalf*,' Gregory said. 'And you see me as one of the rough men.'

'Yes. But that's not what bothers me.'

'Then what does?'

Harry thought about it, finding a way of framing his ideas. 'What bothers me . . . what bothers me is that most people, for most of their lives – for all of their lives if they're lucky – are, well not exactly invisible, but they don't register much in the scheme of things. They live their quiet lives and die their quiet deaths and draw so little attention to themselves that the only ripples they leave when they depart are caused by the tears of those few people who might have loved them.'

He paused and Gregory waited. 'Go on,' he said.

'It feels as though, when people like you, people who, sorry to put it this way, but who live in the underbelly, who spend their lives carving into the bowels of the world . . .' He laughed. 'Lord, listen to me. I think I've drunk a little too much.'

'Go on,' Gregory prompted again.

'Well, when people like you associate with people like us, you make us visible. We lose our anonymity. In a way, we lose our protection, if you see what I mean.'

'I see what you mean.'

'And, frankly, that makes me sleep *very* uneasy in my bed. You reveal a world I don't want to think about. A cruelty I had to acknowledge once and swore I'd try to protect my son from.' He laughed, harshly. 'I couldn't, of course. It coloured every decision I ever made, every action.'

'What cruelty?' Gregory asked.

'My sister was murdered,' Harry said. 'She was just a child. Naomi Blake was her best friend. Naomi escaped and my sister died. It was only three – no four – years ago that we found out what happened to her. I spent most of my life wondering. I spent most of Patrick's life trying to protect him, to make sure lightning didn't strike twice.'

Gregory studied him, waiting silently for more. Gregory knew the value of silence, the need most people had to fill it, but it seemed so did Harry and he said nothing. Gregory sensed that he had relayed all he was prepared to on the matter.

'If you told me to go away and never come back then I'd do my best to oblige,' he told Harry, finally. 'But I don't make empty promises, so I would never promise that you'd never see me again.'

'You're expecting trouble,' Harry said flatly. 'You're expecting trouble to come and find us again.'

Until that moment, Gregory hadn't fully realized this, but as Harry said it he understood that it was true. 'Perhaps,' he said. 'Harry, do you ever get the sense that something is just not right? You may not be able to say why or what, just that it isn't as it should be.'

Harry thought about it and then nodded. 'Since Alec's car crash it's felt like I'm waiting for the storm to break,' he said. 'I think Alec has been too. I think that's why he's been so out of sorts.'

Out of sorts, Gregory thought. Harry, you have a wonderful sense of understatement.

'We've been exposed, haven't we? We're visible now, all of us. We can't hide in the crowd.'

Gregory swallowed the last of his whisky. 'Patrick could never disappear into the crowd,' he said. 'Nor should he. He has a rare talent, Harry. But what he's seen and heard and witnessed will come out in his work, won't it?' He got to his feet. 'I should go,' he said. 'Say goodnight to Patrick for me and, Harry, sleep well. You have at least one of those rough men fighting your corner, whatever comes, and I still hope the storm will pass us all by.'

Harry smiled and there was something sad and knowing in that smile, Gregory thought. 'My friend,' Harry said, 'if the storm breaks over us, then we shall do our best to survive it. I will do everything to protect my son and, though I don't want to think about it, I know he would do the same for me. If trouble comes, then it comes. I've learned enough to know that some things cannot be controlled or avoided.'

Gregory nodded. 'You're a good man, Harry. The sort I'd choose to have at my back,' he said, and then he departed, leaving Harry, the man who was not just an accountant, struck dumb.

SEVEN

I t was getting late, almost nine, and Tess wanted to be off home. She knew that her sergeant did too. But one last review before they left for the day would, she hoped, help bring the case into focus. Be preparation for the morning.

'So, what do we have?' Tess Fuller asked.

'Our victim is believed to be Mr Anthony Palmer. He was thirty-five, unmarried and works for an estate agent in Pinsent. He's the office manager.'

'Was,' Tess reminded her sergeant.

'Was,' Vin agreed. 'He's lived at number five Church Lane, Halsingham, for about seven months. Moved up here from another office of the same estate agency. It's one of these big, countrywide chains.'

'And the owner of the Church Lane house?'

'Is a Professor Ian Marsh. Lectures in International Relations at the local uni. He lets the place through an agency. We've got

our local colleagues trying to locate him, but according to a
neighbour he and his wife are away at a wedding and won't be
back until the middle of next week. And, no, the neighbours
don't have a contact number.'

Helpful, Tess thought. She rubbed her eyes, suddenly exhausted.
She was aware of Vinod's gaze resting thoughtfully upon her and
anticipated his next question.

'I'm fine. Just . . .'

He nodded and glanced back down at his notes. 'I thought we
should do background checks on both of them,' he said. 'Our
dead man and the professor. I've set that in motion.'

'Good. You talked to his colleagues? Anything?'

'No. He came in as a sort of troubleshooter. Apparently the
Pinsent office wasn't meeting its targets. He's been here five
months and sacked two members of staff, demoted another, but
apparently things at the office have started to turn around.'

'But he's not won himself any friends.'

'I don't imagine so, no. But the upshot is, no one got to know
him very well, either. No one could tell me who his friends were,
outside of work. I've got an address book and some numbers on
his mobile; Jaz is working through those now.'

Tess nodded again, approving his choice. 'Family?'

'Jaz thinks she's tracked down a brother, but she's not been
able to talk to him yet.'

'Fine; let me know when she does.' Tess frowned, drumming
her fingers on the desk and wondering if she'd get to keep the
case or if it would be handed on up the chain. As a relatively
new DI, she'd had little experience as senior officer on something
like this. Not that anything like this came along very often – she
was relieved to say.

'What's your take on it?' she asked Vinod. 'You saw the body.'

He grimaced and then nodded. 'Vicious,' he said. 'I mean,
that goes without saying, but . . .'

Tess knew what he meant. 'They enjoyed it,' she said, flatly.
'It wasn't just murder; it was . . . I've never seen anyone that's
been tortured before.'

'I'm glad to say, neither have I. What had he done that they
felt justified in causing so much pain?'

'Could anything justify what they did?' Tess asked sharply,

then waved the outburst away. 'No, I know you didn't mean it that way. But I don't read it that way. I'm not sure it was that personal. It was—'

'Professional?'

'No, not that, either. Professional implies efficiency, doesn't it? I can't see what they did as being all that . . . well, efficient.'

'Not the right word, is it?' Vinod said, aware that she was struggling to find a way to describe what she was thinking.

'No, no it's not.' She sighed and then stretched and got to her feet. 'Look, there's not a lot more we can achieve tonight. Get off home. Hopefully tomorrow we'll have found next of kin and forensics will have something useful to tell us.'

He nodded, knowing there would be long days ahead when the investigation got properly under way. 'I used to go fishing with my next-door neighbour,' he said. 'When we were both kids. His dad used to take us. I remember one day, I got my ankle caught up in some fishing line. I tripped and fell over and pulled the line tight. It bit right into my calf, cut this dead straight line. It drew blood and I was bruised for days after. It hurt like hell.'

'Teach you to clean up after yourself,' she said, not really wanting to think about it. She could see, in her mind's eye, the way the line had cut into flesh, biting its way through as the weight of the body lay against it.

'That's what my mate's dad said,' Vinod smiled. 'He was a stickler for that, making sure we took every scrap of stuff away with us.'

'Pain,' she said. 'The way I see it, it was all about the pain.' She shook her head, trying to dismiss the pictures in her head and she knew that she'd actually be glad to be bumped down the pecking order in this case. If someone else was brought in, Tess decided she'd make just enough noise to save face and then, gratefully, gracefully, just let it go.

Home, for Gregory, was his boat. Currently she was moored a long way off and he felt cut adrift. He'd never been one for bricks and mortar or for a settled pitch, but now he'd have given a great deal to be aboard and heading out to sea.

He'd enjoyed his evening with Patrick and Harry, but at the same time it had served to highlight just how much he didn't belong in their world. Happy to be an occasional visitor; happy, he acknowledged, to count them as friends – that, he found, was a very pleasant thought – but the idea of living in a little house, doing the same job every day, having a routine, now filled him with a kind of dread and while it was true that during his stint in the army he'd had many of those trappings there had always been the assurance of change, of challenge, of difference.

His mind drifted back to the dream he'd had. Four dead with a single bullet. It bothered him that he couldn't find an answer, that none of it seemed to make sense. But it would, he thought. He'd find the sense in it, excavate the meaning and then he'd know what he had to do next. Stay and accept Nathan's offer or go and see what life brought his way.

EIGHT

The murder featured on the lunchtime news, just after Alec and Naomi got back from their Saturday morning walk. A murder in a picturesque village was unusual enough to have made the national headlines and it took a moment for Naomi to realize that this was, in fact, quite local news.

'Halsingham, that's just down the coast, isn't it? A bit inland?'

'It is, yes,' Alec said. 'It was never our patch, but I did a short stint on secondment down that way, drove through it a couple of times.'

He sounded interested, for once, and Naomi felt her spirits lift slightly. 'DI Fuller. Didn't you do a training course with her?'

'Yes,' Alec said. 'I did a couple, actually. But it was a while ago.'

Naomi frowned, her mood crashing once more. It had been a while ago, that was true, but there had been rumours at the time that Tess Fuller and Alec, then both new Detective Sergeants, had been a bit more than work colleagues. Naomi could recall Tess Fuller from her own time in the force, before she had lost her sight. Tess had been, Naomi remembered, small and neat, with dark hair and a pixie face. She was the sort of slight, fey woman who made anyone look big and clumsy, Naomi thought grumpily, and with a reputation for calm and professional competence that had earned her many commendations. 'I didn't know she made DI,' Naomi said aloud.

'About eight, nine months ago,' Alec told her. 'I remember hearing about it. I called her to say congratulations.'

'Did you? You never said.'

'I never thought to say. You hardly knew her.'

'Unlike you.'

'What's that supposed to mean?'

Naomi sighed. Where had that come from, she wondered, this sudden flash of jealousy and irritation?

'Nothing,' she said. 'It means nothing.'

Alec did not respond. The television chuntered on in the background, outlining what little was known about the killing. A country cottage, a tenant no one knew very well. Not formally identified but reported locally as being Mr Anthony Palmer, a local estate agent.

'You want lunch?' Naomi said at last.

'I don't know. Maybe. I can get you something.'

'I can manage.'

'I know you can.'

Naomi sighed. 'You know I'm at the advice centre tomorrow afternoon. You haven't forgotten?' Lately, Alec had seemed confused even as to what day of the week it was.

'No, I remember.'

'You'll be OK?'

It was his turn to sigh. 'Naomi, please stop fussing over me. I know you mean well, but it gets . . . it gets smothering. I'm fine; it'll all be fine. I just need a bit of time, that's all.'

You've had time, Naomi thought. Time for what, anyway? 'What are you going to do with yourself?' she asked.

'I'm capable of keeping myself amused, you know.'

'Apparently.' She gave up and went through to the kitchen, wondering what she actually wanted to eat. It wasn't like Alec to snap at her like that, but then it wasn't like her to snap at him either. She filled the kettle and felt for the switch to turn it on. Back in the living room she could hear that Alec must have muted the television and was now scrolling through his phone book. She could hear the sound of buttons being pressed as he found the number he wanted, then silence as he listened. He must have got through to voicemail because Naomi heard him leaving a message.

'Hi Tess, this is Alec. I just saw you on the television. I . . . um . . . Give me a call when you get a minute; it'd be good to catch up.'

Would it? Naomi thought bitterly. Catch up with what exactly? She heard Alec cross the floor and go into the bedroom.

I'm losing him, she thought desperately. After all we've been through and I don't even think he understands why.

NINE

I t was a while since he'd seen Ian Marsh and Nathan wished this was just the social nicety it was supposed to have been. He'd arranged, weeks ago, that he'd collect Ian from the station so that Kat, Ian's wife, could keep the car. The family wedding had been, for her, a wonderful opportunity for catching up with distant relatives she'd probably not seen since she was a girl, and also an opportunity to show off her own child, now just over a year old. Ian and Kat's toddler was cute and pretty, Nathan thought, but watching her grow over the past year had only served to reinforce the fact that he didn't want kids of his own. He'd be very happy to spoil those belonging to his friends, but he really didn't think he had it in him to be that unselfish. So far as he could tell, children were little leeches – albeit rather fascinating and quite appealing ones – but they sucked you dry nonetheless.

It always amazed him, observing people like Kat and Ian, who seemed to thrive on that neediness.

So, the collection from the station was all arranged; what hadn't been arranged was that Nathan was about to give his friend some really bad news. Nathan had seen the midday news bulletin and recognized the house, even festooned as it was with police tape and filmed from an awkward angle. The funny little porch on the front of 5 Church Lane and the bright pink rose, whose name had something to do with Napoleon, was unmistakable.

Knowing Ian's habit of switching everything off and ignoring the world when he went away, Nathan very much doubted his friend would know anything about the death in his old house.

Parking outside the station was never good, even on a Sunday when there were fewer trains, and Nathan had to circle, twice. He was about to make it a third when he spied Ian emerging from the bargeboard arch. Ian Marsh was bareheaded, his shock of ginger hair sticking out, as it always did, at eccentric angles. His long tweed coat flapped about his ankles. He caught sight of Nathan just as Nathan saw him and lifted a free hand to wave, almost losing the bag slung from his shoulder in the process.

Nathan found he was chuckling at the sight of his old friend. Forever untidy, seemingly chaotic, inveterately clumsy and one of the most acute brains Nathan had ever known – provided someone else told him where he should be and left detailed instructions on how to get there.

He pulled in, holding up the traffic as Ian tossed his bags on to the back seat and then scrambled into the front. 'Train was late,' he said. 'How the devil are you, Nate?'

'I'm good. How's Kat and is Daisy still growing?'

'Like a weed and it's not Daisy, it's Desiree. Kat will have your guts for garters.'

Nathan laughed. 'When's she coming back? I thought I'd take the pair of you out for an adult dinner if you can get a sitter.'

'That would be nice. Wednesday, all being well. Unless she decides to stay on until Great Uncle George goes back to Canada, in which case it will be Friday. But my guess is she'll be sick of them all by then. Family reunions are wonderful in theory—'

'Says the man whose family numbers exactly three, including himself.'

'And which takes nothing away from my point. I'm perfectly happy to borrow my wife's family for a while, but I wouldn't want to live with any of them.' Ian Marsh turned to look properly at his friend. 'So, Nate,' he asked. 'What's on your mind, then?'

Never could fool him, Nathan thought. The only man ever to call him by a diminutive of his chosen name and one of the very few who could ever read him; Ian was the master at that.

'Have you seen the news at all?'

'What sort of daft question is that? Why, what should I have seen?'

'Church Lane,' Nathan said. 'Your tenant, Mr Anthony Palmer. He was murdered there. The police think it happened three or four days ago.'

'What?' Ian turned away and stared out through the front windscreen. 'How?' he asked.

'I have no details yet. I found out a couple of hours ago. I've got people on it, but . . .'

'Nathan?'

It was only ever *Nathan* when Ian was worried, or about to deliver a lecture. Nathan responded to the unasked question. 'I don't see how it could be anything to do with you. You've been out of the game for a while now.'

'Can anyone ever really say that?'

'I'll take you home, then I'll make some calls. No doubt the police will be round at some point. You want me to stay until they've been?'

Ian hesitated, and then nodded, once. 'If you don't mind,' he said. He laughed briefly. 'You know how the sight of a policeman makes me feel guilty.'

'That's because you usually were,' Nathan joked, then regretted his flippancy. Ian was and always had been a man of conviction; it had led him into some very tight corners. 'I could turn around, put you on the next train to Norfolk.'

'Suffolk, and don't think I'm not tempted.'

'Seriously, Ian. Give me your key; I can camp out at your place for a few days, field the questions. You know nothing about the man renting your house; it was done through the agency; you never even met him, did you?'

Ian shook his head. 'But what if it wasn't about him?'

'Then they'd have come for you,' Nathan said. 'You've not lived at Church Lane in months. Why would anyone look for you there? But seriously, Ian, why would anyone come looking for you anyway? You're old news.'

His friend considered that and then nodded. Nathan made the turn into the road leading to Ian's house and swore softly. The car parked outside the house was nondescript, but the woman knocking at the door and man leaning nonchalantly against the wing were anything but.

'Looks like it's too late to turn around,' Nathan said. 'Get your head together and remember – you didn't know the man and you know nothing else either.'

Ian Marsh nodded and smoothed down his wild ginger hair. Nathan could almost hear the adjustment his mind was making, ready for the role he'd have to play. 'I don't,' Ian said. 'That much is very true.'

Tess Fuller turned as the four-by-four drew up in front of the police car and two men got out. One, the younger, paused to take a suitcase and a messenger bag off the back seat. The other stared at her, quizzically. 'Can I help you?'

Tess came back down the path. 'DI Fuller,' she said. 'Are you Professor Marsh?'

'I am, yes.' He extended a hand. 'You're here about Mr Palmer, I expect.'

'You've heard, then.'

Ian Marsh nodded. 'Nathan here filled me in when he picked me up from the station. I must say, I'm shocked. What happened?'

'Perhaps we'd be more comfortable discussing this inside,' Tess said, aware of the twitching curtains and the couple walking down the road slowing down to watch proceedings.

'Of course,' Ian Marsh said. 'Please, come inside.'

The house was unremarkable, Tess thought. An ordinary semi in a pretty ordinary road, unlike the house in Church Lane. Why would you choose to live in this ordinary house when you had a fantastic one available?

'Have you lived here long, Professor?'

'Ian, please. Is your colleague coming in too? I'll pop the kettle on. Nathan, will you stick my things in the study and show the detectives through to the sitting room?'

'Sure.' The younger man opened one of the doors that led off the hall. Tess glimpsed a desk and bookshelves before he dropped the bags on to a chair and closed the door again. 'This way, Inspector.'

'Tess,' she said. She turned to Vinod who had just arrived at the front door. 'This is Vin. DS Dattani.'

'Nathan,' he said. 'I'm just a friend. I picked Ian up from the station. Kat's stayed on for a few days and she's got the car. Come on through.'

He led the police officers into the other room that led directly off the hall. A bay window gave a view on to the privet hedge that shielded the house from the street. Tess sat down on the sofa facing the television and Vin took up position at the other end. The young man called Nathan dropped into one of the comfy looking chairs beside the fire place. It was an open fire, Tess noted. The room was cool. She heard the click of a boiler coming on and the tick of radiators ready to heat up.

'So you knew about the murder,' she said.

'I saw the news report and recognized the house. So I found out what I could before Ian came home. I knew he probably wouldn't have seen anything.'

'Oh, and why is that?'

Nathan laughed. 'Because Ian's idea of a break is getting away from everything. I doubt he even had his phone with him. Anyway, everyone's been busy with the wedding and catching up with relatives; I doubt they'd have paid much attention to the news or made the connection even if they had.'

'Apart from Ian's wife. Kat is it?'

'Kat, short for Katherine. She might.'

'Lucky you watch the news, then.'

Nathan raised an eyebrow and Tess realized that her tone had been a little sharp. There was something about the younger man that put her on the defensive, but she couldn't have said what.

'How long have they lived here?' Vin asked.

'Since they left Church Lane. This was Kat's family home. She inherited after her mum died about a year ago. The plan was to put both houses on the market and buy something bigger, but the market's been dreadful, as I'm sure you know. They moved here – no mortgage – and rented out Church Lane. The plan's still on, it's just been delayed a bit.'

'And I suppose not having a mortgage gives them a bit more to put aside,' Vinod said. He sounded rather envious.

Nathan nodded. 'I suppose it does,' he said.

Ian came into the room at that moment, a tray in his hands loaded with mugs and sugar and a milk carton perched on the edge. 'I know we've got a jug somewhere,' he said. 'But I couldn't tell you where.'

He sat down in the other chair, setting the tray on a little table.

'Please,' he said. 'Help yourselves and then tell me what happened to Mr Palmer. I can't believe anything could happen in a place like Halsingham. Nothing happens there. Ever.'

'Well, I'm afraid something did now,' Tess said. 'Professor – Ian – did you ever meet your tenant?'

'No. I wasn't all that keen on renting the house out, but it made financial sense. Kat set everything up with the agency. She saw his references and all that, but I never really got involved apart from signing the relevant paperwork.' He looked expectantly at Tess and Vinod. 'Do you know who did it? What happened?'

'As yet we know very little,' Vinod said.

'Was there any conflict, between you and your wife, if you weren't keen on letting the house?' Tess asked.

Ian Marsh frowned. 'Why would there be?' he said. 'It's just a house; we planned on selling it anyway.'

'But you had doubts about it?' she persisted, not sure why she was bothering. Habit, she supposed. If you saw doubt, you pushed.

'No, I would have just rather held out for a sale, so we had cash in the bank ready to go if we found somewhere. Anyway, what does that have to do with anything?'

Tess ignored the question. 'You've not been back to Church Lane since . . .'

'Since we moved in here. April. Start of April. Mr Palmer moved in a couple of weeks later. We left the place part furnished; the agency said that was the best way.'

'And you never thought of staying there and renting this place out?'

Ian shook his head. 'No, never. I had no particular attachment to Church Lane, but this place was different for Kat. She just wasn't ready to do that and anyway, there was still so much stuff here. Her parents' things. Kat's mother died just before Christmas but it was a while before she could bring herself to deal with everything. I don't know, it just all worked out so it was better to come here for a while. When Janice was ill, Kat practically lived here for a while. Come to that, we all did, and Kat had started to take Desiree to the nursery down the road and to the mother and toddler group . . . It just seemed like an obvious solution.'

'But you're still preparing to sell this place, despite her attachment?'

Ian frowned at her and Tess knew she was pushing too hard.
Probably to no purpose too. 'I'm letting my wife set the pace, there.
And, actually, I don't think that's got anything to do with you.'

'And you were fine with moving here?' Vinod cut in. 'I mean,
this place, no offence, but it's not a patch on Church Lane.'

'No, it's not,' Ian said coldly. 'But sometimes that's not what's
important, is it? Sometimes it's all about what makes those you
love feel better.'

Vin nodded and Tess glanced through her notebook to see if
there was anything else to ask. Off hand she couldn't think of
anything.

'What will happen now?' Ian said. 'I mean—'

'Well, the house is still a crime scene. We'll get it released as
soon as we can and then . . . I can recommend a specialist
cleaning firm . . .'

'I see,' Professor Marsh said. 'Yes, I see.'

Tess got up and Vinod followed suit. 'I'm really sorry,' she
said. 'This must be very difficult for you.'

'Well, yes, but it must be so much more horrible for the poor
man's family. I can't begin to imagine what they must be going
through.'

Tess nodded. 'Are you likely to be going away any time soon?
I mean, in case we have to speak to you again?'

'No.' Ian Marsh shook his head. 'It's term time, and I'm back
at work tomorrow. That's why I left the car with Kat. It seemed
a shame for her to have to cut the visit short.'

Tess nodded again. 'I see.'

She made sure she had the professor's home number and his
work extension and then left.

'What did you make of the younger one? Nathan?' Vinod
asked as they got back into the car.

'Why? Apart from the fact that he was very pretty.'

Vinod laughed. 'More your area of expertise than mine,' he
said. 'I don't know, he seemed . . . odd.'

Tess shrugged. 'I don't think they're going to be much help,
anyway,' she said. 'It might be worth talking to the wife; she's
obviously the practical one.'

Vin nodded. 'Is it worth getting our colleagues in Suffolk
involved?'

'I think it can wait until she gets back. Any news on next of kin yet?'

Vin shook his head. 'The man we thought was a brother turned out to be an old work colleague who just happened to have the same surname. He reckoned Palmer may have had a half-sister, but can't tell us any more. We'll just have to hope someone comes forward now the name's been released.'

'*Local sources report that the tenant of the house was a Mr Anthony Palmer,*' she quoted. 'I'd like to wring *local sources*' neck, but you're right, we'll just have to see who comes looking.'

Ian Marsh slumped back into his chair and looked across at Nathan. 'That was not fun.'

'I think the police just have that effect on people,' he said. 'You'd best phone Kat, better she hears about this from you as soon as possible.'

Ian heaved himself out of the chair. 'You're right,' he said. 'I'll do it now. Want to make some more tea?'

'Will do.'

'Oh and I picked up some post as I came in. I think there was one for you.'

'Thanks,' Nathan said. He frowned thoughtfully as Ian went off to make his phone call. He'd not used Ian's address as a contact for a long time. When he'd still been travelling a lot, he'd often given his old friend's address as a place to send mail, knowing Kat and Ian would keep letters safe for him. Later, he'd kept the habit when he wanted somewhere neutral for his mail to go to, but not in the past year.

He wandered through to the hall to pick up the letters. Ian was chatting to Kat in his study and Nathan carried the letters through into the kitchen and filled the kettle again. He spread the letters on the table and fished out the one addressed to him.

Nathan Crow. c/o Professor Ian Marsh.

It had, he realized, been forwarded from the house on Church Lane.

Gripped by a feeling of foreboding, Nathan opened the envelope. It contained just a single photograph, taken somewhere that was definitely not England, probably not even Europe. At first glance, he recognized only one person in the picture.

Slipping the photograph back into the envelope he studied the date and postmark. Marseille, just over a week ago . . .

Hearing Ian come out of the study he shoved the envelope into his jacket pocket and turned his attention to the kettle. 'How about I take you to the local pub for dinner?' he suggested. 'I'll bet you've got nothing in the house.'

'Nothing I can be bothered to cook,' Ian agreed. 'That sounds like a perfect idea.'

'How did Kat take it?'

'Upset, of course, and she's going on the Internet to try and find out more than I could tell her. I think she'll come back on Wednesday. I think the family bonding thing is becoming a bit too much of a good thing.'

Nathan smiled and nodded. In his pocket the envelope seemed to burn.

TEN

Naomi volunteered twice weekly at the local advice centre. She'd been doing that since a couple of months after leaving hospital. Her knowledge of the law had made her useful and her willingness to train up on welfare benefits and unemployment legislation made her doubly so. She sometimes thought that, once people had got over the shock, the fact that she couldn't see them actually made it easier for some to talk.

She knew she was doing a good job; knew she was useful; knew she helped to solve a lot of problems for a lot of people – which made it even harder when she realized she could do nothing to help Alec.

Her usual taxi driver, George Mallard, noticed she was quiet as he drove her home from her Monday session.

'How's that man of yours getting on now?' he asked.

George, Naomi thought, was unerring in his ability to pinpoint the very thing she didn't want to discuss.

'He's fine,' she said. 'Well, fine-ish. I think now he's feeling

better he's at a bit of a loose end. He's talked about going back
to university, or retraining for something.'

'Well, he's a bright bloke,' George said. 'I'm sure he could
do anything he set his mind to.' He laughed. 'Just as long as it's
not taxi driving. That's my area of expertise.'

'You know,' Naomi said, 'I think that's about the only thing
he's not considered.'

George pulled up and got out to help her as he always did,
bending to pet Napoleon before checking she had all her bags
and was all right going in on her own.

'I'm fine, George. See you Thursday?'

'Be me or the lad,' he said, referring to his son – still 'the
lad' despite being well into his thirties.

Naomi smiled, thanked him and allowed Napoleon to lead her
up the steps and into the shared hall, then on up the stairs to
their flat. She had the sense that Alec was absent even before
they reached the door. Fumbling for her key, she let herself in
and then called out. 'Alec. We're home. You OK?'

Silence. Emptiness. 'Okaay.'

She released Napoleon's harness, heard his feet on the wooden
floor heading for the kitchen. A moment later, the sound of him
slurping at his water bowl. So Alec was definitely not there then.
Had he been, Napoleon would have gone to say hello before
heading for the kitchen. She crossed to the little table by the bay
window. Beside the phone, they kept a small, digital recorder.
Alec had bought it for them to leave messages on should either
of them ever have to go out unexpectedly. She pressed play.
Alec's voice. 'Hi, love. I won't be long, but I'm just going to
have coffee with Tess.'

That was it. No sense of how long he'd be or when he had
gone, only the unmistakable sense that he'd been happy, excited
even. The depression that had dulled his voice these past weeks
seemed to have lifted.

'Fine,' Naomi said. Trying hard not to mind but minding terribly
'If that's what he wants well two of us can play that game.'

She wondered if she could call her taxi back again. Would
George Mallard already be on another call? She could go and see
Harry . . . except he'd still be at work and Patrick would be off
at uni. Her sister? No, she'd be out on the school run. Who else?

Naomi flopped down in the nearest chair knowing that really she wasn't in the mood to go and see anyone. It was just the suddenness of it. For weeks now, she'd barely left Alec's side and he'd not wanted to go anywhere. It had, she reflected guiltily, been a relief to get back to her twice-weekly volunteering. It had been a break from the intensity of Alec's depression; Alec's lack of motivation. And now, what really hurt was that someone else seemed to have motivated him instead of her. It just wasn't fair. Suddenly overwhelmed by it all, Naomi buried her face in her hands and cried.

ELEVEN

I t had been a while since Alec had seen DI Tess Fuller. She had, he felt, been surprised by his call, but had invited him to meet her at work, promising ten minutes for a coffee.

It felt strange, Alec thought, to be a stranger in a place where he'd once had status and authority. Not at this police HQ, but as part of the same system. He'd been allowed to go past the front desk and up the stairs to the second floor, then someone had met him and directed Alec to wait at the end of the corridor, where a makeshift seating area provided just a modicum of comfort. The offices were more or less open plan, Alec noted, with glass partitions on to the corridor to make the most of the natural light from the windows beyond. He could see Tess through the glass, on the other side of the office, talking to a man in uniform and a woman with a fat folder. She looked no different, Alec thought. Small and pixie like, in tailored black trousers and a light blue top. He knew she used her small size and slight figure to throw people off balance. They too often made the assumption of fragility when that was quite the opposite of the truth. Alec wondered what he was doing here. If he'd really wanted to catch up with his old friend there were many other opportunities he could have taken. And then there was the other why – why was he choosing to catch up with Tess, when there were other colleagues, people he really had been close to in his working life, that he'd all but shunned since leaving the force?

She's still as pretty, Alec thought. But so was Naomi. There had been a time when he and Tess . . . when there might have been . . . But that was long ago and in another place. He didn't really want to rekindle something that hadn't really even got past a kiss or two. Did he?

Alec sighed. The truth was, he thought, that it wasn't really Tess that had brought him here; it was a combination of Tess and the case she was working. It had woken him from the stupor in which he'd existed for the past weeks. It was the first thing that had actually broken through the fog. Sitting in the uncomfortable, low-backed chair at the end of the glass-lined corridor, Alec felt a sudden and acute pang of guilt for that fact. Nothing Naomi or their friends had done in the past couple of months had excited him, had motivated him, and now . . . Did it really take the fact of someone dying to elicit a response?

Just what had he come to?

Alec almost rose and left the building but Tess must have spotted him and he saw her weaving between the desks, heading in his direction. She was smiling.

Alec's heart skipped.

'Alec. What a surprise to hear from you.' She gripped his hand briefly and then released it and glanced at her watch. 'I'm sorry, I can spare you ten minutes, then I've got a briefing. What can I do for you?'

He shook his head, suddenly awkward. 'Nothing, really. I just saw you on the television and I thought, it's been a long time. You know?'

She laughed. 'Let's sit.' She indicated the uncomfortable seats at the end of the hall. 'The coffee in the machine is probably better than the coffee in the office,' she said. 'Can I get you . . .?'

'No, no, I'm fine.' She was keeping him in the public area, Alec realized. He was suddenly and deeply hurt.

'I heard you resigned. I never thought you'd be the one to go.'

'It felt like time.'

'And is it working out? What are you doing with yourself?'

'Oh, you know. Naomi and I, we took some time out to travel a bit, catch up with old friends.' He laughed awkwardly. 'It felt like I'd taken years of missed holidays all in one go.'

'Oh, missed holidays,' Tess sympathized. 'Days off in lieu that you never actually get. I've lost count of the unpaid hours this place has had. I heard you had an accident? Are you all right now?'

'I'm doing OK. My arm took the devil's own time to heal, but I had the plaster off last week. I've just got to have regular physio for a while. It hurts like hell if I drive too far.'

She nodded. 'Well that's good then.'

Tess of old would have demanded details, Alec thought. The Tess he had known would have made sure she knew all about it anyway, would probably have visited him in hospital, or at least sent a card or something.

But that was then, he thought, and now she was trying not to look at her watch, or back through the glass partitions to where she really wanted to be instead of out here talking to an erstwhile colleague now turned civilian.

'Um, this new case? Sounds . . .'

'Um, messy. But, you know, early days and all that. So how's Naomi?'

'Oh, she's fine. We moved back into her old flat, just while we find something we actually want, long term. You'll have to—'

'Yes, I will. Be good to have a proper catch up. I'll call you.'

She was openly glancing at her watch, even though her ten-minute allocation was far from up. 'Alec, I'm really sorry, but . . .'

'No, it's fine,' he said and found that he was actually relieved. It had been a mistake to come. A bad mistake. He walked with her back to the glass door and then continued down the corridor. At the head of the stairs he glanced back, but Tess was already absorbed in conversation and Alec felt himself forgotten.

You really can't go back, he told himself as he made his way down the stairs and passed out through the front office. He was a stranger, not just to this place, which had never been his domain, but to the job, to former colleagues, to a life he had lived most of his adult life. Worse, he felt as though he was a stranger to himself.

The desk sergeant buzzed him through and nodded agreeably. Alec nodded back and stepped out into the busy street. For a brief moment, yesterday, he had felt the old Alec resurface. The old interests piqued and his brain begin to work again. Now he felt himself sink lower than ever.

Empty, numb, Alec got into his car and headed for home.

*   *   *

Patrick really tried to focus on the lecture, but he'd lost the thread some ten minutes in and was now thoroughly mystified. Why the hell had he chosen to do a module on modern architecture, anyway? They had been urged, at enrolment, to try to choose their optional modules from subjects that were unfamiliar, but Patrick had known from the first week that he'd made a mistake. It wasn't lack of interest; it was more that the majority of students on the module were strangers to him and not just in the sense that he didn't know them. Architecture students were not like art students, Patrick decided.

His mind kept drifting back to the weekend and his meeting with Gregory on the Friday afternoon. He had talked about it with Harry that weekend, wondering, like Harry, exactly what the visit meant. In the end, like his father, Patrick had decided that what would come would come and there was little sense in worrying about it and he had gone back to his painting. The odd thing was, Gregory continued to intrude. Without intending to, Patrick found that he had given Gregory's face to one of the figures in his townscape. The grotesques Patrick had sketched in the café peered down into the street and the man looked back. He was carrying Patrick's bag, just as he had on the Friday afternoon, but in Gregory's hands it looked even more crammed and full and awkward and Patrick realized suddenly that Harry must have noticed what he'd been doing these past weeks, carrying an increasing number of his possessions around with him in an effort to feel secure.

Patrick had set his painting aside and gone to unpack his pack, laying his stuff out on the bed, examining each and every piece. The notebooks, the pens, the small toys left over from childhood. Old birthday cards from his mother, for fuck's sake.

Patrick shook his head and began to pack everything back into his pack. Keeping aside his notebooks and pens and a few other small objects, Patrick stowed the rest on the top of his wardrobe and then stepped back to look at it. He could just see the pack, could reassure himself that everything was there, ready to go at a moment's notice. But it was OK. He didn't need it all with him.

He had repacked his university essentials in his messenger bag and then gone back to his artwork.

Now, sitting in the lecture, he felt a little bereft, but also a little victorious – and also utterly bored. His mind drifted back to the part finished work on the desk easel in his bedroom and then to the strange man who had drifted back into their lives. All around him, his fellow students made notes, scribbling frantically and Patrick, completely lost to the lecture now, drew Gregory's face, again and again on the lined sheets of his notebook.

'Professor Marsh?' The young woman standing at his door looked expectant. Did she have a meeting scheduled? Ian struggled to focus and realized that of course she did. Jenny was his ten o'clock tutorial. He'd already propped the door open with one of his heftiest tomes in preparation for her visit.

When had it happened, he wondered, that universities directed their staff to keep their doors open when they had students visit them? Actually, it wasn't an official directive, more of a strong suggestion, 'for your own security and that of our students'.

'So,' he said, trying to recall what she was there for and then, blessed relief, spotting her marked essay on his desk. 'Your essay.'

He glanced quickly at his comments on the cover sheet and then handed it over. 'Not bad,' he told her, noting the slight flush that touched her cheeks as she looked at the mark he had given her and thinking that maybe it wasn't such a bad thing his door was wedged open after all. 'Any questions?'

There were questions, mostly of the *what does this say* variety – Ian knew his handwriting was appalling – and how could she improve her marks?

Ten minutes later she had skipped off, happy, and Ian was left to his thoughts.

He'd done everything he could to find out what had happened to his tenant. Why would someone murder the man? And why in Ian's old house? The fear that this was not coincidence dragged at him, distracted him. He had left that life behind, broken contact with everyone. Everyone except Nathan, and Ian admitted to himself that his reasons for maintaining that friendship was very selfish. He knew that he'd been a big influence on the younger man, had taken Nathan under his wing when he'd been just a diffident, awkward boy. But what if . . . what if . . . what if that contact had brought vengeance down upon him?

Ian Marsh wanted there to be evidence that the man living in his cottage at Church Lane had done something that had led to his death. He wanted public proof, irrefutable and comprehensible, that he had been guilty of some crime, had brought this down upon himself. But so far nothing was forthcoming. The police seemed to know little and were saying even less.

Ian chewed upon his guilt, masticated it, swallowed it down and it lay in the pit of his belly, leaden and rotten.

TWELVE

Some twenty miles away from Ian, Nathan heard his computer chime, telling him that an email had just been received. One he hoped he had been waiting for. Nathan had many contacts; some didn't know that he was the one they were dealing with, but they kept him informed anyway. A little extra cash was still a fine lubricant. He had put out a request on the Sunday for anything on the Church Lane murder, preferably information on how the man had died and if there were any motives or leads the police were not releasing. He knew from experience that crime-scene photos were not that hard to come by. The rest, well, that was harder; it was as though such speculation crossed an invisible line. Usually, by this informant at least, such questions were ignored.

Nathan opened the file, noted that there were several images attached. He checked his security, ran additional virus protection and finally opened the files. He kept this computer purely for such contacts. Nothing that came in via this link ever touched his other systems. Anything that might need to be transferred was sandboxed first and examined scrupulously. Nathan believed you could never have too much security or be too cautious.

He opened the folder and glanced at the thumbnails within. So, crime-scene pics then. Well that would do for starters. He opened the first and scrutinized the scene properly before authorizing payment. Nathan was scrupulous about that too; always pay the messenger and never keep him waiting. Keep the hinges oiled, for you never knew when you might need to open a particular door.

What he saw on the photographs chilled even him, someone hardened to violence. This was nasty, vicious, designed to cause the maximum pain. He zoomed in to examine the way the mono-filament had bitten into the muscle of the upper arms. As the man's weight had sagged against it, the line had cut its way through. In some places, Nathan could see it had stopped only at the bone and he guessed even that would have been marked. He had known of an assassin whose favourite method of dispatch was the garrotte. His material of choice had been this kind of monofilament.

Nathan sat back in his chair and thought about it. He was reminded of something, a rumour, perhaps, some snatch of gossip, but something like this happening before – anyway, he told himself, it stood to reason that whoever had killed this man would have practised their methods.

Gregory might know, Nathan thought. No, most likely Gregory *would* know. It was the sort of information the man collected. Minutes later, he had set up a meeting.

'Is it urgent?' Gregory had asked.

'Why? Do you have a date?'

'I might have.'

Nathan laughed softly. 'I think it's unlikely. Tomorrow will do, but I need your input on something I have a very bad feeling about.'

A moment of silence as Gregory thought about that. 'I have something to do,' he said. 'But I'll see you later tonight.'

'I bought takeaway,' Alec said. 'And a bottle of that wine you like. The one with the goat on the label.'

'Are you apologizing for something?'

'Should I be?' he asked cautiously.

'I don't know.' She heard him move through to the kitchen and fetch plates down from the cupboard. The smell of food reminded her that she'd not eaten since a hurried sandwich at lunch. She'd checked her watch – again – a few minutes before and knew it was after seven.

'I'm sorry,' he said.

'Oh?'

'Yes, for a lot of things. I know I've given you a hard time. I know it's been difficult for you. I know I've been depressed and . . . and all that.'

'And that's suddenly changed? I suppose I have Tess to thank for that.' She realized just how bitter she sounded, but frankly, she didn't care.

'No, actually. I'm still depressed and I don't really know why. I still feel utterly adrift. I'm still finding it hard to want to do anything. Anything. But I want to say I'm sorry and I want to say that I want – need – to do something about it and, yes, I think you might have to thank Tess for that. And if that makes you feel bad I'm sorry about that too.'

He sighed and she heard the creak as he leant back against the cupboard door. 'I don't know what else to say.'

Neither did she, but the smell of the food was getting in the way and she really didn't want to fight, despite the fact she'd spent the afternoon practising for it. 'I'm hungry,' she told him. 'Can we just eat and then, well, whatever.'

'Sure,' he said. 'Sure.'

She heard him scooping food on to plates, pouring wine. She knew he didn't really like wine. 'Why don't you have a beer? I think there's still a couple in the fridge.'

'Sit down, I'll bring you a tray.'

She heard him open the fridge door and peer inside. He always stood and stared into the fridge, even when he knew what he was looking for. It was just an Alec thing. Naomi sat down in her chair by the window. She didn't know what to say and so she said nothing. He set the tray down in her lap and told her where everything was, placed the wine on the small table beside her chair.

'I'm sorry,' he said again.

Naomi didn't reply, she picked up her fork and dug into the food on her plate, suddenly unable to recall what he'd said was where. She wanted to cry, but wanted to eat more and didn't want to talk – at least she didn't think she wanted to talk.

'So, how was Tess?' she managed, trying to keep things normal.

She became aware, all of a sudden, that it was Alec who was crying. That he was sobbing like a hurt child. The dam had broken and the flood had broken through.

THIRTEEN

By the time Gregory arrived, Nathan had printed out the crime-scene photographs and laid them out on the dining table. There were seventeen of them, all focusing on the body, apart from a couple of contextual shots, one taken from the hall and one from the kitchen door. Nathan, who had been to the cottage several times, recognized the scene. A few personal possessions belonging to the victim were the only changes from when he had last been there.

He guessed that these images had been chosen largely for their impact and probably because the photographer did not have access to those taken of the minutiae of the scene. It was possible – likely, even at such a complex scene – that a couple of different photographers had been assigned. That Nathan's informant had access only to certain shots caused Nathan to speculate. He was senior enough to have been assigned the victim to photograph, but not senior enough that he had automatic access to all of the crime-scene images. Interesting, Nathan thought.

He added into the mix the photograph he had been sent, the one forwarded from Ian Marsh's cottage to his new address. He laid the envelope it had arrived in beside the image.

He had just made coffee when Gregory arrived. The older man had a brown paper bag in his hand, emblazoned with a logo Nathan vaguely recognized. Gregory set the bag down on the table. 'Cookies,' he said. 'You should try them. I've brought plenty.'

'Since when do you eat cookies, for Christ's sake?'

'Since Friday,' Gregory said. He didn't elaborate, but was already studying the pictures laid out on the table.

'Recognize anyone?' Nathan asked after a few moments.

Gregory jabbed a finger at the posted photograph. 'The man in the background looks like Michael Caine,' he said.

Nathan peered at the image and laughed. 'He does a bit. It seems a shame, but I think we can discount that as coincidence. Anyway, he's Sir Michael now, isn't he?'

'Probably. Typical, isn't it? He gets to be a knight for pretending to be someone else; you and me, we'd probably get arrested for it.'

'So far as I know, he's never pretended to be someone else just so he can kill someone.'

'Fair point,' Gregory conceded. 'Where did you get this?' He retrieved his coffee, standing back as though surveying the whole landscape of images.

'It had been forwarded to Ian Marsh's place, from the Church Lane address. I used his old house as a letter drop for a while.'

'Presumably before he met Kat.'

'A while before, a while after. Then I thought I'd better stop.'

'Seeing as the pair of you hate the sight of one another.'

'A fact we both conceal from Ian,' Nathan agreed. 'Ian wants both of us in his life, so we called a truce.'

'So you have fun spoiling the kid.'

'Little Daisy. Oh yes, I do.' He smiled, briefly, but Gregory could see that he was worried.

'You know who sent it?'

Nathan nodded slowly. 'I can narrow it down,' he said. 'I only gave the Church Lane address to four people. None of them were operatives; they just did odd bits of research for me, picked up some local gossip, that sort of thing. One of them never sent anything there. Two of them used the address three times between them. One of those is now dead. Nothing sinister, old age got him a year or so ago. The fourth was Annie Raven; she used Ian's address sometimes when she was on assignment and didn't have a place of her own and I've checked with her; she didn't send me these.'

'So that leaves two. Have you been in contact?'

Nathan shook his head. 'I want to know what I'm dealing with before I risk breaking cover; mine or theirs. Anyone you recognize – apart from Michael Caine?'

Gregory nodded. 'The woman in the red dress,' he said. 'And I can make a guess about the location.' He pointed to one of the buildings in the background. A hotel, Nathan had thought. 'I think that's in Marrakesh, but I could be wrong, of course.'

Nathan doubted it. He too had recognized the woman in red, once he'd had time for a proper look. Fifties, white-blonde hair, expensive. 'Last time we met she was calling herself Nancy Todd,' he said.

'I knew her as Michelle Williamson,' Gregory said. 'You think this is a recent picture?'

Nathan shrugged. 'I'm guessing so. The letter was postmarked Marseilles, but North Africa is only a hop from there. I'll work on it. And the crime-scene images?'

Gregory took another swallow of his coffee and then picked up one of the pictures, a close-up view of the injuries caused by the monofilament. He stared at it for a moment and then put it down. 'It brings someone to mind,' he said. 'But he's dead.'

'You sure?'

'Yes. Do the police know how long he took to die?'

'I wouldn't know. Why?'

'Because Mason, the man I had in mind, he could keep someone alive for days. This is crude. The weight of the body on the internal organs, with it hanging like that, would have led to shock, organ failure, death, even without the rope round his neck. He would have asphyxiated.'

'How long?'

'Hours, maybe. At most, and depending on a lot of factors. Whoever did this was in a hurry, but they were also referencing something, sending a message. There are much simpler ways of killing and very much simpler ways of torturing someone for information; we both know that. This is theatrical, excessive.' He pursed his lips thoughtfully. 'I also get the feeling—'

'That they enjoyed it,' Nathan finished.

FOURTEEN

Tess's thoughts drifted to her meeting with Alec as she headed for home. She knew she had been short with him, but hoped he would understand. She was busy, involved, dealing with urgent matters, and a visit from a friend – nice though that might be – was ill timed.

But it was more than that, Tess acknowledged as she closed her car door and headed inside. It was the suddenness that made her feel so put out. Alec had had many opportunities to get in touch with her and, to be fair, they had exchanged a few texts, especially around the time of her promotion, and they had talked vaguely about getting everyone together for a drink some time. But Tess had never quite summoned the enthusiasm to make the date. Alec was someone she had known, someone she'd actually been pretty fond of at one time, but that time had passed and now . . . well, now she wasn't really sure what she felt about him any more. He was an ex-colleague, and probably no more than that.

But what really peeved her, she realized as she dropped her bag just inside the door and headed for the kitchen, was the obviousness of it. Alec was interested in her latest case, not in her. Tess paused at the entrance to her kitchen and bit her lip in irritation. Now, if she was so unbothered about Alec Friedman, why the hell should that bother her?

She made coffee, peered into the fridge to see if there was anything worth eating and in the end resorted to ordering a pizza. Her mother was always on at her to eat better, to take care of herself, but Tess was never domesticated and figured it was probably too late to try now.

She sat back in her favourite chair, enjoying the near silence of her little flat, disturbed only by the faint sounds of the street below and the neighbours above when they slammed their front door, grateful of the respite after a day of noise and disquiet on so many levels. Her mind wandered back to the meeting with Professor Marsh and his strange, attractive companion.

'So what weren't you telling me?' Tess wondered. 'And who the devil are you, Nathan Crow?'

Once the pizza arrived, she settled down with her laptop and another coffee and did a simple search: Professor Ian Marsh + Nathan Crow, not really expecting to come up with much. To her surprise, she found an article about the pair. A photograph of Ian Marsh headed a story about a peace mission in Sudan. Ian Marsh had negotiated with local elders to allow a vaccination programme to go ahead in some remote area Tess could not even pronounce. The report was from a medical journal linked to Médecins Sans Frontières, which she had at least heard of. Three medics were listed in the team; one of them was Nathan Crow.

'A doctor?' Tess asked herself. 'He's a medic?' How old was he, she wondered. She did a search just for the young man and then just for the professor. For Marsh there were articles he had published, a piece about his appointment as Visiting Professor and then another when he took up his current role. Both contained brief résumés of his past work. Diplomatic missions, lecture tours, papers published in what Tess assumed were prestigious journals. A lecture he gave on terrorism, and government security. Another on the role of GCHQ. Tess smiled at that one, wondering if he'd have to rewrite it in light of recent events and revelations.

Information regarding Nathan was thinner on the ground. He was mentioned a couple of times working with the Kurds on the Turkish border, but there was little concrete and Tess wasn't really in the mood to do a deep search. She was curious, that was all, she told herself as she munched pizza and finally turned her attention to anything that might be worth watching on late-night television.

One thing was certain though: both Crow and Marsh had travelled a great deal, and their destinations had not been choice holiday spots.

Across town, Alec and Naomi lay together in bed, bodies curved against one another. They had made love for the first time since Alec's accident. It had been restrained, cautious, as though the bruises of minds and hearts manifested on their bodies, but it was healing too, Naomi thought.

'I felt like I was nothing,' Alec said, remembering his meeting with Tess. 'Kept out in the hall like a random visitor, treated like . . .'

'I know,' she said softly. 'It's hard to go back and be like an outsider. A pariah. I tried it a time or two after I finished, but . . . People were nice enough, but I didn't belong any more and so I stopped going anywhere near the place. I knew I didn't belong.'

Alec raised himself up on one elbow and gazed down at his wife. 'I didn't know,' he said. 'I never thought.'

'Alec, I went through all this five years ago,' she said. 'I know what it's like. Believe me, I know.'

'So, everyone is in position?'

Mae nodded. 'Both teams are set. Look, I can't believe—'

'He's a hard man, your old friend. You'd be surprised at what he'll do.'

'With you pushing him into it.'

'Encouraging, my dear. He owes me. He knows that.'

'But *they* don't. What sort of man risks his wife and kid like this?'

He laughed. 'Are you getting sentimental, Mae, my dear? I never thought I'd be able to make that accusation.' He laid a hand almost tenderly against her cheek. *Almost* tenderly; possessively, she thought.

She moved away from him, brushing the blonde hair back from her face and tucking it behind an ear. 'I'd better go,' she said. 'It's a long drive.' Her coat lay across the arm of the chair and she picked it up, slipping her arms through the sleeves and then adjusting the scarf at her throat. 'I'll call you from the hotel and we'll do a final equipment test.'

He touched her cheek again and turned her face towards him. 'Don't go soft, Mae. Not after all this time. It doesn't suit you.'

She scowled at him. 'I've never let you down. Not you or anyone else that employed me. I won't now.'

'I'd like to think of you as more than an employee,' he said.

'Don't kid yourself.'

She heard him laughing as she left the room. The sooner she was out of here the better, Mae thought. The sooner she was done with this, the better. The sense of unease, of something being wrong was growing again. She'd managed to suppress it for a few days, telling herself that this was just another job and that she'd done worse – both of which facts were true – but she'd rarely felt as though the walls were closing in on her. Not like this.

Reaching the front door, she glanced back towards his study. She could hear him faintly, speaking on the phone. Mae glanced at her watch and then let herself out. A couple more days and she'd be done. She could leave. But no matter how she reasoned with herself, the feeling of dread would not be cast aside or pushed away. It sat, solemn and judgemental at the edge of her consciousness and told her she was a damned fool.

And I can't argue, Mae thought. I'm a fool and this is all wrong and I don't think any of us are going to make it through unscathed. It'll be a bloody miracle if any of us make it out alive.

FIFTEEN

Kat was up early on the Wednesday morning. Desiree had woken at five and wanted to play so rather than wake the whole house, Kat had taken her out into the garden after breakfast and they had tossed a ball around for a while on the dew-soaked lawn. Autumn was really taking hold. The first leaves had fallen from the willow and the horse chestnut had begun to turn golden. This would be the first year that Desiree could kick her way through the crispy leaves. The first year she might actually appreciate snow. The first Christmas she'd really take notice of.

Kat was looking forward to all of that with an intensity she hadn't realized she possessed, not until her baby came along.

'We're going home today,' she told her little girl as she swung her up into the air, enjoying the baby giggles. 'Going to see Daddy.'

'Daddy,' Desi said and looked around expectantly.

'No, he's not here. We've got to go and drive in the car.'

'In the car.'

'Yes, in the car.'

Returning to the house, Kat found that her aunt and uncle were up and bustling about the kitchen. Cousin Sarah lurched down the stairs in her dressing gown, still bleary-eyed. Kat accepted tea, tugged the pink wellingtons from Desi's feet and took off her coat before setting her loose on a still-sleepy cousin Sarah.

'I thought I'd make an early start,' she said. 'I can be back by lunch, do some shopping and get sorted before Ian gets home.' She saw the faint flicker of relief in her aunt's eyes. They loved Desiree, but it had been a long time since they'd had a child in the house and the strain was staring to show.

'Just as you like, love. Need any help with your packing?'

'No, I'm fine. There's not a lot. It's been lovely catching up, though.'

'It has. It's a pity Ian couldn't have stopped over for longer.'

Kat nodded, though she knew that neither her aunt nor her husband could really have coped with that any more than Ian could. He did his best, but he wasn't cut out to be sociable.

She finished her tea and scooped up her little girl. 'Come and help me pack, Desi doo?' She felt her uncle wince. He hated baby talk – which was why she indulged, Kat admitted. She smiled to herself and hugged the toddler tightly and headed up the stairs.

They were on the road by eight forty-five, making good time through the little villages and narrow country lanes. Desiree had fallen asleep almost as soon as the car started to move and Kat, angling her rear-view mirror, smiled at the sleepy, slightly grumpy face. Her hair had really started to grow now and at thirteen months, just toddling and with blonde curls, Desiree was, in Kat's opinion, the most beautiful thing on God's earth – even accounting for the fact that Kat was not a bit religious.

Even if her attention had been fully on the road, it is doubtful that Kat could have reacted differently. She had been driving cautiously, but not slowly on roads she knew well, had slowed for the last bend, but just accelerated again, so that when the tyre blew out, the car was travelling at almost fifty miles an hour.

Kat screamed and slammed on the brakes. She felt the skid begin and desperately tried to pull out of it. Then the sudden shock as the air bag deployed. Stunned and scared and feeling the car begin to tilt, Kat heard her baby begin to cry.

SIXTEEN

Nathan had called Ian that morning and been told that Kat was on her way home. They had arranged to meet for lunch.

'Is that still on?' Nathan wanted to know.

'Yes, she won't be back until after that, I don't expect. Anyway, I've got to be in work this afternoon. If it's OK with you I'll pick something up and we'll eat at my place. I need to do a bit of tidying before she gets back.'

Nathan laughed. 'I'll pick you up from the uni,' he said.

Ian was waiting on the pavement when Nathan pulled up on the double yellow lines. Ian nipped into the car and dropped his bag of shopping down between his feet. 'She left early,' he said. 'So there's a chance she might turn up early. You can see Daisy.' He grinned at Nathan, deliberately using his friend's pet name for Desiree.

'That will be good. She's growing like a weed and every time I see her she knows new words.' He glanced over at his friend, who nodded, satisfied and happy. It was good to see Ian look so contented, Nathan thought. He wondered if he'd ever manage it himself.

The drive to Ian's house was fifteen minutes and they talked about nothing in particular. Old friends catching up, chatting about a documentary Ian had watched on the television the night before.

While I looked at crime-scene photographs, Nathan thought.

He pulled up outside Ian's house and cut the engine. Ian got out. Nathan didn't know what it was that told him something was wrong. Some small sign, some small change, perhaps, but it was there before they walked down the short path to the front door. As the door swung wide, Nathan's sense of wrong-ness was confirmed. Whoever had been there, whatever they had been looking for, they wanted Ian to know it had happened. Books and papers had been strewn across the hall. The desk in the study had been overturned. Light fittings ripped from the wall. Ian stood on the threshold and stared, unable to move.

'Oh, my God. My God.' The house phone lay broken on the floor. He groped in his pocket for his mobile. 'I'll call the police. Call the police.'

Nathan was already moving through the house, checking the living room, then the kitchen. The same level of devastation in both rooms. But there was something else: lying on the kitchen table was an eight-by-ten photograph, two corners held down by salt and pepper pots. The rest of the table was bare, a strange oasis of calm in the midst of chaos. But the image was anything but calm. Kat's face, bruised and scared, stared back at him and she clutched little Desiree close to her breast, her arms wrapped defensively around her child.

Nathan felt his insides freeze. It was a moment before he realized there was something more. A small slip of paper partly tucked beneath the edge of the picture. With the back of his finger, only his nail touching the paper, Nathan slid it out. He could hear Ian's voice on the phone, touched with panic. He looked up as Ian stood in the doorway.

'What's that? What is it? Oh, my God. Kat.'

He stared at Nathan, and Nathan could see the blame in his eyes. 'What did you just pick up? I saw you take something. What did you just pick up?'

'It's nothing,' Nathan breathed softly. 'Ian, I have to go.'

'No, you'll wait for the police. The police are coming. You can't go.'

He tried to block the door, but Nathan simply moved him aside. This was beyond the police; this was beyond any help the authorities could provide. 'I'm going to get them back,' he said. 'Ian, I have to go.'

He ran for the door, keys in his hand, dived into the car and sped away. Ian would never forgive him, Nathan thought, but that didn't matter. If this was his fault, he would never forgive himself.

SEVENTEEN

Tess paused at the door to speak to the uniformed officer. 'The next-door neighbour's taken him in,' he said. 'He's not making any sense, just keeps saying it's all someone called Nathan's fault. He's in bits.'

Tess nodded. Nathan. The younger man who'd been here the other day. She looked through into the hall where two white-clad crime-scene officers moved silently. She glimpsed another in the kitchen. 'Alright to go through?'

One of the CSI nodded and pointed out the designated path. Tess wondered how they'd decided where to put it. The place was a mess, books and torn papers strewn across the tiled floor, soil from the plant that had stood next to the door had already been tracked through into the living room. She made her way into the kitchen and surveyed the broken crockery and shattered glass.

'Is the upstairs in the same state?' she asked.

'It's messy, but not as bad. The kid's room's virtually untouched. I think whoever did this wanted it to have an impact as soon as he came through the door. Or maybe they didn't get time to do much in the bedrooms.'

Tess nodded her thanks.

'Someone had a smashing time,' Vinod said, entering the kitchen behind her. Tess ignored him, her attention fixed on the table, the top clean of everything except that one photograph. She shifted round so that she could see it clearly. Vinod stood close behind her, leaning over her shoulder. She could feel his breath on her neck, hear the sharp in-breath as he looked at the picture. It had been printed, she guessed, on a laser printer that only did black and white. On what looked like cheap photocopier paper, thin and flimsy, but the image needed no embellishment. A woman, clasping a young child very close and very tight, stared out. Her face was bruised, that was clear even in the greyscale shot, and her hair was untidy, clothes dishevelled and the sleeve of her sweater torn at the elbow. It was a picture designed to shock, Tess thought. The details – bruises, and other small signs of violence – deliberately placed to enhance the sense of outrage, of horror. There was something staged about it, the lighting on the woman's face stark and unkind, the room behind them in deep shadow, but for all the artificiality Tess had no doubt that this was for real. The woman's eyes, the way she held her child, the way she had wrapped herself around the little girl – this was a woman frozen in the depths of terror and it was as if her fear reached out and gripped Tess in the gut.

'Fucking hell,' Vinod said softly.

EIGHTEEN

Nathan drove. It was perhaps a full ten minutes before he took any notice of where he was driving to. It was with some relief that he realized he'd switched into auto pilot and his route had been directed home. Or what had passed for home for the past weeks.

He pulled into a road at the back of the flat and approached on foot, cautious and fully alert now. He didn't really expect anyone to be waiting for him. The fact that they had gone after his friend meant they didn't know how to get to him. *They*, Nathan thought. Whoever 'they' were. Nathan had enemies; Nathan's old associates had enemies; the potential list was a long one.

He thought hard. Had he told Ian where he was living? It was unlikely Ian had even asked; it wasn't what Ian did. Even so, it was best to clear out and to do it fast. Not that there was much to take. He headed in through the fire escape at the back of the old house. His neighbours were rarely in during the day and kept to themselves when they were and Nathan often came in the back way. He unlocked the back door and stepped into the kitchen, pausing to listen intently to the house, to his rooms, to the sound of his own breathing. There was little to pack. The computer equipment fitted into a laptop bag, along with the notes he had made on the crime-scene photos, the photos themselves and other bits of paperwork. Clothes and personal possessions went into a backpack. He left everything else where it was, down to the food in the fridge. In minutes, Nathan was gone. He didn't take the time to clean the place down; his fingerprints and DNA were not on record and a place that had been stripped naked of prints and personal signs would be more likely to arouse suspicion than one that looked something like normal in the unlikely event the police should come.

Then he drove again, taking little notice of where until he had left the city behind him and the road climbed up into the hills.

Nathan parked up in a lay-by, in a spot that gave him a view down into a green valley, and only then did he consider his next move.

'This is bad,' Nathan breathed. 'This is really bad.' He reached into his pocket and withdrew the slip of paper he had taken from beside the photograph of Kat and little Daisy. On it there were only two words – a name – but it had been enough to let Nathan know that the message was for him. He closed his eyes and thought about the photographs he had been sent, pictures forwarded from the Church Lane cottage. The picture of the woman in red. As he had told Gregory, the last time he had met her, she had been called Nancy Todd, but she'd used other aliases and Nathan could recall a few. One of them was the name written on that slip of paper.

'Mae Tourino,' Nathan said. 'Mae.'

One thing was for sure, he had to put this right – whatever this was. He had to get Kat and Daisy back to Ian. He had to keep them safe.

NINETEEN

'So what do you know about this Nathan? This friend of yours,' Tess pressed gently. 'How long have you known him? Where did you meet?'

Professor Marsh shrugged helplessly as though it was too hard to recall. 'I was working,' he said. 'On a lecture tour, a summer school. Nathan was assigned to me as interpreter and general factotum. He was still a student.'

'Studying what?' She asked. She could guess from the search she had done the night before, but was reluctant to show her hand yet.

'I don't know. I mean, he was studying medicine. I don't remember exactly what year he was in. I suppose he must have been twenty, twenty-one? Something like that. We kept in touch, we became friends, but . . .'

'Do you have an address, a phone number?'

Ian shook his head. 'There was a gas explosion where he used to live, back in the summer. I don't have his new address. His number is in my phone, but it won't work now. He'll have changed it.'

Tess and Vinod exchanged a glance. 'And why would he have done that?'

Ian Marsh shrugged. 'Because that's what he does. That's what he'll do.'

Tess frowned. The man was clearly falling apart and yet he was also holding things back. Why would he do that? 'You say you became friends. He was a student. Is it usual to become friends with your students?'

Ian Marsh looked puzzled. 'He was never my student,' he said. 'He was my assistant in Germany and then later, in Africa, Turkey, other places. We worked together a number of times. He . . . he . . .'

'He what?' Tess prompted but Professor Marsh seemed to have lost the capacity to respond. He stared into the distance as though seeing something far away.

Or long ago, she thought.

Vinod tried an alternate tack. 'Do you have friends in common?' he asked. 'Someone who may know more than you do about this Nathan?' He frowned 'What did you say his last name was?'

'Crow. His name is Nathan Crow and yes,' Ian Marsh sounded suddenly relieved, 'he's a friend of Annie Raven. Annie Raven the photographer. She's married to that artist, Bob something or other.' He drifted off again and Tess and Vinod exchanged another glance.

'Nathan Crow,' Vinod said what they were both thinking. 'It doesn't sound like a real name.

It seemed almost that Professor Marsh smiled slightly. 'I don't suppose it is,' he agreed. 'He's a storm crow, a messenger of the Morrigan; pecks away at the dead on the battlefield, stealing their eyes . . .' He seemed utterly lost then. Tess watched as he buried his face in his hands and began to weep. It was obvious they'd get no more sense out of him, but there was another question she had to ask.

'Why do you think Nathan was responsible for your wife and

child being kidnapped?' she said. 'Professor Marsh, we need to
know. We need any scrap of information you can give us about
this man. Do you think he took them?'

Ian Marsh, his face still buried in his hands, shook his head
emphatically. 'No,' he said. He lifted his head and the look of
utter despair in his eyes cut Tess to the quick. He's already
buried them, she thought. He doesn't think they're coming back
alive.

'Nathan wouldn't do this. He didn't like Kat much, but he put
on a good show of trying. But he wouldn't hurt her and he loved
Daisy.'

'Daisy?'

'He called her Daisy. Not Desi or Desiree. She was always
Daisy.'

'You can't be sure he didn't do this. You gave us the impression he may have been responsible.'

Ian Marsh sighed. 'Being responsible isn't the same as
taking a particular action,' he said, suddenly pedantic. 'I think
they were taken because of something Nathan did or maybe
didn't do. And I can't forgive that, not ever. He should
have kept clear of my family. He should have kept away from
me. I should never have become his friend. I should never
have let him into my life. So for that, I hold both of us guilty.
Me because I didn't cast him out and Nathan because of what
he is.'

His face contorted, pain and hate fighting for space at the
corners of his mouth and in the depths of his eyes. Tess watched
as he seemed to turn inwards, to shut them out, and she guessed
she'd get nothing out of him now.

'What do you make of that?' Vinod asked after they'd left.

'I think we should go and speak to Annie Raven. I think he
knows more than he's telling. I think he's scared – and not just
for his wife and kid. I think our Professor Marsh is a man who
has looked into the abyss and seen it looking back.'

TWENTY

I t hadn't taken long to find an address for the photographer Annie Raven and by two o'clock, they were on their way. Vinod had been uncharacteristically quiet since leaving the professor's house. Tess could guess what was on his mind, but she didn't think brooding in silence would help. Much better to get it out in the open. Wasn't it?'

'Penny for them?'

'What? Oh, right. I'm not sure they're worth it.'

'You're thinking what might be happening to them,' Tess said. 'The mum and the little girl. You're trying not to think that whoever killed our Mr Palmer might have taken them.'

Vinod shook his head. 'I'm way past that,' he said. 'I mean, it's obvious, isn't it? The two things have got to be related. Whoever killed Palmer came looking for the professor—'

'Or this Nathan Crow.'

'Or him, for some reason we can't get a handle on yet because said professor isn't telling us anything, so now whoever it is has taken his wife and kid. I mean, if that was any normal person and you thought you knew something that could get them back, you'd be spilling your guts, wouldn't you? Only thing you'd be thinking about was what you could do to help.'

Tess indicated to make the right turn the satnav was nagging about and then glanced over at him. 'You're thinking about your sister's kids.'

'Of course I am. Tia's the same age as the Marsh kid. She'd be scared to death.' He shook his head violently. 'It doesn't bear thinking about.'

'Then stop thinking about it.'

'I can't,' he admitted.

'Look,' Tess told him, 'this Annie Raven might have something useful to tell us. Then we start digging into our professor's past. The way I see it is, the only reasons you keep your mouth shut in a situation like this are that you don't give a shit what happens

– and I don't believe that – or you're too scared about what else might happen if you do spill your guts, as you put it. So we keep pecking away at the professor until he gives in, and while we're doing that, we start rooting around anywhere else that might tell us what he's up to his neck in.'

'One thing's for sure,' Vin said.

'What's that?'

'There are at least two teams involved in the kidnapping. Got to be.'

'How do you figure? Oh, the photograph. No way could they have snatched Katherine and the kid and taken their photograph and then got it to the prof's house. It must have been sent to the second team . . . emailed or as an SMS attachment by phone. Then it's been printed and placed at Professor Marsh's house by whoever trashed the place.'

'I'm betting there's nothing missing,' Vin said. 'Whoever did it wanted to create a mess, reinforce the threat. I don't think they were after anything.'

'Well until Prof Marsh is in a fit state to tell us, we'll just have to speculate,' Tess said. But she knew he was probably right. The search had looked like a load of kids had been let loose to run rampage. She'd been to her fair share of break-ins and all looked different, but in a strange way they also looked the same. There was usually some discernible purpose to the mayhem, the breaking, the destruction.

'Looks like we're about there.'

Tess nodded. They turned off the road and on to a track that narrowed as it approached the old farmhouse where Annie and her husband lived. Tess turned again through an open farm gate and into a driveway at the front of an ageing, whitewashed house. It stood squat and square in the middle of a large plot, with small windows and what looked like thick walls. It was not a pretty house, but it had a settled look, Tess thought, as though content with its history and location.

Something nagged at the back of Tess's mind. She'd seen something in the news about Annie Raven; she'd seen a picture of this house, she was sure, but for the life of her Tess could not bring to mind what it was and she didn't think it would have been in an art supplement or anything of that sort. Beyond family snapshots, Tess didn't really have much interest in photography.

The man who opened the door to them looked a little nervous, Tess thought. 'Mr Taylor?' she guessed, remembering that was the name of Annie's artist partner. She showed him her ID and Vinod did the same. 'I wonder if Ms Raven happens to be here. We'd appreciate a word.'

Bob Taylor studied her thoughtfully for rather a long time. She got the feeling he was interested in something other than her identity. Finally, he nodded. 'You'd better come in. We're in the studio. Come on through.'

They followed him into the house and down a short passage beside the kitchen.

'Wow,' Tess said. 'This is lovely.' The studio was a conservatory that ran the full length of one side of the house. Beyond it she could see a high bank, tree covered and fast turning to autumn gold. Tess suddenly understood why an artist would want this unprepossessing little house.

'Bob?'

Tess looked towards the sound of the voice and wondered how on earth she had missed noting the speaker before. The woman was standing beside the window, a red mug clasped in both hands. She was tall and slender with long dark hair and vivid blue eyes. Gorgeous, Tess thought. Beside her, she noted Vinod was suddenly standing very straight; he obviously thought so too.

'This is Annie,' Bob said. 'Annie, these are police officers. They want to talk with you about . . .'

'About your friend Nathan Crow,' Tess said.

Kat didn't know what time it was or how long ago everything had turned into a nightmare. She and Desi had been snatched from their car and thrown into the boot of another. Desiree had screamed and howled, in terror and then in pain as she'd landed hard on the floor of the boot. Kat remembered kicking and biting, clawing at the man who held her, but there'd been nothing she could do; he was far too strong and even if she'd managed to break free of his grasp, there were two others she'd have to deal with. All wore ski masks, but she couldn't recall much else about them, except that they all seemed like giants, with grips like steel, and none of them spoke a single word.

The car had taken off at speed and Kat, not knowing what else to do, had wedged herself as best she could against the bulkhead and gripped her daughter tight.

Desiree had continued to howl, her cries destroying any attempt Kat made to try and listen for clues as to where they might be or how long the journey was.

She fretted that they might run out of air, then fretted more that they wouldn't. That they would have to face what was to come. What were they going to do, these men in masks? Why?

After what seemed like a very long time, the car stopped. The boot opened. Kat was grabbed again and this time thrown into the back of a van, Desi tossed in after her like they were just so much rubbish. Then another man came and grabbed Kat's hand. She felt a pin prick and a sudden pain in the back of her hand. If a pain could taste bitter, this one did. Then nothing until – well, she had no way of knowing how long. She came to in the back of the van, Desi beside her so still she thought the child had died until, holding her close once more, she realized that the little body was still warm and though her breathing was shallow, she was actually still drawing breath.

Kat had wept then. Sobbed until she was exhausted. Her mouth was dry and her head throbbed like she was hung over, and she had wet herself at some point; her jeans were wet and she stank – or imagined she did. Humiliated and so, so scared, she gathered her child close and retreated to the corner of the van, fighting sudden nausea and attempting to shield her child from the worst of the bumps as the van twisted and turned on what felt like a rough road, throwing them first against the bulkhead and then on to the floor.

Again, she had no concept of time, only that it passed. She tried to listen, but could hear nothing apart from the throb of the engine and a radio playing in the cab, tuned, she thought, to a classical station. No conversation, and no outside noise of traffic or changing landscape. A rough road, then a smoother track, then something that might have been a cattle grid. Kat saved those little indicators, tucked them away in the hope they might be useful. Breadcrumbs for when she escaped.

'We will get away,' she promised Desi. 'We will. We will.' Then the van stopped. Hands reaching for them again. A blindfold tied too tight over her eyes. She screamed and kicked and bit, but it was hard to do any of those things with the dead weight of her little daughter in her arms. They half dragged, half carried her into a building. She could hear the change in sound as they crossed the threshold and gained the sense that this was somewhere large. Up stairs that sounded wooden, along a corridor that she sensed was narrow – they turned sideways as though it wasn't a wide enough space for herself and the men on either side. Then a door opening and she was thrown down again. She just managed to twist before she hit the floor, so that Desi landed on her and she didn't fall down on to the child.

The door closed and Kat ripped at the too-tight blindfold, tearing at it with fingers that felt numb and swollen and not her own.

She looked around and found that there was little to see. She and Desi were in a small square room. The walls were black, the floor was black, even the ceiling must have been painted black but she could only guess at that. There was a tiny amount of light shed by what she recognized as a battery-operated camping lantern.

The lantern was set on the floor beside a mattress. On the mattress were blankets and a white nightgown, long sleeved and oddly old fashioned, with a high neck.

'Change your clothes,' a voice said. 'Put on the gown.'

Kat got to her feet. The voice was coming from somewhere above her head 'Who the hell are you? Why have you brought us here?'

'Just do as I say.'

'Why the hell should I?'

She tried to analyse where the voice was coming from. It was soft, she thought, but male, female, she couldn't tell. It sounded faintly distorted as though drifting in and out of focus.

'Your daughter will wake up soon. She'll be hungry. You want her to have food? She'll be wet, uncomfortable. You don't want that, do you, Katherine?'

No, she didn't want that.

Still holding Desiree close, she circled the room, one hand on the walls, trying to guess how big a space it was. She had reached the back wall when the door opened and someone came through. Kat turned, instinctively. A camera flash blinded her and then the door was closed again.

'Now get changed,' the voice told her again. 'And we'll trade. Your obedience for food. I don't want to be unreasonable and I don't really want to be unpleasant. It will be so much better if you just do as you're told.'

Kat stood, undecided. She was sore and cold, her wet jeans clinging unpleasantly.

She laid Desiree on the mattress and slid them off, realizing suddenly that her jacket was gone and she now wore only a t-shirt and a light cardigan. She took off the cardigan, slipped the nightgown on over her t-shirt and then kicked the jeans and sodden underwear across the room. She kept her socks. She had no shoes. Then she pulled one of the blankets around her shoulders and gathered the child close.

Looking up, she tried once more to see where the voice might be coming from. It was silent now, but it had seemed to emanate from everywhere and nowhere.

Kat had never experienced real, unfettered terror, but she did now. The black walls closing in on her, the tiny light – what if it went out? The thin mattress and the coarse blankets and the silence.

She found herself straining to hear. Longing for the voice to speak to her once more. If it spoke, it was at least evidence of someone else there. Someone she might be able to negotiate with. Something she might be able to fight.

Kat didn't want to cry, but found she did anyway. Tears flowing fast and hot down bruised cheeks, finding the cuts and sores from being thrown around in the car and then the van.

She mustn't give in, she told herself. We'll get away. We'll get out of here. Alive.

TWENTY-ONE

They sat around the table in the studio and drank tea. Bob was watchful; Annie thoughtful and cautious; Tess increasingly puzzled. Vinod focused on taking notes and she couldn't guess what he was thinking.

'What about Nathan?' Annie had said. There'd been no surprise, no sense of shock that they were asking – which, in Tess's experience, were the usual reactions. There was no 'what happened to him' question – which was the other, normal response. What is it with these people, Tess wondered. I'm in La La Land here.

'You're telling me you have no means of contacting your friend,' Tess said, increasingly exasperated.

'I'm telling you I can send him a message. I can't tell you when he'll pick it up. Nathan travels a lot. I just send the messages to a drop box and he responds when he's ready. Nathan is a friend; I'm not his keeper or his carer.'

'A drop box?'

'It's like a post office box,' Bob said. 'Only it's online. It's a kind of email.'

'Why not just use ordinary email?'

Annie smiled. 'Because a drop box is encrypted, secure. All ID is stripped from my email and from his response. It uses a combination of public and private keys. Most journalists use something of the sort. We're all cautious about leaks these days.'

'And is Nathan a journalist?'

Annie laughed. 'No. I am, albeit one that works with pictures rather than words. Work has to be sent securely and quickly and from anywhere in the world. Sometimes I have to be careful. The habit is mine, rather than Nathan's, I suppose.'

'And if you contacted him now, told him we want to speak to him, how soon before he got in touch?'

Annie shrugged and Bob laughed.

'It's not funny,' Tess said tetchily. 'A child and her mother are missing and we've got every reason to believe that those holding them are dangerous. Violent.'

'I imagine Nathan already knows that,' Bob said. 'Given the murder, the trashing of Ian Marsh's house and the photograph.'

Tess sighed. She'd told them far too much, desperation and a feeling that she couldn't get a proper handle on events pushing her into revealing more than she normally would. That and, she now realized, Annie's gentle but persistent questions.

'Look,' she said, 'I hope I don't need to stress the confidentiality of all this?'

'I can assure you,' Annie said softly. 'When the full story escapes into the media, it won't be because of us.'

Vinod looked up from his notes. 'And what makes you think—'

'It's too good a story,' Annie said. 'A brutal murder, a university professor, a pretty child. Either your superiors will hold a press conference and release most of what you've told us, or they'll let it slide out into the world, detail by detail. You'll decide that Nathan is the key to all of this and that the more eyes you have looking for him, suspicious of him, the better. So you'll release a photograph of him; emphasize that, for the moment, he's just wanted as a witness. Even suggest that he too might be in danger – which is probably true. Not that there's anything you can do to change that.'

Annie sat back, her gaze fixed on Tess's face. Disturbingly steady.

'And where might we obtain a photograph of this mysterious Mr Crow?' Vinod asked.

It won't be from here, Tess thought.

To her surprise, Annie glanced at her husband. 'The best one will probably be in the wedding album,' she said. 'Would you look?'

'Sure.' Bob left, taking his mug of tea with him.

Tess knew her expression betrayed her surprise.

'How do you know Nathan Crow?' Vinod asked.

Annie tilted her head on one side, surveying the sergeant with that same thoughtfulness. 'We were teenagers,' she said. 'Young teens. I'd just lost my parents and Nathan's were dead too. It was something in common. We became friends. For a while we had the same guardian. He'd been friend to both our fathers so when we were orphaned he took legal charge of the pair of us. You could say we did most of our growing up together.'

'And this guardian. Might he know where Nathan's got to?' Annie sipped her tea. 'I doubt it. He's dead. But I'll tell you why Nathan left in such a hurry. He wanted to be free to act; once you'd started with your questions, he'd have been at least delayed, probably have lost what little time advantage he had. I don't have to tell you that their chances of survival diminish hour by hour.'

Tess almost laughed. This was just too much. 'And what the hell makes you think that Nathan can do what we can't?' she said angrily.

Annie Raven leaned forward and, much to Tess's surprise, she took her hand. 'Because that's what he's been trained to do,' she said. 'Because *you* have to keep it clean, play by rules. Nathan doesn't have to do any of those things. Neither do those men who have Ian Marsh's wife and child. You can't win against people like that unless you make the right play. Unless you are prepared to be as dirty as they are.'

There was a moment of shocked silence. Vinod coughed nervously, obviously thinking that Tess should take charge. Tess withdrew her hand.

'You're wrong,' she said. 'We'll get them. We'll get the wife and child back where they belong and if this friend of yours is in any way responsible, then he'll be brought to book too.'

She sounded pompous, Tess thought, and Annie obviously thought so too. She laughed softly. 'I wish you well,' she said. 'Truly, I do. But you're playing blind.'

Her husband had returned with a photograph album which he laid down on the table. Annie flicked quickly through the pages and selected an image. She handed that back to her husband. 'Bob will copy it,' she said. 'You can have the copy. Don't worry, we've got top of the line equipment: the scan will be as good as the original, or as near as you won't notice.'

'We'd bring the picture back,' Vinod objected.

Annie just looked at him. She closed the album and set it aside. It was very clear that she was impatient for them to go.

'You realize I could charge you with obstruction,' Tess said. Oh God, she was just sounding pompous again.

'For doing what?'

'I don't believe you. I think you'll be in touch with Nathan the moment we leave.'

That earned her a raised eyebrow and a considered look. 'Do you want the photograph?' Annie said. 'Because I could insist you come back here with a warrant.'

'That won't be necessary,' Vinod said. 'Ms Raven, we're grateful for your help, but you can understand we're concerned. Two innocent people have been taken and—'

Annie Raven held up a hand and Vinod fell silent. 'Sergeant Dattani, I know all about innocent people being punished for things others have done. Believe me. So does Nathan. But the only guilty parties here are whoever took the mother and child and whoever ordered it done. Can you think of one justifiable reason for doing that? Even to punish someone or to obtain information or to send a message? I think you'll agree with me that nothing anyone had done could justify such an action, could excuse this threat to innocence, as you would term it? No, so this is not Nathan's fault; this is not Nathan's guilt, and neither, presumably, is it Ian Marsh's. The only people responsible for this action are those that carried it out.'

Bob Taylor had returned with the picture. He set it down on the table and Annie examined it before handing it over. There were four people in the picture. Annie, looking amazing in a fitted red dress; Bob Taylor, his gaze fixed adoringly upon his wife, and two other men. 'That's Nathan,' Annie said, indicating the younger of the two.

'The other one's my brother,' Bob volunteered. 'He was the best man.'

Annie was on her feet now and signalling it was time for them to leave.

'We may need to speak to you again,' Tess said.

Bob coughed nervously and then handed her a business card. 'That's my lawyer,' he said. 'He handles the business side of things for me. If you want to speak to us again, then please call him first and set up a meeting. I'm . . . I'm getting quite particular about who comes to my house these days.'

* * *

'What the hell just happened?' Tess stormed as they drove away. 'Who the hell do they think they are?' She slammed the heel of her hand into the steering wheel. The car jerked sideways.

'Watch it,' Vinod said calmly. 'You'll have us in the ditch.'

Tess glared at him. 'You think I handled that badly.'

'I think we both did. I think Annie Raven is used to catching people off balance. At least we know what this Nathan Crow looks like.'

'That's if she's not spinning us a yarn. She volunteered her friend's picture a bit quick.'

'Crows and Ravens,' Vinod said. 'Is there a Magpie some-where? A Jackdaw? They've got to be made-up names. I mean, who'd call themselves after a corvid?'

'So, we do a background check on the whole damned lot of them. Annie Raven and her husband; Ian Marsh; this Nathan Crow.'

'You want me to get Jaz on to that now? She and her team are still working their way through paperwork from the Palmer murder. Best they broaden their search now.'

Tess nodded. 'Do that and see if you can grab them a couple of extra bodies to assist.' Not that this is likely to stay my case, she thought. This is much too big, especially now.

She could hear Vin speaking on the phone, getting updates and then talking to DC Jaz Portman. When he got off the phone he confirmed her thoughts.

'A Major Incident Team is being formed,' he said. 'There'll be a briefing when we get back.'

Tess nodded, not sure whether she was disappointed or relieved. 'Who's heading it?'

'No one knows yet. Superintendent Chase is organizing every-thing that end. Looks like we'll get shunted sideways though.' He sounded bitter.

'There'll be plenty to go around,' Tess told him. A sense of deep foreboding gripped her. She remembered the crime scene, the sight of Anthony Palmer hanging from that beam, the mono-filament eating its way into his flesh. She tried not to imagine the pain, but couldn't help herself. Whoever had done that to Palmer now had a woman and a child.

TWENTY-TWO

Annie had done what she always did when she wanted to think: she had wandered out into the garden and stood beneath one of the scrubby old oaks which, though they were well past their sell-by date, neither she nor Bob could bear to take down. Bob watched her, sipping a new cup of coffee. The visit had shaken him up; the last couple of months had been peaceful and wonderful. Annie had seemed content, had been working part-time teaching a photography course and Bob had slowly resumed his painting. It was the memory of the episode preceding such peace that set Bob so much on edge. The man who had tried to kill him and the other, equally frightening in his own way, who had stopped him. Bob had glimpsed what had been Annie's world and he didn't like what he had seen.

He saw Annie start back towards the house and sat down at the big table in his studio to wait for her. Knowing whatever it was had been resolved, he worried as to *how* it had been resolved. Shrugging off the old coat she wore, she sat down opposite him.

'He hasn't been in touch to ask for my help and he hasn't told me what's going on,' she said. 'That means Nathan doesn't want to be found, not even by me. He's gone deep and for that he needs other help. I'll send him a message about the visit, but that's all I can do.'

She reached across the table and took his hand as she had Tess's earlier. 'I'm not about to get involved in this,' she told Bob.

He lifted her hand and kissed the palm. 'Of course you are,' he said. 'If he needs you. You'd never walk away from someone you love. I know that and I respect it. Nathan is family. He's a brother to you. I wouldn't dream of blackmailing you, of making you choose; you know that.'

Annie squeezed his hand. 'And Nathan knows that too, about you.' She sighed deeply and rubbed at her eyes with her free hand. 'He's gone after them, after the child mostly. He won't rest until he finds her.'

'You know most kidnap victims don't survive, don't you?'

'I know the statistics, Bob. Death usually happens in the first hour. Sometimes, I think, that's a good thing. But this is no ordinary abduction. They'll keep the wife and kid alive. That way they keep all of the control. If Ian Marsh thinks his family is dead they'll have no means of keeping the pressure on.'

'You think this is about Professor Marsh, not Nathan?'

'I don't know,' Annie admitted. 'It could be either; could be both. Nathan specializes in upsetting the wrong people, but from what I know of Ian Marsh, he's not been so far behind.'

'You've not mentioned him before.' Not that it meant anything. There were a lot of things Annie didn't talk about.

'I don't *know* him. I've met him twice, but not in any, you know, work context. Nathan brought him to an exhibition – he brought his wife too, come to think of it. And I met him once when Nathan gave him a lift somewhere. I was in the car.'

'But you know *about* him.'

'I know he worked as a diplomatic aide – and you know as well as I do that can mean anything from him being the man who makes the coffee to the man who disposes of the bodies. He speaks several languages, but Nathan first met him when he needed an interpreter. I don't remember what language. Nathan said he facilitated medical access on a couple of occasions, but we didn't talk about him. He was part of Nathan's life I had no involvement in. Nathan likes him, that's all I'm really sure of. Apparently he got sick of the travelling and probably the getting shot at, so he shifted into academia. That must have been a decade ago. Nathan was only in his early twenties when they met.'

'And so the idea that someone might take his wife and child because of something he did?'

She shook her head. 'It's possible, of course. I think most of what he did was legit and transparent. According to Nathan, he's got a conscience, has Professor Marsh – or at least, he did have.'

'What do you mean?'

Annie shook her head and for a moment Bob thought she would refuse to answer. She had always tried to keep him out of what he thought of as her other life. He saw her considering what she should tell him. Finally she said, 'He did a lot of work with injured kids; worked all over the Middle East trying to get medical programmes off the ground, negotiating and coercing when he had to. Truth is, Bob, I don't know, but maybe he did something, got himself mixed up in something that meant certain pressures could be applied.'

'And you think someone now wants to make him pay?'

'I think it's possible. But I don't think he's been in any position to tread on toes for a very long time. Whoever is doing this, they knew they'd also draw Nathan in. I guess that's at the very least a bonus.'

Bob squeezed her hand. 'Annie, he's survived worse, I'm sure. He'll come through.'

She smiled. 'I know. Bob, I wish this could all just go away, you do know that, don't you?'

He kissed her hand again. 'We play what we're dealt,' he said softly, 'and if the best we can come up with is a pair of twos, then we just have to bluff that bit better. I love you, Annie. Better or worse, remember?'

'Better or worse,' she agreed and hoped fervently that it would be the former.

TWENTY-THREE

Naomi's taxi dropped her off after her second afternoon at the centre. Alec wouldn't be there; he'd already warned her of that. He'd decided he wanted to do his next hospital appointment alone.

'It makes no sense for you to just sit around in the corridor waiting,' he had said.

'Then maybe you should let me come in. I am your wife, Alec.'

'I know, it's just . . .'

He didn't finish and she didn't argue, too worn out and angry to bother any more. Naomi didn't know if this sudden show of independence was a good thing or signalled the deepening of the rift between them, but she didn't have the energy to try and figure it out or to ask him more. Instead she called the advice centre and made herself available for another two-hour slot.

Letting herself in the communal front door, she sensed at once that someone was there. Napoleon whined in recognition.

'Hello? Someone there?'

'Hello, Naomi.'

Gregory? What on earth was he doing here? 'You'd best come up,' she said. 'You know you shouldn't come here. Anyone could see you.'

Gregory laughed. 'Except the person I came to visit.'

'Oh, we're doing irony now, are we? Come on in; Alec won't be back for a while.'

'Where's he off to?'

'Hospital,' Naomi said shortly. She led the way into the flat and released Napoleon from his harness. He turned immediately to get his share of fuss from Gregory. 'Tea, coffee?'

'Whatever you're having.'

Naomi nodded and went through to the kitchen. She filled the kettle and switched it on, got mugs from the cupboard, using the time to gather her thoughts. She liked Gregory in an odd kind of way, but she could not help but see him as a storm crow, presaging trouble.

'You want to carry your mug through,' she said. 'I'm fine with one; I have this tendency to spill two.'

She felt him come into the kitchen and reach past her for the coffee and she was suddenly very conscious of his presence. Of his scent and height and . . . she pushed the thought aside, knowing it had arisen only because she felt so neglected by Alec just now.

'So, not to seem rude, but why are you here? I thought you'd have left the country or something by now.'

Gregory laughed softly. 'That would have been the sensible option,' he said. 'But no, life doesn't always allow for the sensible options. Truth is, Naomi, I've got a problem and I think you might be able to help me with it.'

'Me? I doubt that. What the hell can I do?'

'You know a woman called Tess Fuller. She's a DI.'

'I know what she is,' Naomi said. A little too sharply, she realized and realized too that Gregory would have heard. 'Alec knows her better; he's actually worked with her. What about her anyway?'

'There was a murder—'

'Church Lane. Mr Palmer? The tenant.'

'That will be the one. This DI Fuller, she's heading the investigation.'

'And?'

'And things have got complicated. It's not just a murder any more.'

Naomi listened as he filled her in on the kidnapping, Nathan's involvement, their speculation as to what might be at the heart of things. 'So, as I say,' Gregory continued. 'We've got problems and I need your help.'

'To do what?'

'Well, for a start, how good is this Tess Fuller? What sort of problems are we likely to have?'

Naomi laughed. 'And I should tell you, because . . .? No, forget that, silly question.' She'd tell him because she owed him, Naomi knew that.

'She's good,' she said reluctantly. 'Thorough, efficient and imaginative and that often tips things. She can put herself in the position of the victim, the perpetrator, imagine what they would do. She's very young for a DI and she's very new, only got the promotion about eight months or so ago, but from what you're telling me, she's the least of your worries.'

'Why?'

'Because she'll be sidelined. This is too big for the locals to handle. Her superiors will already be creating a Major Incident Team. They'll pull in experts from wherever they need them. Tess will still work the case, but she won't be the senior investigating officer; she just doesn't have the experience or the clout.'

'We thought that might be the case.' Gregory said. 'But she'll still know what's going on.'

'And she still won't tell me.'

'But she might talk to Alec? You said they were friendly?'

Naomi groaned. 'Gregory, what do you want from me? Look, they are friends, once they were even close friends, but she won't divulge—'

'Not even if he's involved.'

'Involved? How? What do you mean?'

'Naomi, she's looking for Nathan; she's already spoken to

Annie Raven; she'll dig and dig deep and it won't take long before Clay's name comes up, before Alec's name comes up. True, he was peripheral, but he was still involved; his aunt was still involved.'

Damn Molly Chambers, Naomi thought.

'She'll see him as a source, an opportunity . . .'

'And you want to do the same,' Naomi said flatly.

'We all want the same thing,' Gregory said. 'To get Katherine Marsh and her kid back safely.'

'And the likelihood of that is . . .?'

'We believe it's still possible. A dead wife and murdered kid aren't such good leverage as a wife and kid you can hurt and maim. The dead don't suffer.'

Naomi felt the chill of his words penetrate. 'That's awfully close to emotional blackmail,' she said.

She sensed him shrug his shoulders. 'Whatever it takes,' Gregory said.

By the time Alec returned home, Naomi had made up her mind. She would help if she could, but there was no way she was going to force Alec's involvement in anything. If Tess made the connection and came asking questions, then so be it, but she'd had enough of the worry, the danger, the violence that people like Gregory brought with them.

At least, that's what she told herself.

But the ghosts of her past crowded around her after Gregory had left. Her best friend from childhood, taken and murdered; those she had encountered in her working life whose lost voices and lost lives called out to her. Those dead and wounded she had adopted on behalf of others.

'Those we have lost are the ones who shape our lives the most,' Molly Chambers had once told her. 'They make us fearful and they fill us with courage because we know what we have already faced and therefore what we can face again.'

About that, Naomi was not so sure, but then Alec's adopted aunt was a tough old bird. Tough and brave and compassionate and Naomi knew she would have no hesitation. For Molly there would be no debate. Gregory would ask and she would help in any way she could, no matter what the potential cost.

'Well I'm not Molly Bloody Chambers, am I?' Naomi stated angrily. Her voice seemed to bounce around the empty room and Napoleon came over to her and laid his head against her knee. She stroked him, absently, her mind drifting.

They'll be so scared, Naomi thought, and she knew then that any resolution made would just fall apart when it came down to it. She could not just stand aside if there was a way of helping to find Katherine and her baby girl and she wasn't much bothered which side of the law that involved.

TWENTY-FOUR

'So, what do we have?' Nathan said.

'Resource wise, not a lot. We can access computer equipment and there are about half a dozen people I figure might help out at short notice. But you say you don't want anyone involved . . . Nathan, the two of us can only do so much.'

Nathan paced, his forehead deeply furrowed. 'We have to assume that we can't trust anyone,' he said. 'That everything is compromised.'

'You're trusting me,' Gregory pointed out. 'A lot of people would think you are off your head for doing that. And you can trust Annie.'

'No, leave Annie out of this. I've almost got Bob killed once; I'm not about to risk that again.'

'As I remember it, that wasn't exactly your fault, and besides, that's for her to decide, not you.'

Nathan waved his words away.

'I still have contacts,' Gregory said. 'So do you. Anything we get we treat with extreme prejudice, check it out before we move, but like I say, we can't cover the ground alone.'

Nathan dropped into the old armchair beside the bed. They were using one of the old safe houses Clay's organization had set up. Only a handful of people had ever known of its existence and most of them were now dead. Even so, Gregory knew they couldn't risk staying here for long. There were still threads linking this place back to other times and other actions and spider-web thin though they were, he and Nathan now both had a price on their heads and it wasn't just the authorities that were after them. The police didn't bother Gregory; at most he viewed them as an inconvenience. But having allied himself with Nathan, Gregory had become a target; the big question was, who were the potential shooters?

As though reading his thoughts, Nathan said, 'I have no claim on you. If you upped and left, I'd not hold it against you.'

'I know. But that's not what I do.'

Nathan nodded and Gregory knew it would not be mentioned again. Gregory had made his decision. 'The woman in the photographs you were sent,' he said. 'That's all we've got so far. We start with her and work back to the source. Someone's leaving you a trail. The question is, who? And are they friend or enemy or something in between? Or just shit stirring?'

Nathan smiled. 'There's a hell of a lot of shit to stir,' he agreed. 'But you're right; we start with Michelle Williamson, or Mae Tourino or whatever she's calling herself now, start with what we know and who might have sent those pictures to me and what they are trying to tell me.'

'Pity they couldn't have included a note,' Gregory said. 'I hate bloody cryptic clues.' He picked up his coat and started for the door. 'We need food,' he said, 'and I want to get a look at the newspapers and I'll pick us up a laptop and a wi-fi dongle. I can't be doing with those little phone screens.' He paused and turned. 'Incidentally, whose picture did Annie give them?'

'Mine,' Nathan said.

'What? For real?'

'It was the wisest move,' Nathan said. 'Why aggravate the situation? Ian Marsh has pictures of me, so do half a dozen other people. Usually I'm off in the crowd somewhere, but remember, I've got a respectable side, Gregory. I live my life in plain sight most of the time.'

Gregory nodded briefly and then left. He often forgot that about Nathan and Annie, that they had public faces. He was so used to being the invisible man that it was an odd thought to be otherwise. He closed the door quietly and stood in the dark outside of the little cottage. The curtains had been drawn and no light escaped from the blackout linings. From the air, it would be possible to pick up an infrared signature that would define the cottage as being warmer than the surrounding air, but nothing would be visible from the ground unless you got up really close and it was so remote, up the winding little lane, that few would come anywhere near. The farm a couple of miles distant might realize someone was in residence, but it was understood that there were always people mad enough to holiday there, even late in the season.

Even so, Gregory was uneasy. The threads were there. Once upon a time this had been a safe house for other organizations; anyone digging might just find a reference to it. Or was that being paranoid?

Gregory got into the car and started the engine. It seemed far too loud in the twilight silence. Had he always been paranoid, Gregory wondered, and then knew the answer to that was probably yes. He also knew that paranoia was what had kept him alive this far, and he was not about to drop the habit any time soon.

Two things really bothered him and he felt they were starting to bother Nathan too. He hoped so, but realized that the young man was presently too personally embroiled to have the perspective Gregory would normally have expected. One thing that was niggling at Gregory was the photograph. Who had sent it and why? On its own, Gregory might have dismissed it as just one of the random bits of intel that fed back from informants all the time. Someone saw someone, noticed something unusual, remembered something and they forwarded it on. But then the same woman had been referenced in the kidnapping. The little slip of paper left beside the photograph of Kat and Desiree.

Gregory didn't like it. To his eyes, it was almost like overkill; someone was ensuring Nathan would see the right clues, take note of the right scraps of information. And Nathan was emotionally entrapped enough that it was working.

Someone knew all the right buttons to press and was currently pressing them all at once.

He drove slowly towards the main road, pausing at the junction. The road was clear; empty at this time of night. He wondered where he'd manage to find a takeaway at this time of night and in such a godforsaken spot. Turned left, just because.

Nathan, Gregory decided, was in no fit state to be playing this particular game. Had he been in a combat situation, Gregory would have sent the younger man back, well behind the lines, authorized some compulsory R & R, while those with clearer, more detached heads sorted the problem. But he didn't have that luxury right now. Nathan was right at the heart of the situation – involved, emotional, unreliable – and Gregory would have to compensate for that, create his own game plan and focus on harm minimization, not just for the victims but also for the operatives.

Having made up his mind, Gregory felt better. He'd raise his suspicions with Nathan, of course, and he felt certain that Nathan would agree with him; that it all looked too easy, too suspicious. But Gregory was also aware that reason would not be Nathan's greatest strength right now and no matter how much he agreed that Gregory was right, it might not be a consideration when it came to play.

Gregory shrugged. That was fine. He could compensate. He'd been doing this sort of thing forever. His mind wandered back to his dream. Not to the bodies in the room now, but to that moment when he had lain on that thyme-fragrant hill and had been momentarily distracted by the hawk as it began to swoop.

It had been the blink of an eye, less than a heartbeat, but still too much; still too long.

'Focus,' Gregory said. 'One of us has to keep the goal in focus. Otherwise, the way I figure it, we'll all end up bloody dead.'

TWENTY-FIVE

Beyond all expectation, Kat had fallen asleep. She woke when the door opened again and something was dropped on to the floor. By the time she'd moved, the door had closed.

Kat stared at the bag that had landed close to her mattress. It was a standard black dustbin bag, knotted at the neck. In the dim light shed by the lantern, it was impossible to make out more.

Beside her, Desi snuffled and showed signs of waking up. Kat pulled the other blanket over her and went to investigate. Inside there was bottled water, food, disposable nappies. Pyjamas for the child.

Kat picked up the lantern and searched for the door. She could just discern the outline, black against black, but there was no handle, no means of opening, no sign of a lock. She clawed at the edge, but there was nothing to get hold of and reason told her it would be fastened tight from the outside anyway. Glancing back at Desiree, horribly aware that the child would be left in darkness if she moved far from the mattress, Kat stepped cautiously past the door and along the walls, again trying to define the edges of this new world. In the corner of the room was a chemical toilet and she thought she felt a flow of air from somewhere above her head, but could not be sure.

At least, she thought, whoever was holding her and her baby, they weren't planning on starving them and she didn't have to pee on the floor or in a bucket.

Why the hell, she wondered next, was that so important? But somehow it was. She had to look for hopeful signs, had to be convinced that they would get out of here, alive and unharmed. Had to stay strong. Ian would have realized they weren't home; he'd have raised the alarm. People would be looking for them. She tried not to think that Ian wouldn't even know where to start looking; no one would.

Desi started to cry, a thin pained wail that had Kat flying to her side. She grasped the child close, rocking her gently. Desi was wet and her nappy was also soiled.

Kat felt in the plastic bag and found the nappies and, to her relief, a pack of wet wipes. She cleaned her child up and changed her, discarding the wet tights and the dress. Desi had vomited, she now realized. It horrified Kat to think that her child might have choked on her own vomit, been unconscious and unable to turn her head or sit up.

The anger somehow made her feel better, for a brief moment. The reality crashed in on her again. Where were they? How long was the food meant to last for? Had they been left alone in this place? The thought of that scared her almost more than the idea that someone was watching, spying on them. The men who had grabbed her and manhandled them both. Drugged them and brought them to this cell.

She looked at the food in the bag. Sandwiches, some fruit, some chocolate bars. Water. When would they be fed again?

'Okay.' Kat breathed. She had to think, she had to be ready, she had to listen and try and work out a pattern, should anyone come back and open the door again. She had to try and work out where that voice had come from and if the little draft she thought she had felt was real or just imagined.

She persuaded Desi to drink some of the water. The child was obviously feeling as miserable and hung over as Kat had when she'd first woken up. She clung to her mother and howled plaintively.

And Kat sat on the thin mattress, with her back to the wall, facing the spot where she knew the door to be and rocked her gently. 'I'll get you out of here,' she promised, over and over again, saying it like a mantra and willing herself to believe.

TWENTY-SIX

Tess and Vinod arrived back at the police headquarters to join the first meeting of the Major Incident Team. DCI Branch – someone Tess had heard of but never met – had waited on their arrival before making a proper beginning, but it was obvious he was already up to speed.

'Anything useful from Annie Raven?'

'We got a photograph of Nathan Crow, the man who was with Ian Marsh when—'

DCI Branch nodded. He already knew who Nathan Crow was. 'Genuine, you think?'

'I don't see why not.' She paused and propped her bag on a side table, withdrew the photograph. 'It's from their wedding. Bob Taylor and Annie Raven.' She pointed. 'The best man is Taylor's brother. That's Crow. I don't see why she'd bother to lie about it; we could check with other guests, make life difficult for her if she lied. I'm betting it's the genuine article.'

Branch nodded. 'Get his face isolated and copied after the meeting,' he said. 'We'll get it distributed and consider releasing it to the press.'

Tess opened her mouth to object that they had no evidence on which to launch a man hunt.

'As a witness, who may also be in danger,' Branch said.

Tess shut her mouth and went to join Vinod.

Standing at the front of the room, Branch introduced himself and the half-dozen people who had come with him. A list was being distributed, with names, ranks and brief notes on previous cases. Tess made her own notes anyway. Writing something down fixed it for her in a way that merely reading it never did. She was called to the front in her turn to give everyone a run down of the case so far and their interview with Annie Raven. She produced the photograph of Nathan Crow.

'We don't know how he fits into the picture at the moment. DC Jaz Portman and her team are running background on everyone involved.' She looked at Branch meaningfully. 'If you can spare someone from your team to assist that would be useful.' He nodded, but didn't agree. Tess moved on. His lookout, she thought, but she knew what could happen all too easily; people reported to those in their usual chain of command. Two unfamiliar groups grafted together could sometimes mean that people got left out of the loop unless proper liaison was set up from the start. Someone had to keep the book, be a central point. But of course, she chided herself. He knew that.

'I don't think she was exactly straight with us,' Vinod was saying and Tess realized she had missed the question and who had asked it. She was dog tired, she realized suddenly – not that she could use that as an excuse.

'In what way?'

'I don't know. Omission rather than commission,' Tess said. 'She was cautious, wary and not just in the way everyone is when the police come to call. It was almost as though she'd just developed the habit. Her husband too. He's directed all new communication through their lawyer. He said he was getting to be particular about who he let into his house.'

Branch frowned. 'Seems a little extreme.'

'Maybe not.' It was Jaz, glancing through her notes. Branch gestured to her and she stood up, faced the room. 'I started to run basic checks, just to see who we were dealing with. This

Bob Taylor is a pretty famous artist and his wife is a photo journalist. Top flight. Mostly war zones. She's been in some tight corners according to what's available online, so the wariness might just be professional caution. But there's more. She and this Nathan Crow were under the guardianship of a man called Gustav Clay. They grew up together.'

Tess nodded. 'She told us that.'

'But this Gustav Clay. He died a couple of months ago. I got hold of a guest list from his funeral service; it reads like a who's who of the diplomatic corps and foreign office and I don't just mean from the present lot. His obit. describes him as a career diplomat and from what I can gather he wasn't just embassy staff. I reckon this guy was a real-life spook.'

A ripple of laughter through the room and Jaz flushed.

Branch held up a hand for silence and nodded at Jaz. 'Copy what you have into the main folders,' he said. 'I expect new material to be made available as it comes up and copies laid out on that table over there. And I expect everyone in the team to update themselves even if it's outside of your immediate brief. Right, do we have anything else?'

Jaz sat down and Tess could tell she was deflated. 'It kind of fits,' Vinod muttered. 'All the rest of the cloak and dagger stuff we've been getting hints of all day.'

Tess nodded.

Branch was speaking again. 'About half an hour ago we got our first concrete lead. Katherine Marsh's car was found on a side road about ten miles from her uncle's house. Half in a ditch and on a bend known locally as an accident black spot. It seems that several of the locals had spotted it earlier in the day; they'd checked no one was still inside and phoned it through, but as I say, it's a spot where the local farmer is used to finding tourists who'd skidded off the road, so the connection wasn't made. What also slowed things down is that her uncle was certain she'd have taken a different route. Time was wasted following that up.'

'Which has really pissed Branch off,' Vinod commented.

Tess nodded. It pissed her off too. Time had been lost. Far too much time.

'So, our game plan is this: DS Fields will join DC Portman and her team on the background, and will be the voice for that team. DI Fuller and DS Dattani, you'll be travelling down to Suffolk tomorrow morning to interview the family, look at the route Katherine Marsh took and liaise with the CSI on scene. Report back to me by phone at noon and then we'll decide on your next move. Best make an early start; it's a long drive. You'll also be responsible for keeping Professor Marsh informed. The two of you had first contact with him, I understand?'

Tess nodded.

'And he's refused the services of a liaison officer.'

She nodded again. 'We tried to get him to stay with a friend, but he won't be budged. I've made all the arrangements for the phone intercept.' She glanced at her watch. 'That should be in place by now.'

'I'll chase it up,' Branch said. 'You and Vin get off home and get some sleep. You're expected down there by eight.'

God, what sort of time would they have to start out? Tess wondered. She nodded again. 'Sir.'

There were a few more loose ends to tie, but Branch dismissed them shortly after that. Tess glanced again at her watch. She was wondering. Why had Katherine Marsh chosen that route? Why had her uncle been so certain she had gone the other way?

Ian Marsh answered the phone on the second ring. His voice was tense and dry.

'They found the car,' Tess explained. 'No, I'm sorry, I don't have much more to tell you than that. I'm heading down there.' Something prevented her from telling him that she wasn't leaving until the morning. She just knew he'd want her to be going now, would take comfort from that little deception. 'I was wondering about where her car was found. Her uncle was certain she'd take the main roads, and the search was focused on—'

Ian Marsh laughed softly. It was a hollow sound. 'Oh, lord,' he said. 'He was a worrier, always. Kat said it was like Little Red Riding Hood's mother telling her to keep to the path. Always keep to the path. Kat never did. She grew up in that neck of the woods, knew the roads like . . . Well, she'd always nod and smile and make him think she was taking his advice but she never did. She likes the back roads, the country tracks. Said they were prettier and more interesting to drive.'

Tess could hear the man's voice begin to crack. 'I'm so sorry,

Professor Marsh,' she said softly. 'We'll find them. I promise you.'
But he had hung up on her. Retreated into his world of pain. Tess
thought about ringing him back but what could she say, what could
she do? The best she could do for him now was to go home, get
what sleep she could and get ready for the long drive in the morning.

Naomi lay awake, thinking. She'd gone to bed early with a
headache and listened to an audio book for a while. She still
missed the act of turning pages, the smell of familiar, oft-read
favourite books. The simple pleasures of browsing bookshops
and libraries. Now her choice of titles was dependent on others
and it just wasn't the same. She'd loved picking up an unknown
author or an unusual subject.

She could hear the television on in the other room. Alec was
watching a film that involved a lot of bangs, crashes, shouting
and explosions. But she was pretty sure he'd be in the other
room, watching television, whatever was on. They had lived so
much in one another's pockets these past months that personal
space was an almost forgotten luxury and since his accident,
Naomi had instinctively kept even closer, her desire to protect
suddenly almost overwhelming. These last few days seemed to
have facilitated the crisis she knew would come; they had also
highlighted their mutual need for quiet time alone, even if only
a flimsy stud wall and a painted door divided them.

What to do about Gregory? What, if anything, was she likely
to find out? Alec still ached from what he had taken as a personal
snub from Tess and what Naomi knew was only an inevitable
consequence of their changed relationship. Alec was no longer
an insider, no longer privy to the secrets and the contact and the
intimacy of the job. And it *was* intimate, she thought, in the same
way that any group who faced mutual threats or problems with
really significant consequences were intimate. You bonded with
your own kind and the inevitable segregation that followed on
from separation, be it voluntary or not, was inevitably hurtful in
a way that those whose workmates were just casual friends would
never understand.

She found she was thinking of Kat and the child. She'd not
spoken of any of this to Alec. He had been so busy with his own
thoughts that it would have felt almost like an intrusion and,

besides, she was really not sure how he'd react to Gregory's request. The policeman part of Alec was still not just wary of Gregory but also suspicious of him – and with good reason. Gregory and Alec's version of law and the right had probably not been even on nodding terms in years. But he also had reason to be grateful to the man and Naomi knew that would have rankled.

'Where are you?' Naomi said softly. 'If you're alive, are you cold or hungry, are you in the dark? Are you in pain?'

She tried to stop, but her thoughts ran away with her, visualizing the worst.

She had done this before, Naomi thought. A long time ago, when Naomi had just been a little girl, scared for a friend who had disappeared without trace and blaming herself for the loss, she had tried to imagine what might be happening. The truth was, her friend was already dead. She had felt, then, that the world blamed her. Harry's sister and her best friend. Just snatched away, never to return.

Was Ian Marsh thinking like that? Was he imagining, dreading, torturing himself with what might have happened, just as Naomi had when someone she loved had been taken away, and as she did now about a woman and child she had never even met.

Sleep wasn't going to happen and she no longer wanted to listen to her book. She got out of bed and found her dressing gown, went to join Alec with his film and the crashes and bangs and loud explosions, hoping that the noise would somehow drown out the voices in her head and the pictures that swam behind her sightless eyes, more vivid and intense than anything she had ever seen in her sighted days.

TWENTY-SEVEN

Ian Marsh had returned home. There had been offers to call someone, offers of help from neighbours he had barely spoken to until today, offers of a police liaison officer. Ian had rejected them all. The local Suffolk police were already at Kat's uncle's place, trying to piece together what had happened from that end, so Ian was spared the task of telling them that their niece and her child had been abducted. He'd have to talk to them later, he knew. Field the inevitable questions about why they had been taken and what anyone could possibly want from a university professor and his wife and child. Ian was not a rich man; comfortably off, yes, and with property worth a good amount against which he could probably raise money for a ransom, but they were hardly obvious targets. Not if you looked at it through normal eyes anyway.

But that was the trouble, Ian thought. So much of his life was hidden, kept secret even from Kat. Especially from Kat.

She knew he'd travelled abroad a great deal, that he'd worked for various relief agencies, lending his skills and expertise, especially when, as a younger man, the adventure of it had appealed to him. But the Professor Marsh she knew – the almost forty, respectable, ordered and safe Professor Marsh – what could he possibly have done that meant someone took his wife and child in punishment?

The phone rang and Ian was in two minds: should he leap for it, seize it in case it was the abductors, or should he ignore it in case it was Kat's aunt or uncle seeking information he didn't have?

Reluctantly he raised the receiver from its cradle to find it was neither. It was Tess Fuller telling him that the phone tap he had agreed to would be in place in the next hour or so and asking if he was sure he didn't want someone with him. He was surprised the intercept on his phone had taken so long to set up, knowing how physically easy it was in these digital days. He said so, heard Tess pause as though surprised and remembered that most people would not consider that. Most would still think of a phone tap as a physical thing; men and equipment staked out at the professor's home.

'We still have to get authorization,' she said. 'You shouldn't be alone. You should go to a friend, a relative, or get someone to stay with you.'

'There is no one, really. I don't have family. Not apart from Kat and Daisy.'

'Daisy?' She seemed curious that he'd used Nathan's pet name for the child, especially as Ian was so angry with Nathan.

Ian closed his eyes and cursed inwardly at this second mistake. 'I can't always get my head around Desiree,' he said.

'I see,' she said. 'Look, you've got my number; call me if you change your mind or if you just need to touch base. I've got to warn you, there's not likely to be much I can tell you; we're still feeling our way.'

'No, I understand that,' Ian said. 'I'll be all right.'

He stood in the hall and looked around at the devastation left by whoever had put that photograph on his kitchen table. Fingerprint powder and a chemical scent he could not immediately identify added to the sense of this being a place he no longer recognized. Bending, he picked a couple of the books off the floor and then a sheaf of papers. He should tidy up; Kat hated it when things were a mess.

He clutched the books and papers close to his chest, trying very hard not to weep with rage and frustration. Wishing he could tell DI Fuller that he couldn't phone a friend because he really had none. Not close friends that would understand what he was going through. The closest he had was the young man who'd brought him back to this mess some seven hours before. Who had 'fled the scene' as that sergeant, Vinod or whatever his name was, had put it.

Ian knew that Nathan hadn't really run away, just as he knew that Nathan would never deliberately do anything to endanger any of them. But how do you explain that to someone who knew nothing of the likes of Nathan Crow, knew nothing of the life Professor Ian Marsh had led before time and age had pushed him back into respectability?

Slowly, almost reluctantly, but because it was something to do and he had to do something, Ian bent and gathered up another book and a further sheaf of papers. He carried them through to his study and dropped them on to his desk. Then went back for more.

When Kat came back it would be to a clean and tidy and welcoming house. There would be no trace left of what had happened. There would be nothing to remind her. She would bring Desi in and they would settle down together on the big sofa and he would hold them both so tight, for so long.

'Please God give me another chance,' he whispered to a deity he had long since stopped believing in. 'Give me back my wife and child. Punish me but let them be all right.'

He wandered upstairs and stood at the door of Desiree's room. Not much had been disturbed in here. Her cot was untouched, her collection of soft toys still sat on the chest and her little night light glowed in the plug socket. He tried to picture his daughter there, sleeping softly in her bed or scampering up to him, arms raised to be cuddled. Ian turned away, overwhelmed by a sudden feeling of loss and shame. Instead, he went into the room he and Kat shared. Her mother's room, down the hall, was bigger, but neither of them had felt right moving in there and so they had remained in what had been the guest room, using the family bathroom rather than the master with its en-suite. He had come up here just after Nathan had left, a sudden impulse to check what had been done in the rest of the house drawing him into their sleeping space. That most intimate and private of places. A mess had been left here too, whoever had come in and wrecked their house seemingly enjoying the process. Bedclothes had been dragged on to the floor and drawers opened, their contents tipped out, but it was a half-hearted, done-for-effect sort of messiness. Unimportant and causing only nuisance. And he had seen it. Like the photograph on the kitchen table, this had been laid out in solitary splendour on his wife's pillow. Her mobile phone. The green light at the bottom corner telling him that there was a message.

Hesitantly, Ian Marsh had picked it up and opened the message screen. Two words. *Say nothing.*

Then there had been the hammering on the door and the police had arrived and he had been ushered out and taken care of. Given gallons of tea and sweet biscuits he'd normally have refused.

'They're good for the shock,' his neighbour told him. 'You can't beat tea and biscuits for a shock.'

Or for anything else, Ian thought. At least according to your average Brit. A cup of tea, a sit down and a sweet biscuit: the empire had been founded on that principle, hadn't it?

And he'd not dared to look at the phone again. Instinctively, he'd slipped it into his jacket pocket before he'd opened the door and he'd failed to mention it when the police arrived. Failed to mention it again when they'd gone through his house, looking for clues, or whatever it was they did. Not mentioned it when Tess and Vinod had talked to him. Not spoken of it when he'd told the neighbour he wanted to go home and she had fussed around, offering to cook him some dinner and inviting him back for a breakfast he knew he'd never eat, even if he accepted.

He took it out now, Kat's little mobile in its bright pink case, and stared at it intently. There had been no further message and when he tried to send a return text it just bounced back.

It wasn't meant to be like this, Ian though desperately. Something had gone seriously awry. Something had . . .

What?

He lay down on the still rumpled bed, his face resting against Kat's pillow, her phone in his hand and closed his eyes. Despite everything, or perhaps because he could no longer bear to be conscious of it, Ian Marsh fell asleep.

TWENTY-EIGHT

'It's a life skill,' Harry had said. 'You may never get to like it, but it's a useful thing to be able to do.'

And so they had found Patrick a driving instructor and he had embarked on the acquisition of this essential ability. And Harry had been right; he didn't like it. Two driving instructors later, Patrick had changed his mind. He knew he would never be a natural driver, but he was at least gaining a degree of competence.

The first instructor had enthused that 'boys of your age always get it quickly; most pass first time.'

Three lessons in and Patrick had already undermined his faith.

The second had been patient enough, at first, but had also had expectations that Patrick knew he couldn't meet – conversational ones this time. Constant questions about potential girlfriends and ambitions and pop music completely flummoxed him. He wasn't much good at casual conversation at the best of times, even with people he knew well, and trying to have in-depth conversations about bands that Patrick didn't know or girlfriends that he didn't have while trying to remember what gear he was supposed to be in or which side of the steering wheel the indicator switch was on had just reinforced Harry's prediction that he might not like driving.

The third instructor had been different. She was a middle-aged lady in tweed skirt, sensible shoes and with a penchant for lavender cardigans. Harry had been very doubtful, but Patrick figured she couldn't be any worse than the first two. He would happily have given up and so far as he was concerned, this was his last shot. He told her that at the start of the first lesson, knowing he sounded defensive and probably brattish, but was frankly past caring what she might think of him.

'I'm just really bad at it,' he said. 'Everyone tells me I should be good at it. Apparently boys of my age always pass first time or something.'

She had laughed at that. 'Really? That's the first I've heard. Let's just see what you *can* do, shall we, then we'll talk about the best way for me to help you do it better.'

Patrick had stared at her, then realized that he was being rude and looked away, but it had been the start of better times so far as the driving was concerned. She had questioned him gently and calmly about what he liked to do with his time, made no assumptions, not tried to be some kind of pseudo teenager, and finally sorted out how to get him to remember which was his right and left hand.

'I'm dyslexic,' he told her almost apologetically. 'Dyspraxic too. That means—'

'You find it hard to orientate yourself physically and sometimes you get left and right mixed up or you transpose whole physical spaces. And you are maybe a bit clumsy at times.'

Patrick nodded.

'My granddaughter has similar issues,' she said. 'Patrick, which hand do you draw with?'

He held up his right.

'So your drawing hand is your right hand. If I say turn right, then you turn in the direction of your drawing hand, OK?'

It was such a small thing, but it made an enormous difference. When he finally confided that he didn't know when to change gear, she encouraged him to listen to the engine, to hear the engine in the same way he'd hear music, with an underlying rhythm and a changing tone. More than that, she was totally unfazed if Patrick chose not to speak. Few people, Patrick thought, could really deal with silence and it was a relief to find someone that didn't insist on constant conversation when he was trying to focus on getting his hands, feet and brain all pointing in the same direction.

The upshot was that he was making progress and she was even talking about booking him in for his test. When he felt ready – which, he told himself, would not be for a while yet.

'The best preparation,' she said, 'is for me to get a friend of mine, another instructor, to take you out just as if it was a driving test. I'll sit in the back, but I won't say anything. When you can cope with that, then we'll think about the test properly. You're a good little driver, Patrick. You just need to believe that enough to cope when I'm not there.'

They ended the Thursday morning lessons just outside the university so Patrick could get straight to his lecture.

'Are you enjoying it any better?' she asked him.

'Not really, but I'll stick with it, see what happens. And this is just my foundation year, so I suppose it's all about finding out what I do and don't like.'

'You'll be staying here for your degree?'

'I think so. I know everyone says you should leave home and stuff, but I'm not sure I'm ready for that.'

'Some people fly the nest early,' she said. 'I did, but I think generalizations are terribly overrated.'

Patrick smiled at her and then got out of the car and fished his bag from behind the seat.

'Less to carry today,' she remarked.

Patrick flushed. 'I left all the stuff I didn't need at home,' he said. 'I guess I don't need the "just in case" stuff so much after all.'

She just nodded and Patrick wondered what she really thought about him. He had the awful suspicion that his driving instructor actually understood a lot more about him that he would have liked.

Hitching his bag on to his shoulder, Patrick started off round the corner to his entrance. He found that he was looking out for Gregory and slightly disappointed not to see him – though, he told himself, there was absolutely no reason why the man should have been there. He had thought long and hard about why he liked Gregory so much. Was it because the older man inhabited a world Patrick had only glimpsed; one that was exciting and alien?

That was inevitably part of it, he had decided, but certainly not a big part. On the whole Patrick had no desire to see any more of that world. He was certainly no proto maverick, not about to run off and join the army or the foreign legion or whatever people like Gregory did when they were Patrick's age. He decided in the end that the appeal was that he and Gregory were oddly alike. They both had difficulty in navigating the ordinary, basic stuff that most people took for granted. They both felt they were on the outside of things, like watching the rest of the world through a plate-glass window. People on the other side of that window waved and encouraged them to come over to their side, but Patrick – and he felt Gregory too – never could seem to find the door.

TWENTY-NINE

Tess and Vinod arrived half an hour late for their meeting. Despite the satnav, they had become confused in the narrow lanes and had to back track twice. The uniformed officer leaning against his car seemed merely amused by their apologies.

'It's tricky round here,' he said, his accent seeming both round and flat to Tess's ears. 'You got to know the roads.'

The car had tipped on to its side in the ditch. The driver's side front tyre was shredded and skid marks on the road revealed Kat's fight for control.

'Blow out?' Vin asked.

'Mebbe. But I reckon not and the CSI would seem to agree with me.'

'What then?'

'Mun took a pot shot at 'er,' the officer said.

It took a moment for Tess to translate. 'Someone shot her tyre?'

'Surely looks that way. Doubt she was going fast round that bend, not if she knew the road. She'd ha slowed and took it careful, but a tyre gone and even at a reasonable kind o' speed she'd have left the road.'

'They've found the bullet?'

'What was left of it. Found it this mornin', figured I'd tell you when you got here, seein' as it was new information.'

Tess looked around her, trying to figure out where such a shot might have been taken from. The landscape was flat and low lying. Hedgerows divided fields, the odd tall tree breaking the rhythm. She looked down at the skid marks and the direction of travel. Vin was just a breath ahead of her.

'That oak over there?'

'That's the way I figure it. Got a team coming along in a bit to take a look-see. You want to wait around or come back down after you've talked to the family?'

'We'll come back,' Tess said. She crouched down to look at the ruined tyre. It would have been a difficult shot, she thought. And somehow this latest revelation made the whole thing even more sinister. She had checked in with the team earlier that morning: so far there had been no contact, no demands, only two calls logged to Ian Marsh. One had been her own call to him the night before and one made by Kat's uncle just after.

She peered into the car, noting the car seat in the back of the small, four-door saloon. The driver's door and rear passenger door were both ajar.

'The doors were open when the car was found?'

'They were; one of the local farmers admits to fully opening the front door, just to check there was no one inside, but he reckons they were both ajar when he got here. We got his fingerprints and hers. The mother's. Got them from the uncle's place. There's no more to be had on the door handle. Wore gloves, I suppose, whoever took her and the babby.'

Tess nodded. 'When are the CSI team due?'

'Another hour, I reckon. I'm hanging on here. You get off and talk to the family and I'll give you a bell when they get here.'

Tess nodded, thanked him and when Vinod had asked for better directions for getting them to their next destination, they left.

'Hell of a shot,' Vinod said, echoing Tess's earlier thoughts. 'And why no ransom demand? Why no more communications? I don't get it, Tess.'

'Neither do I. I've got a very bad feeling about this – I mean over and above the fact that a mother and child are missing and some poor bugger's already dead. It feels all . . . screwed up.'

He nodded. They had come to a junction. The satnav told them to go left; local knowledge to the right. Shrugging, Vin ignored the satnav. 'It's a bit flat round here,' he said. 'We took my sister's kids to Great Yarmouth one time and I thought Norfolk was flat, but this seems like it was ironed.'

A couple of miles on and he turned into a wide farm gate and up a short gravel drive. 'This would be it,' he said. 'Ready?'

To meet grieving family? Tess thought. Never. But the door had already opened and a pale woman with soft grey hair stood on the threshold. Here we go again, Tess thought. More pain, more grief and the thought nagged at her that in truth it had only just begun.

THIRTY

K at had no notion of what time it was. She tried to work it out. She was hungry and so was Desi and they'd both slept for a while, but she wasn't certain if that meant that night had passed or if they were now into another day. She'd heard no sound outside of their cell for some time now. Had no sense that there was anyone nearby. Sometimes, straining her ears, she thought she heard the sound of water and once, from very far off, the sound of a train.

Had they been left alone?

She changed Desiree and gave her more water and one of the sandwiches. She ate the second. She was still hungry, but cautioned herself that she must make their small supply of food last. Desi couldn't go without, but she could. She was more worried about the water. Surely they, whoever they were, would come back, would not just leave them there? Kat sought comfort from the fact that they had been given food and supplies already. That was a good sign, wasn't it?

'Go home?' Desi said hopefully. 'Car?'

'We'll go in the car soon,' Kat promised.

Desi got up and toddled off, evidently looking for something to play with now she was up. She stopped at the edge of the faint circle of light shed by the lamp, and turned and looked at her mother as though expecting her to do something about it. Why were they in the dark, where were her toys? Why were they here?

Desiree was too young to elucidate all of the questions Kat saw in her expression, but they nevertheless filled her with despair.

What if the light went out, if the batteries failed? What if they were left in the dark, without food, without water, without . . .

No, she told herself sternly. She would not be without hope. She had to keep that alive, otherwise she'd never keep herself and her child alive. She had to believe that someone would come to bring them more food and drink and she had to believe that someone would come and find them.

Kat got to her feet and took Desi's hand, picking up the lantern in her other and together they patrolled and examined their confines.

Wooden walls, Kat realized. But thick and solid. Experimentally, she kicked hard at one of them and got nothing for her trouble but a throbbing foot. A wooden floor. She felt along the join between floor and wall. A strip of wood sealed the gap between. She lifted the lantern high, but could not see the top of the walls surrounding them. The battery lamp supplied just enough light to illuminate the two of them and a small circle. There just wasn't sufficient strength to see much above Kat's outstretched arm when she held the light above their heads.

Desi didn't like being left in the dark down below. She wittered and clung to her mother's leg.

'It's OK, baby,' Kat soothed. She lifted the little girl into her arms and continued with her pacing, trying to get some sense in her mind of how much space they had, or if they were fully enclosed, above as well as below. She got the odd sense that there was no ceiling on their effective box. That the ceiling was high.

Their brief journey ended once more by the door. She could barely feel the gap and could only just make out where it was when she held the light very close. But again, when they had passed the far corner, where the chemical toilet had been positioned, there had been that small sense of air moving. Of a draft, or at least a change in pressure.

She sat down on the mattress again and searched once more through the bag that had been left, laying everything out on the floor. Assessing how long she could make it last.

Desi, of course, spotted the chocolate and Kat allowed her a couple of squares.

Nappies, wet wipes, three packs of sandwiches left, now they had eaten one. Bottled water, three apples. Four assorted bars of chocolate. And batteries. For a moment Kat forgot her rage and thanked whoever it was for the gift of light.

Then her heart sank again. There was so little really. She could eke it out, but Desi had to be fed, cared for and Kat was suddenly afraid that no one would be coming back. The stuff in the bag had a hurried, unplanned, ad hoc look to it. As though someone had rushed around, grabbing stuff off the shelves and shoving it into a bag without much planning or thought. She examined the packaging more closely, looking for brand names and price tags. She didn't recognize the logo on the sandwich wrappers and the price labels were white, generic, applied by one of those pricing guns Kat had seen shop assistants using in smaller shops that didn't bar-code everything.

'A garage, maybe,' she mused aloud. 'What do you think, Desi? Does it tell us where we might be?'

Did it tell her anything about the men who had snatched them?

She put their little stash of belongings back into the black plastic bag and tied the neck – both to stop the toddler from treating it as a toy and also to protect it from chocolate scavenging. She took a closer look at the mattress and the blankets and the clothes they had been given.

The mattress was old, springs working their way through in places. But it was clean and didn't smell. The blankets were also old with small holes here and there. They looked like the camping blankets her parents had used when she was a little kid. Those had been green and khaki, warm, slightly coarse and bought from the old army and navy store, and these looked the same. They'd obviously seen a good deal of use.

Her nightdress must have belonged to a much larger person than Kat. It hung on her and reached her ankles, and it too was well worn, a brushed cotton dotted with tiny flowers, the sort of thing Kat's Nan had years ago. Desiree's pyjamas were likewise brushed and warm, and a bit big for her, but they were clean and ironed and, when Kat sniffed at them, she could still catch the scent of wash powder and floral softener.

Where had their own clothes gone? Kat hadn't thought to look for them before, but she did now, lifting the lantern and examining the floor where she had thrown her jeans and Desi's wet tights. They were gone. When had they been taken? When the bag had been left? When the photo flash had gone off and blinded her? No, that had been before she had changed her clothes.

'Sing.' Desiree demanded and Kat obliged, singing every nursery rhyme she could think of, clapping and playing pat-a-cake and Incy Wincy Spider. Making her baby laugh despite everything.

And as she played, the thought began to grow. Someone had planned this, obviously. Someone had found this place, wherever it was, to hold them in. Someone cruel and in control had brought Kat and her baby here. But someone had felt bad about it too. The food, maybe even the mattress and the clothes. Had they been part of the original preparation? Increasingly, Kat didn't think they had. She believed – hoped – that it was because someone had wanted to help her and Desi. Someone wanted to give them a fighting chance. Kat clung to that thought, that idea. We've got to get out of here, she told herself as she patted Desiree's little palms for the umpteenth time. I'm not going to let my child die.

THIRTY-ONE

'Hello, Billy,' Gregory said. 'Long time no see.'

The man called Billy tensed as he heard the familiar voice and then did a stupid thing. He decided to run, taking off across the yard as though the Devil himself was in pursuit.

He managed half a dozen paces before Gregory brought him down. 'Something wrong, Billy. I thought you'd be happier to see me.'

He dragged the man to his feet and back into the poky little office he had been heading towards before Gregory had scared the sense out of him.

'I don't know nothing.'

'You don't know what I'm asking yet.'

'I still don't know nothing.'

Nathan followed them inside and locked the door. The first employees weren't due for another half-hour or so, but there was no telling when someone might decide to get in early. Even if they worked for a scrote like Billy.

'I don't have to tell you nothing. I've got people coming. I'm a respectable businessman, you know.'

Nathan laughed softly. 'Sit down, Billy,' he said.

Gregory eased him into a chair and stood back, looking at Billy Harding. 'So, you've taken over from the old man,' he said.

'I'm straight now. He retired, handed the business over. You got no call to be coming here like—'

'We just want some information,' Nathan said. 'Then we'll be on our way. Vanish from your life as though we'd never been.'

Billy stared at him. 'Who the hell are you?'

Nathan perched on the edge of Billy's desk and glanced around at the dusty shelves, the stacked folders and the slightly cleaner, clearer desk opposite with a computer on top that was obviously the domain of whoever did the actual work while Billy 'managed'. 'Still in the removals business then?'

'I run a legitimate show. No funny business now.'

'Apart from the odd overseas consignment,' Nathan said.

'No. I don't get involved in any of that. Not now.'

'Ah, I was forgetting. The last time didn't go so well for you, did it? Two men dead and you in the hospital for, what was it, four, five months?'

Billy tore his gaze from Nathan and focused on Gregory as though he suddenly decided that might be a safer option. 'Tell your friend. I know nothing. I do nothing. Not now.'

'And as long as you keep it that way, we won't be bothering you,' Nathan assured him. Billy refused to look comforted. 'We just want to find someone. A woman. Someone you used to know, before you went straight and legit and all that.'

'I don't know any—'

'Mae Tourino. Or you might have known her as Nancy Todd or even Michelle Williamson, or maybe even another name. She's not known for her consistency.'

Billy was shaking his head violently. Gregory stopped him, holding on to his scalp, twining his fingers into the man's gelled hair and keeping him still. 'You're sweating and sticky, Billy. That's not very pleasant, you know.'

Nathan slipped of the desk and put a hand into his pocket. Billy strained to get away, as far away as possible from whatever he was about to produce. His relief on seeing just a photograph was almost comic, Gregory thought.

'This woman,' Nathan said. 'The woman in red. You've done business with her. I know that. I'd like to find her, Billy.'

Billy Harding tried hard to shake his head again, but Gregory's hold was too strong.

'She'll kill me.'

'She isn't here. We are. What's the greater threat?'

'I don't know where she is. I just know where she was.'

'Where and when?'

'She did a job for Franks, that's all I know. Two, three months ago. Then she dropped off the face of the earth. He's been after her, came looking here. He don't know where she is neither.'

Nathan glanced at Gregory. 'Do you think our friend here is scared enough to be telling something close to the truth?'

'I think so,' Gregory said. 'You want me to make sure?'

'Might as well. Though hold off a moment.'

Nathan withdrew another picture from his pocket and showed it to Billy. 'Look,' he said. 'See this, Billy.'

The sound Billy made assured Nathan that he was paying full attention. 'Someone did this, Billy, and the man took a long time to die. But I can do worse. I can make it last longer. Think about that; think about how much it's going to hurt if I find out you're lying and have to come back.'

'I don't know his name,' Billy Harding yelped. Nathan's gazed shifted briefly to meet Gregory's.

'So what *do* you know, Billy?'

Billy's shaking had turned violent now. He struggled and whined and tried his damnedest to get away. Gregory continued to hold him tight. Thoughtfully, Gregory took one of Billy's hands. 'Choose a finger, Billy. Which one do you use the least?'

'I told you. I don't know. I telled you all I know. Franks will know. Franks knows who he is and what he done.'

Gregory dropped him abruptly. 'As we say, Billy, we can always come back,' he said. 'If you haven't been straight with us.'

'True, we can always come back,' Nathan agreed.

They left then, Billy Harding a trembling wreck in his office, waiting for his employees to arrive and not quite believing he had got off so lightly this time.

THIRTY-TWO

'**D**id Katherine seem unhappy or worried about anything?' It was a standard question but was met with bewildered looks.

'We'd had a lovely weekend,' her aunt said. 'It was such a long time since we were all able to catch up.'

'It was a family wedding, I understand?'

'Yes. A cousin. Not a close cousin, but you know . . . we thought it would be a good opportunity to get everyone here. Some of the older relatives, well, you don't know if . . . you know . . . It might be the last time and . . . there was little

Desiree. It was the first chance to see her properly for a lot of
people. Kat took such a long time to settle down . . .'
    'Mum, she's only thirty-seven. It's not that old these days.'
    'It was still a surprise,' Aunt Christina said. 'She was always
so set on her career. We never thought she'd find a man she
wanted to stay at home for.'
    'I think she plans on going back to work,' her cousin objected.
    'If she comes back.' It was the first time the uncle had spoken
and the whole party fell silent and turned to look at him.
    'Bert, you can't say a thing like that. You can't!'
    'But I'm right, aren't I?' he challenged. 'The chances of getting
either of them back unharmed are practically nil.'
    'It's hard to say,' Tess placated. 'Each event, each kidnapping
is so very different.'
    'I'm talking statistics here. People don't come back.'
    Tess looked at Vinod, wondering how best to respond to Bert's
statement. She wanted to argue, but it was a difficult thing to
fight against. He was right, of course, but most families clung
to the idea that they and their loved ones would beat the odds.
Especially this early in an investigation.
    'You thought she'd take a different route away from here,'
Vinod asked. 'Why was that?'
    'Because that's what I always tell her to do. It's logical.'
    'Kat doesn't like being told what to do,' his wife stated. 'And
maybe if we'd realized that they'd have found her car a bit sooner.
Instead, you were so bloody certain she'd have been a good girl
and listened to her uncle—'
    'And if she had listened to me, stuck to the busier routes, she
and that baby might still be with us. They might have made it
home. Instead of which—'
    'You always have to be right, don't you?'
    'Please,' Tess almost shouted. 'This is helping no one.'
    Aunt and uncle had the grace to look shamefaced. 'You asked
if she had any worries,' Kat's cousin said. 'Do you think she
did? Do you think she'd been threatened?'
    'We've nothing to indicate that,' Tess admitted. 'But I
just wondered if, being among her family, she might have
mentioned something. Professor Marsh says he can think of
nothing—'

'Professor Marsh,' the uncle snorted. 'And when's he likely to have noticed anything?'

'Bert. Please!'

'You don't like Professor Marsh?' Vin asked.

'I don't dislike him. I've just got no time for academics in their ivory towers, that's all.'

'How did they meet?' Tess asked.

'Kat worked in HR at the university. I'm not sure how exactly they got together, but I know they met there. It's funny,' the aunt went on, 'but he was so unlike anyone she'd ever dated before. She'd always gone for the flashy ones, you know.'

'And you think they've been happy together?'

Christina smiled. 'Oh yes. He loves her and she loves him and there's little Desiree now.' Her lips trembled and her eyes filled with tears. 'She's just a baby. Just a baby girl.'

They left soon after that, Tess feeling there was nothing to be gained from more prodding and poking at their collective pain.

'What do you make of all that?' Vin asked.

'Oh, I think every family has an Uncle Bert,' she said. 'I don't get the impression any of them really took to Ian Marsh, but they accepted him because he was Katherine's choice. I don't think we can read anything else into it.'

Vin nodded. 'Back to the crash site?'

'May as well. Hopefully the CSI will have arrived and have something useful to tell us. Anything positive would be welcome right now. Then we ring the boss and await further instructions.'

'And find somewhere to get some lunch,' Vinod said. 'I'm starved.'

Jaz had decided to take a lateral approach to her search and had called up all unusual abductions happening in the past six months. Many she had discounted straight away – parents taking children abroad figured heavily, but didn't seem relevant, unless something really changed and they suddenly had reason to believe that Kat Marsh had run off with her little girl.

She ran a search both of official files and of the broader Internet and media reports, knowing that sometimes a different perspective could throw up interesting results. Jaz was acutely aware that her own profession was trained to see incidents in a particular way, your average journalist in quite another – and don't get her started on social media. By midday she had about a dozen reports tagged for further inspection.

Meanwhile, her colleagues had been looking for instances where monofilament had been used either as a murder weapon or as a means of torturing or restraining a victim. Jaz would have made bets on the number being low, but by lunchtime, they too had a clutch of examples and one in particular that seemed to merit a further look.

DCI Branch had arranged for everyone actually in the building to come and update him at twelve-thirty and so they gathered in the conference room. Branch put Tess on speaker phone. The line was bad. She was standing in the middle of a field, she said. And the rain had started an hour before, swept across the open country on a sharp wind.

'CSI found a slug in the engine block. It had gone through the tyre and deflected upward into the vehicle. It's pretty bashed up but it's gone to ballistics. There's what might be some traces of the shooter in the tree across the road from the bend where she went off the road, but nothing very conclusive. However, it looks as though someone knew she'd come this way, waited for her and blew out the tyre.'

'You've spoken to the family?'

'Yes, but apart from the fact that the uncle didn't really approve of Ian Marsh, there's nothing more to tell there.'

'Any reason for the dislike?'

'He doesn't like academics. Look, unless you've got anything else for us to do, we'll grab something to eat and we can be back for the main briefing.'

'Do that,' Branch said.

He looked out at the handful of officers gathered in the conference room. 'Any thoughts?'

There was a moment of silence, then DC Fields spoke up. She had been working with Jaz on the background search and had come up with the other murder. 'It seems like overkill,' she said. 'And I don't mean just the tyre being shot out. It seems like someone wants to get someone else's attention.'

'Except there's been no follow up,' Branch said. 'No threats, apart from the implicit one in the photograph. No demands.'

'Perhaps we're not the ones that are supposed to hear,' Jaz said quietly. 'Look, I'm not sure what I mean, but maybe there's a message in all this that's not meant for us. Someone is seeing it and reading it loud and clear. To someone this silence is really a shout.'

Branch nodded again. 'You could be right there,' he said. 'And you've found something that makes you certain of it?'

Perceptive, Jaz thought. Not bad looking either. She found herself sneaking a look at his ring finger. It was bare, but, she reminded herself, that didn't always mean anything.

'We've come up with a couple of connections, or possible connections,' she said. 'But I think we'd like a bit more time making sure these aren't just wild geese before we share.'

Branch raised an eyebrow and then looked from Jaz to his more familiar colleague, DC Fields. She nodded. 'Something's coming together,' she said. 'But the pattern isn't showing yet. We'll have something worthwhile by the briefing or we'll have moved on.'

'We should have pushed him further,' Gregory said. 'You know he'll be on the phone to Franks by now.'

'Of course he will. It doesn't matter. I'm not keen on taking Bernie Franks by surprise anyway; he tends to overreact.' Nathan laughed briefly; mirthlessly. 'I doubt your friend Billy knew much more. I didn't want to overplay our hand. He thought we'd come to ask him about the dead man as well as Mae; if we'd carried on he'd soon have realized we didn't know shit.'

Gregory nodded, conceding the point. 'So, we go and see Mr Bernie Franks,' he said. 'You ever do any work for him?'

Nathan laughed as though the idea was absurd. 'You think Clay would have let me lower myself to that?' he said. 'Clay was fussy about what I did. Annie too.'

'So, no lowlifes below a certain pay grade,' Gregory said. 'None of your ordinary, common criminals. Didn't stop him putting you both in the line of fire though, did it?'

Nathan shook his head. 'We did what we did. He had us well trained.'

Gregory sensed that the conversation was over. Nathan was

still oddly sensitive about his erstwhile guardian. Had he cared about Clay, he wondered? He figured it was a difficult question and that Nathan himself probably didn't know the answer to it. Clay had been in *loco parentis* for both Annie and Nathan since they were just kids. That had to count for something.

'How did you meet Mae?' he asked.

'Would you believe at an embassy party? Clay had taken us with him, me and Annie. He often did, liked to show us the sights, and I think he wanted us to be prepared for the roles he'd got planned. Clay was ambitious for us. Anyway, I was seventeen and she was bloody gorgeous. Gregory, I was smitten and Clay knew it. He paid her to look after me for a few days.'

'Seriously?'

'Seriously. Rome,' he added. 'It was Rome. I'm guessing she must have been, what, forty? Gregory, I think I was a little bit . . .'

'In love?' Gregory asked.

Nathan shook his head. 'I don't think I've ever been in love,' he said. 'I watch other people, try to understand what they feel and sometimes, like those few days with Mae, I think I get close. Then I get bored. I lose interest and it's like someone flicked a switch, turned the feeling off. It's not meant to be like that, is it?'

'I don't think so,' Gregory said. 'I'm not sure I'm the best person to ask.' He hesitated, then said, 'But there are people you care about. People like Annie. Like the prof and his family.'

'You see, I think that's where you're wrong, or at least that's where *I'm* wrong. Annie, yes. I think I do love Annie. We shared such a lot over the years. Went through so much loss together and it's like we're locked together, tied up by memories and actions and just being around, you know. But the rest? No, it's not love, Gregory; it's possession, same as it was with Clay. Clay drew people into his charmed circle, he claimed them, made them his own and would do anything to protect them – so long as he didn't get bored or they didn't step over some invisible line. I don't think I've got an invisible line, but I'm not going to rule the possibility out. But I know I do the same thing as Clay. I mark people as mine, for whatever reason, and I protect them, do all I can to keep them safe, because . . . because I've claimed them.'

'Sounds cold,' Gregory said. 'I'm not sure you're that cold.'

Nathan thought about it. 'I hope not,' he said. 'But I suspect I am. I suspect I substitute possession for love – but, you know, I suspect there are a lot of people out there doing exactly the same thing. They make believe they love when the truth is they only possess. They say, "You're my wife, my daughter, my son. You're not doing x or behaving like y because that's not what a child of mine does."'

'You don't like people very much, do you?'

Nathan was silent for a moment, then he said, 'When I was fourteen years old, a group of men broke into our house. They shot my father and tortured my mother. Then they raped her. I came home and walked into the middle of it. Thankfully, they were too busy to hear me come in. I took one of the guns from my father's cabinet and I walked into the room and I shot three of them before they even knew I was there. The fourth man . . . Anyway, Clay found me later, and he saw what I'd done, and he understood. He took me under his wing, as they say. I owed him for that. But I paid my debts.'

Gregory stared out of the car window watching the rain fall across grey fields. It was one of the few times Nathan had talked about his youth. He found himself thinking about Patrick and the difference between the two. Life had shut doors on both of them in different ways, but Patrick seemed to have coped by feeling *more* than was normal. Nathan had decided to feel less.

Gregory's own parents had been a mystery to him, just as he had been a mystery to them. They'd been good, honest, ordinary people, hard working if a little unimaginative. His mother had understood from very early on that Gregory was different. His path would be his own to tread and she would probably never understand it. So she'd done all she could to deal with the parts of his life she could control: made sure he had the best education she could manage, always turned up to parents' evenings and provided him with whatever kit he needed, even though that strained the family finances. He'd always been well fed and clothed, cared for, though not understood. He bore her no resentment for that; he'd not been the child she had expected to have. Neither did he resent the fact that when he'd announced, at seventeen, that he wanted to join the army, she'd been unable to hide her relief.

They'd kept in touch for a while, but, like his teachers and his school friends, such as they were, it was as though they'd just been his caretakers until he could take care of himself.

It was sad, he thought. She'd have made a good mother, had she had the right child.

'I met Mae in Singapore,' he said. 'Michelle, she was then. Turned up on the arm of some Soviet big wig. It was just after the wall came down. Gorbachev was making eyes at Maggie Thatcher and the Cold War was in its last throes. So that was before you got your mucky paws on her.'

'My paws were never mucky.'

'Unlike you, I never got close. I think we exchanged three words. But she was like the rest of us. A player. Everywhere you looked, there was Mae, blonde, brunette, redhead. Always on the move, always with an eye for the next big thing. Age is a cruel thing, Nathan. Age and time.'

Nathan laughed. 'Are you getting sentimental?'

'Only occasionally. Nostalgic, maybe. Ever think the world is too complicated now? I find myself craving simpler times, when I had a fair idea of what I was against and who I'd have to kill to keep the status quo.'

'It was never simple,' Nathan said. 'Never black and white, not really. It was always Technicolor messy.'

Maybe he was right, Gregory thought. Outside the day was still a misty grey, damp and cheerless, but the fields were gone now and the road was widening out. Grey buildings replaced faded, wintry trees. They'd spend the night in one of the chain hotels where no one remembered anyone and then move on again. Tomorrow, they'd be seeing Bernie Franks and, hopefully, another piece of the puzzle would be joined.

He thought about Katherine Marsh and her child, wondering again what was really going on and where they were tonight.

THIRTY-THREE

I t was the silence that was so oppressive, Kat thought. Church
Lane had been quiet, with thick walls keeping what little
country noise there was at bay, and for a while she had found
that oppressive too. But then she had grown used to the creaks
and groans of old timbers, the cry of the fox across the fields, and
sometimes an owl, off hunting in the twilight. She had learned
to map the noises and understand them and the sense of isolation
had diminished as a result.

She had been glad, though, when they'd moved back to her
old home. She liked to hear the sounds of the occasional car in
the street and her neighbours in the garden. It wasn't intrusive
– no loud music or screaming kids; it wasn't that kind of street.
But it was familiar and ordinary and kind of cosy.

Sitting now on the old mattress, her child sleeping at her side,
Kat found she was straining to hear . . . anything. She'd identified the sound of water – occasional and unclear, lapping rather
than running or flowing – and the sound of a far-off train. Once,
she thought she had heard a car door slam, but there had been
no sound of an engine, so she was no longer sure. She listened
for the sound of someone coming back. Willed it and feared it
and couldn't decide which was worse; that her abductors would
return or that they wouldn't. That she'd be left alone with Desi
and they would both die here, slowly starve. She was rationing
the food and water, ensuring Daisy drank and ate, but keeping
her own intake to a minimum. She had thought about just not
eating or drinking, but reason had prevailed. If she collapsed,
what would her daughter do?

She tried not to think what would happen if no one came and
brought them more supplies. The thought of her child, hungry
and thirsty, tore at her; the thought of Desiree dying of hunger
or thirst was one she kept pushing determinedly away – but it
kept returning, haunting her.

Desi's breathing was soft and even and Kat rose carefully,
took the lantern and walked the perimeter of their cell once
more. The batteries were going, she noted. She had two more
sets, but that was all. As she had done already several times,
she glanced back to make sure her child was still sleeping and
then turned off the light. The darkness closed around her, like
some solid thing.

Kat began to count. She knew it would take her eyes time
to adjust to the dark. Would take time to tell if the darkness
was as entire and thick as it first seemed. If she could see
anything . . . didn't that mean that light might be seeping in
from somewhere?

Three times she had tried this same thing. Turned out the light.
Counted to fifty and then one hundred, waiting for a glimmer
– of light, of hope, of anything.

Three times there had been nothing. Only the heavy, pervasive
black.

Kat looked up, hardly daring to believe. It was so slight she
thought she might be mistaken. But no, it was there. High up
there was a tiny hint of light – a window, maybe?

Kat's heart beat very fast. She moved back a step or two,
moved to the side, shifted forward slowly, trying to get a sense
of where the light was coming from and how high up it might
be. She realized, abruptly, that this meant there was no roof
to their cell. That the light was coming from a window in a
wall, outside of this box they had been forced into. If she could
climb up . . .

Desiree woke and began to whine, scared by the sudden dark.
Kat switched the lantern back on.

Could she get out? How high were the wooden walls? Higher
than she could reach, she knew that. Even standing on the chemical toilet, she'd been unable to touch the top.

But there was light, Kat thought. There was a window. She
had no idea how she might make her way out, even less how
she'd get Desiree out, but even so, it was a tiny hope.

Kat picked up her little girl and hugged her tight, soothing
her. There had to be a way. She was not going to just stay here
and die.

THIRTY-FOUR

Thursday lunchtime and Jaz and her colleague returned to their little cubby hole of an office and shared sandwiches and chocolate and discussed what they had. The two other officers that had worked with them for part of the morning had been dragged off, one to help with the house-to-house enquiries and one to help hold the line against the sudden rush of reporters who had invaded the professor's quiet street. There had been little in the way of an official statement yet, but Jaz knew that something as big as this would never be kept quiet for long and the link with the earlier murder would be irresistible. The papers and television news would be full of it for a few days. A quick Internet search told her that it had already gone international.

'If he's got any sense he'll move out,' Fields said.

'And what if the kidnappers call?'

'Then it'll go straight to call divert. We'll pick up.'

'True, but . . . I don't know. I think if I was him I might want to be there. I wouldn't want to be on my own, but leaving would feel like running away, somehow, or like deserting them, you know?'

Fields nodded. 'I see what you mean. Hope neither of us ever have to find out what we'd actually do,' she said. 'Right, what have you got? You show me yours and I'll trade mine.'

We both sound far too cheery, Jaz thought guiltily, but the truth was this was the part of the work she loved doing. 'You first.'

'Well, I've got this,' Susan Fields said. 'But I don't know if it's relevant. I did a search for the use of monofilament, either as a murder weapon or associated with and there are a few instances where fishing twine or similar has been used to tie someone up, usually just because it was available. Mostly, the killings were impulsive. I think it's fair to assume there was some planning in this one – even if they went after the wrong man, and I think that's something we've got to think about seeing as how the professor and his family have been targeted again.'

Jaz nodded. 'OK, so anything that might link more directly?'

Her colleague hesitated. 'I don't know, she said. 'It's a bit far-fetched, maybe, but . . . Look, I'll just show you the crime-scene photos and you can tell me what you think.'

She brought up two images on to the twin screens in front of her. One was familiar; the kitchen at Church Lane and the body of the estate agent hanging from the tie beam. Jaz winced, unable completely to control the revulsion she felt. She looked at the second picture. It seemed to be an old factory or ware-house of some kind. The body had been hoisted up higher this time, on to some kind of gantry, the arms bound, the body stripped to the waist, the same deep marks on the torso.

No rope, Jaz noted, but apart from that the similarities were striking.

'This looks old,' she said. 'It's not a digital image.'

'No, but there's been a drive to put old case files on the system, going back through the nineties, and this is one of those. We're lucky. It might have taken an age to trawl through the paper files, though we may still have to do that.'

'So, who died and who did it?'

'Well that's the thing. I didn't find this on the system. It's not a police file. I did the same kind of lateral search you're doing because, I figured, it would be the kind of thing the media would love if they picked up on it, but this is a bit of an oddity. It was taken in East Berlin in 1994, so just a few years after the wall came down and reconstruction was just getting under way. There were a lot of empty warehouses; a lot of deserted industrial buildings. Contractors moved in to dismantle an old steel works and they found this.'

'And the dead man?'

'Well according to the online translator – and my very poor German – the article says he was ex Stasi.'

Jaz stared at the two pictures. 'If we can access this, then others can too,' she said. 'It could be just coincidence. I mean, this is, what, twenty years time difference?'

Susan Fields nodded. 'Like I said, it's a stretch, but . . .'

Jaz nodded, understanding what she was saying. The two scenes bore so many similarities but differences too and she thought that wasn't just because of the difference between the industrial and domestic settings. 'What's the context for the article?' she asked and from Susan Fields' grin knew she had asked the right question.

'Well this picture is from a book written in the late nineties about the reconstruction of East Berlin. There was a chapter about what happened to the Stasi records and this was included. But the picture and some of the material for the chapter came from a PhD dissertation written a few years before – the student gets a credit in the chapter heading. So I chased up the student paper and you know how it is sometimes – I chased the rabbit down the rabbit hole and found that the original source was a now defunct local news sheet. It wasn't even an official newspaper. Apparently, just before the wall came down, there was this mass movement in East Berlin, loads of these little pamphlets springing up all over the place. The Stasi would close one down, make some arrests and another one would spring up. Most were just photocopies, passed out to friends and then left wherever. This PhD student went round collecting as many as he could. He found that a few actually survived the fall of communism, like the one this picture appears in. No one came forward to claim authorship and the paper vanished completely after ninety-six. I guess there wasn't so much to protest about. Whoever he was, he called himself The Gadfly – only in German:– *die Bremse*. Gadflies bite and irritate people, apparently.'

'And the author of the PhD dissertation?'

'Well, I did manage to track her down, but she died in a railway accident a couple of years after she got her doctorate.'

'Convenient,' Jaz commented. 'And the author of the book?'

'Is still around, working as a journalist in Bremen.'

'Might be worth getting in touch,' Jaz said.

'So, what do you have?'

'Well, mine is more recent at least. I did a search for abductions that seemed out of kilter. You remember the Gilligan and Hayes thing, the two human rights lawyers who were killed a couple of months back?'

'I do, but I don't see—'

'Truthfully, neither do I. It was just on my weird list. But I did a bit of checking anyway and a familiar name came up. Gustav Clay. Wasn't he the guardian of our mysterious Mr Crow?'

'And Annie Raven,' Susan Fields agreed. 'But what's his link to Gilligan and Hayes?'

'Well, that's the thing. He's mentioned in some of the cases they dealt with. He was a diplomat of some kind, we know that, but he seems to have become a consultant after he retired. To be honest, it's all a bit vague. All I've got is the odd news report when what they did made it into the news. But like you said, once you start chasing the rabbit . . .'

'And your rabbit hole led where?'

'Well, you know how Gustav Clay's house was supposed to have been blown up because of a gas leak and the said Mr Clay was believed to have died in said explosion?'

Susan nodded.

'Well. There's a problem. On day one, because Clay was high profile, it was being looked at as a possible terrorist act. There are reports that Clay's two dogs were found in the garden, shot to death. And there's no mention of finding a body in the wreckage.'

'It might have taken a while to find him.'

'True, but by the following morning. First thing the following morning, all reports are talking about a gas leak. The dogs are suddenly killed in the explosion and their owner is found inside. There's only one reference to the dogs being shot and that's put down as being a mistake made by an inexperienced fire officer.'

'Odd mistake to have made,' Susan commented. 'Do we have a name for said fire officer?'

'We do,' Jaz said.

'Then you'd better go and talk to him. I'll hold the fort here, chase some more rabbits.'

THIRTY-FIVE

Toby Parks was off duty and a bit disturbed to find a police officer on his doorstep. He was even more disturbed to find out what she had come for.

'Look, I was probably a bit green; didn't know what I was seeing, all right? I'd only been on the job a few weeks. The explosion at that house was the biggest thing I'd attended and I got a bit carried away by my own imagination, yeah?'

'Is that what you really think? Or what they've told you to say?' Jaz challenged.

He had the grace to look uncomfortable.

'Look, I'll keep this as off the record as I can. We're looking into a murder and a kidnapping. A woman and her little girl.'

He frowned. 'How can that have anything to do with the explosion?'

'We don't know, yet. We don't know if it is, but there are links, names that have come up in both cases, so I've got to look into it. And the early newspaper reports said—'

'Said I was a stupid bugger who couldn't tell the difference between dogs that had been shot and ones that died in an explosion.'

'I'd have thought the difference was an obvious one,' Jaz suggested.

Toby sighed and flopped down in one of the big armchairs in his tiny living room. The space was dominated by a TV and a games console. Two big chairs filled most of the remaining space. He was single, Jazz guessed.

'We were first responders; got there before the police. The place was in bits and we were told there'd been no one home so far as anyone knew. The whole place was an inferno. A couple of us went round the back, just to check how far from the wood it was, make sure the fire hadn't spread and there were no outbuildings to worry about. People store some odd stuff in outbuildings; you can't be sure what you'll find. Anyway, the whole place was surrounded by this high wall and there's, like, lawn all round the house, so a natural fire break. Which was lucky. But the explosion had sent burning debris out even past the wall, so I called that in and then started round the back. And that's when I saw the dogs. Irish wolfhounds or something. Big buggers. Stone dead. One had half its head missing. The other had a hole in its chest big as a fist. So I called that in too and then got back round to the front. Me and two more fire crew were dispatched to take care of the secondary fires in the wood. The rest of the crew made a start on the house. A few minutes later two more fire trucks arrived and so did the police and an ambulance, just in case, like, and later my division manager came and looked at the dogs. It took a long time to get the fire under control and these journalists turned up, a TV news crew, and I got talking to them.'

'You'd been told to make a statement?'

He shook his head. 'No, and I got it in the neck for it later. But I'd been stood down – I mean, I'm the least experienced of the team, so I'd been put in charge of all the back-up jobs while the big boys went and played with the fire. And I just got chatting, like, and I told them about the dogs, about how it seemed, you know, a bit strange, like. And then I noticed this other police car turn up. And they came up and took charge and cleared the journos off and next thing I know my boss is calling me all sorts of idiot for talking to them and how I'd no idea what I was seeing and I should never say anything without clearing it with him first. I thought I was going to get the sack.'

'But you are certain of what you saw?'

He nodded awkwardly. 'Yeah, I'm sure. Someone shot those dogs. But look, I don't want to get involved in any of this. I've got a job I like and I want to keep it, right?'

Right, Jaz agreed. She left shortly after, Toby obviously now very uncomfortable with his revelations and regretting them. She hoped she wouldn't have to get him to repeat the story at any time; she had the sneaking suspicion he'd deny it all.

THIRTY-SIX

The evening briefing was in some ways depressing. There had still been no contact from the kidnappers of Katherine Marsh and her daughter. No real progress had been made; house-to-house enquiries had thrown up no reports of strangers in the street or unusual activity and it was, as someone commented, the sort of street where strangers stood out like a sore thumb and a lot of the residents, either older people or young parents, were around for much of the day.

The fact that Katherine's car had been shot at raised a shocked murmur among the team but wasn't immediately helpful. Jaz and Susan's digging led to speculation and debate, but everyone agreed it was hard to see how it all fitted together.

Jaz reported back on her conversation with Toby, the fire officer. 'Can you get him in to make a statement?' Branch asked.

'I can get him in,' Jaz said. 'But he's obviously been told to keep schtum and he'll now have had time to regret talking to me.'

Branch nodded. 'Well, if it becomes relevant, we'll bring some pressure to bear.'

'There is one other thing,' Jaz said, feeling somewhat deflated. 'I mean, it's not a lead, exactly, but it might be a source of information. We had all the Gilligan and Hayes stuff sent over. Officially, the investigation is still open, but there's been nothing new really since day one. But there's an ex police officer involved. A local guy.'

'Oh? Who, and how involved?' Branch asked.

'His name is Alec Friedman, was a DI. He quit a few months ago, but he was used as a consultant on the Gilligan and Hayes thing. Apparently his aunt was involved in some way – though I can't tell you how because some of the details are missing.'

'Missing? I thought you sent for all the case notes.'

'I did. Some of it has been, what do you call it, redacted.' She held up the sheets she had printed off to show him. 'Look, bits are blacked out. I phoned through to find out why, but was just told it came from above – and I don't think they meant God. Anyway, I spoke to a DI Barnes, who was involved in the Gilligan and Hayes thing. He couldn't tell me much, but did suggest I speak to this Alec Friedman.'

'Alec?' Tess said. 'I don't see . . .'

'You know him?'

'Yes. I used to know him well.'

'Then you should be the one to talk to him, I think,' Branch said. Tess nodded.

'Did DI Barnes say who authorized his involvement?' Branch asked.

Jaz grinned. 'Oh, that would have been God as well,' she said. 'Barnes said Mr Friedman was far from happy. He wanted to stay retired. There was something else he said too, or sort of said. I asked him if he'd heard of Gustav Clay and he just laughed, then he said we should ask Alec about his car accident.'

'He didn't elaborate?'

'No, he was out at a scene so I only talked to him for a few minutes, but I don't think he was happy even to do that.'

Branch frowned and nodded. 'OK,' he said. 'Well, keep on digging and maybe try to persuade DI Barnes to come over and have a chat. Now, media management. What's happening on scene?'

The meeting broke up soon after that. Tess caught up with Jaz as they were both leaving. 'This Barnes, did he say anything more about Alec? Is his name in the case notes?'

'Not that I could see, and no, like I said, he was busy on scene. He could only spare me a couple of minutes.'

'Or only wanted to.'

Jaz shrugged. 'Maybe. Isn't Alec Friedman that friend of yours who came into the office the other day?'

'He was,' Tess said, wondering now if it had been such a random coincidence as Alec had made out.

THIRTY-SEVEN

Kat's mobile phone vibrated in Ian's pocket. He took it out and stared at the screen. He pressed the button and lifted the phone to his ear. 'Hello. Kat?'

'Katherine can't come to the phone right now.'

Ian's legs turned to jelly. He dropped down into the chair, his heart thumping in his chest and his mouth suddenly dry.

'I want to speak to my wife.'

'Sorry, can't be done.'

'Why are you doing this? You promised me they'd be kept safe.'

'And so they have been. So far.'

'No. You lied. You said you'd get Kat and the baby out and I'd be joining them. You said—'

'And I kept my word. Pity you didn't do the same. Ian, you have only yourself to blame for what has happened to your wife and child. We had a deal; you reneged on that deal.'

'No. I didn't have what you wanted. I couldn't get what you wanted. I thought I'd be able to, but—'

'And that's my problem? How? A deal is a deal. You became greedy, Professor Marsh. You'd got yourself a glimpse of something and you wanted more.'

'It wasn't like that!' Ian shouted desperately. 'I couldn't . . . Look, give me a chance. A few more days, that's all I need. You can give me that.'

'Can I, Professor? Look at it from my angle. You gave me guarantees; I in turn gave others guarantees. You don't keep your end of the bargain, then neither can I, and that makes me look bad. I have a reputation, Ian. You're spoiling that for me.'

'A few more days,' Ian begged. 'I just need a few more days.'

There was a moment or two of silence as the other man considered the option and Ian allowed himself to hope. 'Forty-eight hours, Professor. Fail me and I'll have to get what compensation I can in other ways.'

'What do you mean?' Ian asked, but he thought he knew. He couldn't bear to know.

'Forty-eight hours. No more.'

The phone went dead. Ian knew it would do him no good to try and call the number back, but he tried it anyway, desperately searching through the menu for the number of the last call, finding it unknown. In a fit of sheer frustration, he hurled the phone across the room and then hurled himself after it. What if he'd broken it? What if he'd smashed this last link to his wife and child? What if . . .?

The phone in its bright pink case had hit the arm of the chair and fallen to the floor. To his profound relief, it was unharmed. Ian stared at the screen, willing it to ring again, knowing that it would not. Eventually, he put it back into his pocket and just sat, his back to the wall, his head full of terrible thoughts. He knew he had killed them, Kat and little Daisy, just as directly as if he'd plunged a knife into their hearts and twisted it and, oddly, finally acknowledging that filled him with a new resolve. There was nothing he could do for them now, so he had to move on, put all thoughts of guilt and pain aside.

The priority now was simply to save himself.

THIRTY-EIGHT

On the Friday morning Tess arrived at Naomi and Alec's flat just as they were leaving for their morning walk. 'I can go on my own,' Naomi said.

'No. No, I don't think so. If you want to talk to me, Tess, you can tag along.'

Naomi could hear the irritation in his voice, the upset still hanging on from his visit to see his old colleague earlier in the week. Naomi understood; she doubted Tess would.

'Okay,' Tess said slowly. 'Well, I don't mind tagging along. I've just got a few questions to ask you, if you don't mind.'

Beside her, Naomi felt Alec shrug. 'Ask away,' he said.

Tess waited until they had reached the promenade before beginning. Naomi paused, expecting Alec to take up his usual position on the sea wall, but much to her surprise, he came down with her to the sea's edge and Tess had no option but to follow.

'We've been talking to a DI Barnes,' she said.

'Nice for you,' Alec returned. 'He's a pleasant man.'

'You were involved in that Gilligan and Hayes thing a couple of months back, apparently.'

'Indirectly. Why?'

'Because what happened then might impact on this current kidnapping. And the murder.'

Alec shrugged. 'Well I'm sure Barnes will help in any way he can. I've resigned, you know.'

'But it makes me wonder, Alec. When you came to see me the other day, you were very interested in the murder of Anthony Palmer. Why was that? Was it really a coincidence, you suddenly turning up like that?'

Alec laughed shortly. 'Why wouldn't it be?'

'Because the last thing you were involved in, and this, it seems they are all hooked up together somehow and—'

'And when I came to visit you the other day it was genuinely just a wish to see an old friend. No one knew of the supposed connection then, did they? And I wasn't involved. My aunt was, again, indirectly . . .'

'That would be Molly Chambers. The old lady who had some killer blow his brains out on her landing.'

'Molly does have that effect on some people,' Naomi said. She knew she shouldn't have but it was just too much to resist.

'Molly Chambers, yes,' Alec said. 'She became involved because on the site where Gilligan and Hayes died in the back of that van, she happened to have some of her stuff in storage and there was a suspicion that her locker had been tampered with. Molly isn't the easiest of people to handle. I liaised, you might say.'

'Liaised. Right. So maybe you can tell me why, when we sent for the file, half of it had been, shall we say, removed.'

'I resigned,' Alec said again. 'Tess, I'm out now. I can't tell you any more.'

'Not even about the car crash you were both involved in?'

'What about it?'

'An accident? Really?'

'My brakes failed. We were on the crest of a rather nasty hill. The weather was bad. I did all the right things, took my foot off the accelerator, went down through the gears and was about to switch off the ignition when my dear aunt Molly got impatient and pulled the hand brake on. Had she waited a few seconds more, I'm sure it would all have been fine; as it was we skidded off the road and rolled three or so times down the hill.'

Alec's voice was very controlled, but Naomi could feel him shaking; he still found it so hard to talk about those last few moments before the crash. In truth, he didn't recall a lot about it, but Molly did and Molly had spared him no detail.

'We survived,' Alec said. 'There's not a lot more to tell.'

A beat of silence and then Tess tried another tack. 'What do you know about a man called Gustav Clay?'

'Career diplomat, friend of Molly's and her husband. Died a couple of months ago. Why?'

'In a gas explosion. At his house,' Tess pursued.

Alec hesitated for a moment too long. That wasn't what happened, Naomi thought. Tess would notice his hesitation.

'Presumably,' Alec said,

'Alec, what are you not telling me?'

'Tess, I'm telling you this is nothing to do with me.'

'I spoke to one of the first responders. He told me Clay's dogs had been shot and the house rigged with explosives. He was also told not to talk about it, that the official line was that this was a gas explosion.'

'I wasn't there, Tess. How the hell would I know?'

'And what about Nathan Crow, or Annie Raven?'

'Annie Raven is a photographer. I don't know Nathan Crow.'

'But you know the name?'

Alec sighed. 'Tess, no. No I don't. My only connection to any of this is an aunt and she's not even a real aunt.'

'So maybe I should go and talk to her?'

Naomi laughed. 'That, I'd like to see,' she said.

'What Naomi means is that Aunt Molly is a tough nut to crack. She'll talk to you if she wants to. If not, you don't have a cat in hell's chance of getting anything out of her. Anyway, you can't – she's not here. She's done the sensible thing and flown south for the winter.'

'Where?'

'Tess, I don't know. She sent us a postcard from Seville a week or so ago. Where she's gone from there is anyone's guess. She's an independent old bird and she's got the money and the wherewithal to go where the hell she likes and probably will.'

'But she must have told you . . .'

'Why? The only person she ever consulted in her entire life was Edward. Now Edward's gone, I don't think she consults anyone but herself.'

Tess seemed about to argue, then changed her mind. 'Well, I'll have to go and see this DI Barnes, then.'

'You can talk to him; doesn't mean he'll be able to add anything,' Alec said. 'Tess, I'm not being obstructive or awkward, I'm just telling you this: if all this does link back to the likes of Gustav Clay, then it goes well above your pay grade.'

Tess spent a few more minutes trying to extract other details. Then she left, storming off up the beach. Naomi could hear the crunch of her boots on the pebbles as she made her departure; the frustration in each step.

'Well, I don't think that did much for your future friendship,' she said.

'You don't have to sound so pleased about it.'

'I'm not. I didn't mean to. Look, she upset you; I'm allowed to be pissed off with her for that.'

Alec took her hand. 'What do you make of all this?' he asked.

'I don't know. I think we should just keep our heads down and hope the storm misses us this time. Alec, what do *you* make of all this? Is it connected?'

'Probably. But you're right. We're best keeping to the sidelines. I'm curious, though.'

Naomi laughed. 'Of course you are. So what do you want to do about it that isn't really doing anything?'

'Why didn't you tell me Gregory came to call?'

'How did . . .?' She withdrew her hand from his, suddenly uncomfortable. 'I'd have told you; you just didn't seem in the mood to want to know, that's all.'

'George Mallard gave me a call, said he saw someone hanging about when he dropped you off. People are protective of you, Nomi.'

It was a long time since he had used the diminutive of her name. 'George had no right to be checking up on me.'

'No, probably not, but his heart is in the right place. People care about you and when people care, they don't always do the diplomatic thing. So, what did he want?'

'To see if Tess Fuller had told you anything. He and Nathan are trying to get the wife and kid back; Gregory reckons the police don't know what they're getting into.'

'And he's probably right.'

'So he wanted me to keep my ears open in case Tess told you something and you told me.'

'I think that's unlikely now,' Alec said.

'We know she's made some links, maybe we should tell Gregory that. I don't know. Chances are there'll be nothing else. She's really got the arse with you.'

She felt Alec shake his head. 'Tess will be back,' he said. 'Tess is tenacious and she can't bear to think anyone is keeping things from her. She is terminally nosy.'

'I hope not,' Naomi said. 'I may not actually like the woman, but from what I've seen this year, terminal nosiness can be a real deal.'

THIRTY-NINE

B ernard Franks was not a man to cross. Despite knowing that, Nathan had managed to cross him on numerous occasions and had done so with impunity. Until recently, he'd been protected; no one touched one of Gustav Clay's people. Now though, Nathan realized he was walking into the lion's den and not even armed with a whip and chair.

'I should go with you,' Gregory said.

'You should wait in the car. You and Franks are like matches and petrol fumes. I can do without the pair of you upping the ante.'

Gregory shrugged. 'He tried to have me killed.'

'Of course he did. That's what he does. Not that you're one to talk.'

'There's a difference,' Gregory objected. 'I don't subcontract.'

'And that makes you morally superior?'

'In the eyes of some people.'

Nathan looked closely at Gregory, trying to decide whether or not he was joking. He decided, on balance, that he probably wasn't. The older man had some odd sensitivities.

'If I'm not out in ten minutes, come and fetch me,' he said.

'A lot can happen in ten minutes. Make it five.'

'Gregory, a bullet takes a second.'

'He won't shoot you,' Gregory said. 'He rarely shoots people.' He leaned forward and fiddled with the radio, looking for something classical, Nathan guessed.

Nathan got out and headed into the pub that was Bernie Franks' domain. This, he thought, could be a really bad idea.

At the bar, he ordered a pint though Nathan actually rarely drank beer. He stood, sipping at it, knowing that his presence had been noted and Bernie Franks would either deal with him in person or send a message with someone who would. The mirrors behind the bar gave him a view of most of the pub lounge. Last time he'd been in here it had been a real spit and sawdust place, but Franks seemed to have attempted gentrification. There was carpet on the floor and the pool table that used to stand slap-bang in the middle of the room had been moved to an adjoining space. A board behind the bar even advertised food and guest beers. But there had been no gentrification of Bernie Franks.

'Business must be good,' Nathan said as the shadow blocked the light from the window and Franks loomed into his mirrored view.

'That's because I'm particular about my clientele.'

Nathan set his beer down and turned to face Bernie. 'One question and I'll be out of your hair,' he said.

'Why should I answer any?' Bernie spoke with a surprisingly soft voice. There was a drawl to it that Nathan had always thought of as West Country via Mississippi. Annie reckoned it was from trying to emulate American Gangster and not quite making it.

'Because you're curious,' Nathan said. 'If you weren't curious, you'd have sent an emissary.'

Franks smiled, the large mouth splitting wide. 'An emissary,' he said. 'I'll remember that. Hear that, lads, you're all my emissaries from now on.' He laid a great paw of a hand on Nathan's shoulder and leaned in. 'I heard about old Gus,' he said. 'Heard he had the right idea and tried to take you down with him.'

'It seems to have crossed his mind,' Nathan agreed. 'But I've forgiven him. No point in holding a grudge. Billy told me to come to you,' he went on.

Franks narrowed his eyes. 'So I understand. Maybe you could tell me what he would do that for.'

'Because at the time he was shit scared. I think the present danger trumped what you might do to him. He said you might be able to tell me where to find Mae. That she'd been doing some work for you.'

The grip on Nathan's shoulder tightened. He tried not to react but knew Franks would feel the tensions in his muscle as the fingers dug in.

'Mae is a free agent. She comes and goes.'

'But you were looking for her, Billy said.'

'Billy doesn't know dick. I looked for her, then I stopped looking. She was otherwise employed. Understand?'

Nathan nodded. He'd not expected an easy run, but so far it wasn't so bad. Franks could have flattened him – or worse – and chucked him out into the street or into the canal at the rear of the pub.

'Bernie, get one of your . . . emissaries to feel in my jacket pocket. There's a couple of photos in there you'd be interested in seeing.'

Bernie Franks laughed. 'You selling mucky pictures now, Nathan?' He nodded to one of his men who fished gingerly in Nathan's pocket and laid the envelope he found on the table. Another nod and the man emptied the envelope on to the bar. Bernie Franks turned his attention towards them, his fingers still practising a Vulcan death grip on Nathan's shoulder.

Nathan fought to keep his voice steady. 'You recognize anything or anyone, Bernie?'

'I thought you'd got just the one question,' Bernie said, but there was an unease in his voice, barely there, but enough for Nathan to catch. He scraped the pictures off the bar with the hand that wasn't torturing Nathan and handed them to one of his associates. Bernie was silent as the pictures were passed around and finally placed back on the bar.

'So what's this then, Nathan?'

Bernie lowered his head to Nathan's level and peered into his face. His breath reeked of beer and breath mints.

'Who's Mae running with these days?' Nathan asked.

'Hell should I know?'

'You said she was employed. Who by, Bernie?'

Bernie released Nathan so suddenly that he staggered back a pace or two. He caught a glimpse of Gregory, standing in the doorway. Five minutes must have been and gone, he thought. It felt like a good deal longer.

'I'll answer two questions,' Bernie said. 'Just for old times' sake. Because you were old Gus's boy. And you can tell me one in return.'

Nathan could have sung with relief. Instead, he nodded cautiously.

Bernie stabbed an enormous finger at the picture of Mae Tourino that Nathan had shown him. 'That bloke there, the one that looks like Clint Eastwood gone to seed, he's one of Rico's. Rico Steadmann,' he added as though Nathan might not know to whom he referred.

'That unlucky bastard –' he poked the same finger at the crime-scene photo of Anthony Palmer – 'had the misfortune to cross said Rico Steadmann. Stole something or didn't do something. Fucked if I know. Five or six years ago, maybe a bit longer. Rico lost him, but I remember the stink it caused. Looks like he found him again.' Bernie grinned again.

'And your question?' Nathan asked politely.

'Why you want to know?'

'Because he was killed in Ian Marsh's house,' Nathan said. He saw Bernie's eyes narrow.

'And how is the Prof?'

'Not so good. You must have heard, someone snatched his wife and child.'

Bernie's eyes were now a slit. 'Seems he's pissed someone off then.'

'It does.' Nathan waited, wondering if Bernie knew anything more; if he'd tell if he did, but the big man simply reached across for Nathan's beer and took a long drink.

Nathan took it as his cue to leave. His shoulder was throbbing and he knew it would be black with bruises, but it was a small price to pay. He had a new direction and two new pieces of the puzzle.

Gregory stood in the doorway until Nathan reached the car and only then did he join him. Nathan rubbed gingerly at his shoulder as they drove away. Classical music now filled the car. 'Do we have to have Mahler? I can't stand the man.'

'Which just demonstrates your lack of class. So, what do we know that we didn't before Bernie wrecked your trapezium?'

'Two things. Linked and surprising,' Nathan said. 'Mae's working for Rico Steadmann and the man killed in Ian's house was not as innocent as anyone thought. Five or six years ago, according to Bernie, he did something or stole something, or otherwise pissed Steadmann off big time, then disappeared. It looks like it finally got him killed.'

'And if Steadmann's involved there's another link,' Gregory said.

'What?'

'His one-time mentor was Mason, the bloke I told you about, whose weapon of choice was wires and monofilament.'

'Right.' Nathan nodded. 'Steadmann know you killed him, does he?'

'I would think so,' Gregory said quietly. 'He was the one who put out the hit.'

FORTY

Tess was still steaming mad when she arrived at Ian Marsh's door, having run the press gauntlet at the road end. She tried to quiet her irritation when he opened the door, his expression suddenly hopeful as he saw it was her.

'Any news?'

'Not exactly, Ian. I'm sorry. But I have some questions, some possible leads. I need you to fill in some details if you can.'

Ian leaned forward and peered out past her. The house itself was well hidden from the media press at the end of the street, the high hedge providing a modicum of privacy. 'How long do you think they'll stay? They ambush my neighbours every time one of them leaves the house.'

'We've got officers keeping them in order,' Tess soothed. 'Maybe we could move you out for a few days? Put you up in a hotel?'

Ian Marsh shook his head. 'I don't want to go anywhere else,' he said. 'This is Kat's home; Desi's home. I won't leave it until they come back. That wouldn't seem right.'

Tess nodded but she didn't really understand the logic.

'Come on in. Your sergeant not with you today?'

'No, he's organizing the press conference for later. It'll be on the midday news, Ian, so you need to be prepared for more interest for a while.'

'There have at least been no phone calls. I thought the media would have – but of course, the phone calls are all intercepted, aren't they?'

Tess nodded.

'I mean, I appreciate that, but what if the kidnappers call and you don't know who they are? What if they want to talk to me and they end up talking to a police officer? I mean . . .'

'Ian, our people are trained for this. It will be all right. If anyone calls you'll get to talk to them, hear anything they have to say, I promise you.'

He sighed, then led her through to the living room she and Vin had sat in before. He'd tidied the place up after the break-in, Tess noted. Even cleaned the fingerprint powder. She wondered if every time he went into the kitchen he still saw that picture lying on the table. His wife's scared face staring up at him, the child clasped tight in her arms. She sat down on the sofa and withdrew her notebook.

'Tell me what you know about Gustav Clay,' Tess said.

For a moment she thought Ian Marsh was going to deny knowing him. His face clouded with confusion and then annoyance. Then he seemed to make a decision. 'I knew him,' he said. 'I can't say I liked him much but he was useful, I suppose.'

'Useful?'

'In the work I was doing a few years ago. That's how I knew Nathan too. Clay knew everyone, could open doors I certainly couldn't. There was a conference on the future provision of international medical aid. Not the emergency care, the crisis management stuff that makes all the headlines; the conference in Damascus was all about vaccinations, preventive medicine in the developing world, that sort of thing. It's not, strictly speaking, my field, but I'd delivered a paper earlier in the year on the political instability in Sudan and the effects that was having on rural communities. I reprised my paper at the conference, alongside dozens of other speakers. Nathan acted as my interpreter and we'd all go out together to eat in the evenings.'

'And this was, when?'

'Oh, goodness. Eight, nine years ago. Nathan was still a student. He'd been working through the summer with one of the medical relief agencies. He wasn't fully qualified then, of course, but he knew enough to be useful.'

'You mentioned he trained to become a doctor.'

'Um, yes, he was training anyway. He never completed his internship.'

'And you say Gustav Clay could open doors?'

'He had the contacts. High level diplomats and ministers, that sort of thing. It's one thing reporting on what needs to be done for the people on the ground; it's quite another being able to navigate the political corridors and actually getting anything implemented. Then it really is a case of who you know and not what you know. Clay was good at that sort of thing.'

'So,' Tess wondered, thinking of Gustav Clay's connection to the human rights lawyers Gilligan and Hayes. 'Would you say Clay was a humanitarian then?'

She was unprepared for the burst of laughter from Ian Marsh. Once set off, he seemed unable to stop. Tess watched, horrified, as the man sought to regain control. He wiped his eyes on the back of his hands. 'Excuse me,' he said. 'Hysterical, really.'

She wasn't sure if he meant his behaviour or her question. 'I'm not sure I understand.'

'Clay was a bastard,' Ian Marsh said. 'He was useful only in as much as it amused him to be, or because he could see an advantage in it. Clay liked his public face to be clean and well scrubbed, but he spent his whole life wallowing in shit.'

'I'm still not sure I understand.'

'Look,' Ian Marsh said and his tone was suddenly angry. 'Do you have anything to tell me about my wife and child?'

'Not yet. I'm sorry.'

'That's all I'm interested in.'

'Knowing the background—'

'What background? I knew Clay and his people for a brief while almost a decade ago. After which I went into academia and there I've stayed. I met my wife five years ago; we married, we had a child. Clay did not figure in any of that, so there is no background.'

'And yet you kept in touch with Nathan Crow,' Tess said.

'Which was my mistake. I should have cut all ties. I should have exorcised the whole damned lot of them from my life, but I didn't. Too bad.'

'And yet you seem to blame Nathan Crow in some way for your wife's abduction,' Tess reminded him.

Ian Marsh's gaze fixed on her face. His eyes, blank and cold, made Tess want to shiver. She suddenly wished that Vinod was there with her. His sensible, practical presence would have been a secure touchstone; instead, she felt suddenly adrift and just a little afraid.

'Go and find them,' Ian Marsh said. 'Find Kat and Desiree. That's your job, that's what you are meant to be doing, not sitting in my house, asking stupid questions, making stupid allegations.'

'Professor Marsh. Ian. I'm not making allegations and I am doing all I can to find your family. We all are. But we have to follow every lead that presents—'

'I'd like you to leave now,' he said. 'I want you to go.'

Tess got to her feet and headed for the door. She was seriously unnerved by the sudden coldness in his tone. She glanced back from the front door. Ian Marsh was standing in the middle of the living room, just watching her. All trace of the affable, disorganized professor she and Vinod had first met seemed to have melted away; a core of something harder had been left behind.

FORTY-ONE

'Once the Cold War thawed,' Gregory said, 'there were a great many people suddenly without pay or occupation and a great many weapons suddenly available and suddenly very cheap. Through the nineties a good proportion of both surfaced in the Balkans, or in Africa, or found themselves nice little earners fighting for whatever faction was hiring, smuggling people, drugs, arms, anything else that could be fitted into a box. The cream were hired by other intelligence agencies.

'Others faded away into the background. Someone once estimated that if you added up all the casual informants, all those on the payroll part-time, all those officially employed, the Stasi had one informant for about every seven people in the general population. Most just got themselves lost in the background because that's where they'd been all along.'

'And this Mason?'

'Went freelance. Some would say went rogue. He killed a number of his old colleagues, murdered a fair few what you'd term innocent civilians too. Rico Steadmann found a place for his expertise in his already extensive organization. Rico's father was slowly handing over control but by the time the old man died, Mason already had his feet well and truly under the table. Rico, who'd looked to this man for guidance, shall we say, soon began to realize that he was about to become surplus to requirements. So he ordered the hit and I took the contract.'

Nathan frowned, his mouth quirking with amusement. 'Back then, weren't you an official employee of HM government?'

'I might have been.'

'You were moonlighting?'

'I did it on my own time. My extra-curricular activities never got in the way of the day job. Truth was, Nathan, he had it coming. I'd have got around to it some time, even without the extra incentive. The man was ripe for extermination.'

Gregory's mouth had set in a harsh line, all humour gone. Nathan thought about asking further, then decided against. Friendship should only trespass so far.

'So,' he said. 'Our next move.'

'Is to get some grub and then do our research. Steadmann's one of the old brigade. He knows us, knows our methods, and besides, we might not want to object to his killing of Anthony Palmer or whoever the man really was, so what's the point in upsetting people we don't have to? All we want is to get Kat Marsh and Daisy back. The rest is not our problem or our concern.'

Nathan nodded. 'You ever think that Annie might be right?' he said. 'That we should just buy a farm or something and settle down. Shed the complications?'

'Didn't Ian Marsh try that?' Gregory said. 'Fat lot of good it's done him.'

FORTY-TWO

The press conference at Friday lunchtime had led to a flurry of calls, but generated no new leads. A few people claimed to have recognized Nathan Crow and spotted him at the end of their road, but there had been nothing that seemed worth the follow-up that would be required to check out the sightings. Most of the calls had related to drivers who'd spotted the car in the ditch. Of those, only one seemed really significant: local police, driving the route, had estimated that Kat would have reached that spot around nine-fifteen and the driver, from a nearby farm, told them that the nine-thirty news had just come on when he passed the car. He had stopped, checked for casualties and then driven on.

'So we know she was taken before then,' Branch had told his team on the Friday evening. 'And if the locals are right, she'd have reached that point about a quarter of an hour before. So we've got another bit of the timeline.'

Much good it's going to do us, Tess thought. It's confirmation of something we thought, not additional information.

'The farmer who drove by,' Vinod asked. 'Was he usually about at around that sort of time?'

'Apparently, yes, so he was either very lucky, or whoever ambushed Kat Marsh knew his habits and knew what window they'd got.'

'But no one could know what time she was going to leave her uncle's house.' This from Jaz.

'I think we have to assume someone was watching. I think they also must have known the route she'd choose, which implies they knew a great deal about Katherine Marsh. I think we've also got to assume that there were various fall-back plans, just in case she broke with her own habits or decided to leave at a busier time of the morning. I also think that if the driver of that car had been in the way, whoever took Katherine and her child would have simply seen them as collateral damage.'

Jaz nodded. She was looking at her notes and Tess wondered if she'd found anything new. She was still stinging from Marsh's dismissal of her and still a little shaky too. The man had unnerved her.

'Could the family be involved?' she asked. 'Professor Marsh, the uncle. Is there anything . . .?'

'Nothing as yet. But we're obviously not ruling it out.' Branch looked keenly at Tess. 'Any particular reason for raising this now? You saw Marsh earlier today, didn't you? Anything to report?'

'I asked him about Gustav Clay and he says that he knew the man but had no contact with him for years.' She shrugged. 'I don't know; he seemed a bit off today. Angry, frustrated.'

'He's waiting for news. I'd be surprised if he wasn't.'

Tess nodded and made no further comment even though Branch paused, waiting for her to elaborate. 'I spoke to Alec Friedman too. He wasn't helpful.'

'You want to bring him in?'

Tess was surprised. 'For formal questioning? Any particular reason why I should?'

'Only that something's evidently pissed you off. I'm assuming it's either Alec Friedman or Professor Marsh or both. If it would make you feel better, haul them both in.'

There was general laughter and even Tess joined in, feeling herself relax for the first time since she had been to see the Professor.

'They're both holding back,' she said as the laughter subsided. 'I'm just not sure why.'

FORTY-THREE

The weekend passed with frustrating slowness and by Monday morning, with no new information and no contact from anyone, Tess was determined she was going to have another crack at finding out. Alec, she decided, might well hold the key to some of this and her first impulse was to go and harass him on the Monday morning. Reason and a busy schedule put that on hold. She'd wait until she finished for the day, spring a visit on him that evening, sit on his bloody sofa and refuse to go until she got some answers – though knowing Alec and Naomi, she thought ruefully, they'd be just as likely to ignore her and bugger off to bed as they would be accommodating.

She spent an hour fielding calls from Kat Marsh's relatives, from the press, wanting updates post press conference, then helped man the general phone lines for a while, reassuring members of the public that kidnapping wasn't usually something that went viral; thanking those who just felt they had to call to send good wishes to Katherine Marsh's family, and note down the few new sightings that had come in about Nathan Crow. Most seemed to be the 'certain I saw him on the telly, at the end of our road, in the pub on Saturday night' routine that were rarely worth the time it took to write them down, but all had to be checked out, just in case.

At midday Tess willingly surrendered her place on the phones. She understood why DCI Branch insisted they all take a turn with the routine stuff; it kept everyone grounded, everyone involved and gave staff who might otherwise suffer from banality overload a break, but that didn't mean she had to like it.

On Monday afternoon, Naomi went to do her usual stint at the advice centre. She was busy, as usual, and not entirely surprised when the centre manager put his head around the door and asked if she could squeeze another client in before she went.

'I know you're meant to be going, but . . .'

'No, it's OK; give Alec a call for me will you? Tell him I'll be a bit late.'

She heard voices out in the hallway and then the door open and close once more.

'Hello, Naomi,' a familiar voice said.

'Gregory? What the hell are you doing here?'

'Seemed like the easiest way of getting to see you at short notice. I didn't want to come back to the flat.'

'So you're my extra appointment instead.' She wasn't sure whether to be annoyed or pleased, but that was often her response to Gregory. 'I'll give you twenty minutes. That's it.'

'Right you are. So, what do you have to tell me?'

'What makes you think I've got anything?'

Gregory said nothing. He just waited.

'And what do you have? Are you any closer to finding them?' Naomi demanded.

'So far, no. We have a few leads and a network of people out looking. We'll get there.'

'You think they're still alive?'

'As I said before, I think they'll be kept alive. Yes.'

'Alec knows you came to see me.'

'Your taxi driver friend saw me when you opened the door. I was surprised he didn't come to check on me.'

'I'm glad he didn't.'

'I wouldn't have hurt him. But Napoleon there must have reassured him. Tail wagging like a bloody jack hammer.'

'I sometimes think that dog has no taste.' She could hear him now, his tail beating a steady rhythm on the lino. 'Tess Fuller came to talk to Alec. They've made a link between the kidnapping and Clay and the Gilligan and Hayes kidnapping, or at least she thinks there may be one. My guess is she was fishing. My other guess is they don't know a damn thing about a damn thing.'

'Right,' Gregory said. 'She mention what she thought the link might be?'

Naomi shook her head. 'No. Look, what probably happened is this. Someone did some digging into Prof Marsh's background, probably looking for Nathan Crow too. Clay's name came up, so they dug into Clay's record. That was bound to lead them to Gilligan and Hayes; Clay used them on occasion, I believe . . .'

'And opposed cases they brought on other occasions. So yes, there'd have been a paper trail.'

'It's my experience that at this stage of an investigation anything that can get followed up does. She mentioned speaking to DI Barnes – you remember him?'

'Yes. And that led her back to Alec and Molly Chambers, I'm guessing.'

'It did. Tess is annoyed, though, because a lot of the information she wants has been redacted. No one is telling her anything.'

'Good,' Gregory said simply.

'Look, you do know this isn't a pissing contest, don't you? There's a woman and kid out there, probably both scared half to death. Frankly I don't give a damn who finds them. You don't gain any prizes for game play, Gregory. Just for results. If you have anything, anything at all that might help the police—'

'I don't,' he said shortly. 'And I'm not losing sight of what's at stake here. Believe me.'

Naomi said nothing. She wanted to believe him. 'Do you think Marsh is involved?' she asked, not sure where the question had come from.

'Nothing to say he is, but nothing to say he's not, either. But what motive would he have?'

'None that I can think of.'

'And that's the problem. There's no motive for this that any of us can think of. Marsh has been involved in nothing out of the ordinary for years. The only contact he has is Nathan and if someone is after Nathan there are more direct routes.'

'So . . .'

'So, I'll give you a number to call if anything comes up from your end.' She heard him tapping on a screen and a moment later heard her own phone receive a text.

'Where's Molly Chambers, by the way?'

'Lord knows,' Naomi said. 'She's taking a winter holiday.'

Gregory chuckled. 'I only ask because her house has been empty for a few days and I wondered when she might be back. We've got a date at some posh restaurant she knows. I think she wants to chat about old times.'

'I can imagine,' Naomi said drily. 'Right, you've had more than your twenty minutes and I'd best get off; my taxi will be here and George will be getting very suspicious if he sees you again.'

'I'll be in touch,' Gregory said. 'Just keep your ears open.'

The man in the dark suit had arrived mid afternoon and been ushered into Branch's office. Jaz had seen them through the window as she'd passed. The man talking, Branch listening. He didn't look happy, Jaz thought. She wondered who the man was; the suit looked expensive and he had an air about him of someone used to being in authority.

A little after four Branch and the stranger emerged and came over to where Jaz was working.

'This is Charles Duncan,' Branch said. 'He's going to give you his phone number and you'll be responsible for copying him into anything you've turned up already and anything more you find out. You'll fax over a full set of notes each afternoon after the end-of-day briefing.'

Jaz was temporarily thrown. 'Do we even have a fax machine any more?'

Branch smiled. 'Apparently there's one in the storeroom, back of the front office. I'm sure you'll cope.'

'Can't I fax from the computer?'

'I'd prefer you to do it from the landline,' Charles Duncan said. Jaz nodded, not sure what else she could say.

Charles Duncan left soon after and Branch came back to Jaz's desk.

'Who the hell was that?'

'He's apparently from the Home Office,' Branch said.

'Which means?'

'Which means you copy him into everything we have every day. Think you can handle it?'

'What's going on, Boss?'

'That,' he said heavily, 'is apparently not for us to know. Oh and Jaz, this is your responsibility, you understand. I'll deal with Susan, but you keep it to yourself otherwise. Any problems, you come to me. Got that?'

'Sir.'

He returned to his office and Jaz could see that he was rattled – and annoyed. So, she thought, spooks in the past and now spooks in the present. What fun – I don't think.

FORTY-FOUR

Evening visitors were rare. As autumn drew on, Naomi relished that sense of cosiness, closing the curtains, listening to the often strong wind off the sea and of settling snug and warm inside.

Tess arrived just before eight and neither Naomi nor Alec were particularly pleased but neither were they particularly surprised that she had come back for another shot at getting information. Naomi could hear, though, that she was upset and stressed and frustrated and she felt a modicum of sympathy for the other woman.

'Look,' Tess said. 'I'm sorry, but I need to know. What the hell is going on?'

'And I told you. I don't know.'

'Alec, please.'

Silence filled the space between them. Outside the wind howled, flinging rain against the windows. Somewhere, Naomi, thought, Gregory and Nathan were searching. Somewhere a woman and a child were . . .

'Alec,' Naomi said.

He sighed. 'I'll make some coffee.'

'I don't want any coffee,' Tess said. 'I don't want platitudes or excuses or mealy mouthed crap. I want to know what you know and I'm going to sit here until someone tells me what the bloody hell is going on.'

'What makes you think we know anything?' Alec said.

'You know a damned sight more than I do. OK, tell me about Gustav Clay. Start with that. When did he die and how and who shot his dogs?'

'I don't—'

'Come off it, Alec. Remember I've spoken to one of the first responders, a young fire officer that everyone is now trying to fob off, tell him he didn't see what he knows he did. Look, I'm all in favour of national security or whatever the latest excuse is, but I can't do my job while everyone is keeping me in the dark.'

Alec sighed and sat back in his seat beside Naomi. She felt him making his decisions, the arguments, that were never really that ingrained anyway, dissolving and departing. She tucked up her feet on the settee and leaned into his shoulder. 'He didn't die in the gas explosion,' she said. 'He shot his own dogs, we think, and set the place to explode. The entrances were booby trapped with trip wires. The explosion was meant to kill others he knew would come looking for him.'

'Who?' Tess demanded. Her voice was shaking. 'What others?'

'Well, among them, Nathan Crow,' Alec said. 'Look, I can't tell you a lot because I don't know it all. Clay felt that Nathan Crow and Annie Raven had betrayed him. He was used to getting his own way, to being in control. In the end, he set a trap for Nathan and went after Annie in the worst way. He tried to kill her husband. Thankfully, they were ahead of him and someone got to Clay before he got to Bob Taylor. He died in Bob's studio. But you won't get anyone to verify any of this. The mess was cleaned up and that was that.'

'*I'm quite particular about who comes into my house these days,*' Tess said.

'Sorry?'

'Something Bob Taylor said. I guess that's what he meant. So, this Gustav Clay. He was some sort of spy?'

'More a spy master, I think,' Alec said. 'Though I'm not sure that does him justice. Someone described him as a spider, sitting at the heart of a worldwide web. He was everywhere and had been, I think, since the start of the Cold War. Maybe before.'

'So, how does that fit in with the Marsh kidnapping and the murder of Anthony Palmer?'

'Maybe it doesn't,' Alec suggested. 'Maybe this is more personal. Maybe you've seen what you think is a connection and you're pushing it because you've got nothing else?'

'I don't believe that,' Tess said stubbornly. Then, 'Maybe. I just don't know. And after the Cold War?'

'I think for some people it never ended,' Naomi said. 'It just shifted location. First to the Balkans and then to Africa and the Middle East, but from what I've been told, the greatest threat now is from franchise terrorism. That's been the real game changer.'

'Franchise? I don't get that. And who told you?'

'Franchise terrorism is exactly what it sounds like,' Alec said. 'If you bought a business franchise for, say, a coffee shop, then your shop would as far as possible be identical to the same franchise coffee shop down the road or in the next town. You'd operate in the same way, decorate your shop in the same way, use the same beans, same recipes, same packaging.

'Franchise terrorists work in small groups. They are affiliated to the main organization, whatever that might be, trained, given the same instructions, the same manuals – the same packaging, if you like, but in the way that any individual coffee shop is an individual business opportunity, managed and organized independently, with its own staff and its own customers.'

'Like the Al Qaeda cells everyone talks about. Yes, I get that.'

'So far as I understand it, the intelligence community has had to change dramatically to keep up. Cold War intelligence was as much about the mutual bugging of embassies and keeping a lid on dissent as it was about spies. Surveillance was person based. Informants in your workplace or block of flats or in the café or on the bus.'

'As opposed to the electronic chatter that everyone shouts about today.'

'Well, that existed, there was just less of it. But this country has always been at the heart of monitoring. The Americans have had listening posts here for decades. The NSA can't spy on its own citizens from US soil, so it's done so from here. Anyway, the change to the franchise model meant that the intelligence service had to switch to a similar formation. It had to be mobile and independent and autonomous in its decision making, pretty much like the groups it is pursuing.'

'Someone I knew said the Cold War experts were now seen as dinosaurs,' Naomi said. 'That the new generation are all mammals. Warm blooded and fluffy on the outside but still as dangerous. He reckons the mammals are doing their best to eliminate the dinosaurs.'

'And Clay was?'

'A dinosaur, I suppose,' Naomi said. 'But one with his claws so tightly dug in that anyone who came close to dislodging him would be ripped to shreds.'

FORTY-FIVE

Tess got a call early on the Tuesday morning. There had been a sighting of Nathan Crow that seemed worth following up. Vin arrived at her front door half an hour later and she finished her breakfast toast in his car. He'd brought coffee for both of them and a large flask of chai and a tiffin box of snacks and sweets for later. 'Mum thought we might appreciate them. It's quite a drive. I stayed over last night,' he explained.

'Not a great way to be spending Diwali,' Tess said ruefully.

'We all went to see the lights last night and everyone's piling round for a meal later, so I won't miss out. You'd be very welcome, you know.'

Tess smiled. 'Thanks,' she said. 'I think I'd like that.' It would be an opportunity to dress up and she knew from experience that the welcome would be warm and the food great. 'Where are we going, anyway?'

'Leeds, fortunately just the outskirts of.'

Tess groaned. 'I always get bloody lost in Leeds.'

'Which is why we have satnav.'

'And we are going to see . . .?'

'One Bernie Franks. Reckons Nathan Crow visited his pub.'

'And we believe him, because . . .?'

'Because he left something behind. Two photographs. The enterprising Mr Franks had them scanned and emailed to us. One was of the crime scene in Ian Marsh's cottage.'

'What? How? Did this Nathan Crow take it?'

Vin shook his head. 'No, I doubt it. It's a ringer for one of the crime-scene photos. Crow got hold of it somehow. We might have a leak; we might have a hacker. That's one for internal affairs to sort.'

'So, this Bernie Franks. He's a pub landlord? Why would . . .?'

'He owns a pub, there's a difference. My tablet's in the glove box. There's a file on the desk top. I grabbed what I could before I came over. Bernie Franks is one of the old-fashioned "Hard Men", from the looks of it. Armed robbery, intimidation, protection . . . Anyway, he's semi-retired according to the locals. Keeps a few of his boys around for show; it's rumoured he hires them out on an ad hoc basis. Takes a cut.'

'So his word is good because . . .'

'Well, apart from the photographs, precisely because he's been around for a long time. He knows a lot, has seen people come and go, get locked up, get dead.'

'And why would he shop Nathan Crow to us?'

Vin laughed. 'I asked that too. The local DS I talked to reckons Franks will do anything for devilment. But it occurred to me—'

'That Nathan Crow is too canny to have left anything behind by accident,' Tess finished. 'You think he arranged this with Bernie Franks?'

'Um, don't know what to think. About any of this, if I'm honest. I know you shouldn't think like this, but you know what really gets to me? I don't like any of them. I mean, you can usually empathize with the victims, with the families, even with the people you interview on the periphery of it, you know?'

Tess nodded.

'But Ian Marsh, I mean the guy is so cold, somehow. It's like he's going through the motions. And that Crow guy – it's like he's superior, or thinks he is. Same with that photographer and her husband. It's like they think they're special, somehow, you know what I mean?'

'I know what you mean,' Tess said.

'And I keep thinking about Katherine Marsh and her little girl and wondering how the hell she got mixed up with someone like Ian Marsh in the first place. And I don't quite know why I feel like that about him. He's a nice enough man, comes over as ordinary and helpless and scared and . . . But it's like there's something else going on, you know?'

Tess nodded again, remembering her last meeting with Professor Marsh. He had scared her, she realized now. Not by anything he'd really said or anything he'd really done, but just that . . . what had Vin called it? That undercurrent.

She glanced up from the files she had been perusing on Vin's tablet. 'Well,' she said, 'you might be glad to hear that Bernie Franks looks like he's just a good old-fashioned villain.'

Vin laughed. 'I don't believe that,' he said. 'He'll have his secrets and his undercurrents just like the rest of them. I've been chatting to Jaz,' he said. 'She reckons we got a visit from a mysterious man in black the other day. Reckon's Branch was most put out.'

Tess squinted at him. 'Johnny Cash?' she asked.

'What? No and not Will Smith either. And no, we've not had any UFO sightings. Home Office, Jaz reckons. She's having to send regular reports to him on the QT.'

'Not so much on the quiet if she's telling you.'

'Jaz likes me,' Vin said. He grinned. Truth was he liked Jaz too and Tess wondered why they didn't just get on with it and become the item most people wrongly assumed they already were. 'The Gustav Clay connection, I suppose. Vin, what do you make of Ian Marsh?'

'You really don't like the man, do you?'

She shrugged, not sure why she held back on telling her partner what had happened on the Friday. The unease she had felt; the sudden change in the professor's demeanour.

FORTY-SIX

Naomi had arranged to meet Patrick in town on the Tuesday morning, a day he had only one lecture. They'd spend some time shopping and meet Harry and his mother for lunch. Alec had said he'd try to join them.

Naomi valued her friendship with this son of her oldest friend and it wasn't unusual for them to do things together, but the invitation to shop had come out of the blue and she guessed there was something on his mind. George Mallard's son dropped her outside the new shopping centre that had opened up in the spring.

'Looks like he's already here.'

'He would be. Patrick is as punctual as his dad.'

'Maybe I could get him to give lessons to my two. I have to tell them we're leaving immediately half an hour before we go anywhere.'

He helped Naomi from the car, checked that she'd got a lift home and then drove away.

'Hi,' Patrick said. 'Thank you for coming.'

'Pleasure,' Naomi said. 'So what are we doing this morning?'

Patrick slipped his arm through hers. She'd left Napoleon with Alec, knowing Patrick was more than capable of looking after her and that it would probably be easier with just the two of them in the shopping crowd.

'Three things,' Patrick said. 'One I really need your help with and so does dad. It's Gran's seventieth in about ten days' time and we want to get her something special, so we could do with some advice.'

'OK. And the other two things?'

'Well, one is a uni assignment. I've chosen to do a mini module on portraiture. It's one of the optional things and I thought I'd get on better with something that was kind of less abstract. I would like to paint you, if that's all right. We're supposed to be exploring our subjects. I thought I'd rather explore someone I know.'

Naomi laughed. 'You know how I hate having my photo taken. I think being painted is going to be much worse.' She could sense his disappointment and said hastily, 'But for you, yes, of course, that's fine.'

'Good.' Patrick relaxed. 'I'll make it as painless as I can. The third thing is Gregory.'

'Gregory. Right. Harry mentioned he'd appeared. I've seen him too. Is he upsetting you?'

'What? Oh, no, nothing like that. He's fine. I like him, actually.' Patrick took a deep breath and then said, 'He knows this artist I really admire. He's called Bob Taylor and I wondered . . . I wondered if you thought it would be out of order if I asked Gregory if he'd ask Bob Taylor to maybe look at some of my work.'

Wow, Naomi thought. *Of all the things I thought you were going to ask.*

'I mean,' Patrick went on, 'I know it's maybe an imposition but there are things he does . . . there's this kind of ethereal quality to his work and I don't know how he does it. He just seems to catch the moment, the second, like he's frozen it, you know what I mean. I knew his work before, but after Gregory mentioned him, I took a better look.'

And you were star-struck, Naomi thought. 'Ask him,' she said. 'Does he know this Bob Taylor well?'

'I don't know. You don't think he'd mind?'

'I think if he thought it was inappropriate he'd tell you. Gregory is very direct.'

'True. OK, thanks,' Patrick said. 'Now what the hell are we going to get for Gran's birthday?'

'So, did we actually gain anything from that encounter?' Tess asked.

'Two photographs and a positive sighting.'

'From a career criminal who may or may not be yanking our chain.' Tess sighed and leaned her head back against the seat, closed her eyes. 'We know there's a leak,' she said. 'That's a photo from the crime scene. Question is who and why.'

'And that's a problem for Internal Affairs. Why is this Nathan Crow looking for that woman, do you reckon?'

'I'm betting Bernie Franks knows,' Tess said wearily.

'And he's not saying. This Nathan obviously thinks it's all connected with the Marsh kidnap. Maybe she's involved? Maybe she killed our man Palmer. Maybe we should both go back and talk to your mate Alec Friedman.'

'Maybe we should,' Tess agreed. Maybe that's all we've got – a whole load of maybes.

Bernie Franks waited for a few minutes and then called Rico Steadmann.

'I've passed the pictures on to the police, like we agreed,' he said. 'They seemed more bothered that someone had got hold of crime-scene evidence. I think Mae's a new thing for them, but you should watch yourself, Rico. She's a loose cannon these days. Unpredictable.'

'She's never been predictable,' Rico told him.

'Anything else?'

'No, I don't think so. I can take it from here. Oh, yes, one more thing. You've got cameras at that place of yours?'

'Security cameras. Yes.'

'The man with Nathan Crow. I'd like a look at him. Could be someone I know.'

FORTY-SEVEN

'So, where do we stand?' DCI Branch rubbed his hands together in anticipation. A couple of people laughed; others settled more expectantly into their seats. Jaz, a little late for the briefing, slipped through the door and stood just inside.

'Still no next of kin for our Mr Palmer,' Tess said. 'We talked to his work colleagues, here and from his old workplace, but all they can tell us is that he kept himself to himself and didn't socialize. Nothing in the Church Lane house to suggest he had family. Not even photographs – and that's the other thing. Everyone else in the estate agency, here and back where he worked before, had work-related pics on their phone. Nothing untoward, just random stuff when they'd been out together. Apparently Mr Palmer never went out with anyone. The only time he socialized with the group was last year at the Christmas party and he didn't get much choice in that one: his old boss organized for a bit of a do after they'd shut up shop for the afternoon. And from that we've got this.'

Branch took the picture and looked puzzled. It was a group shot – ten people in various states of celebration. Silly hats and full glasses much in evidence.

'Middle of the back row,' Tess said. 'You can just about make him out. He's trying not to be there.'

'Can we enhance it?'

'Technical services are doing what they can. But it does make you wonder about him. Anthony Palmer doesn't seem to have left much of an impression. We didn't even find a driver's license at the house.'

'But he drove a car.'

'And according to Swansea, never actually applied for a photo license.'

'Passport?'

Tess shook her head. 'Of course, whoever killed him could have cleared the place of anything personal, but we found no trace of a search, never mind anything being taken.'

'If the search was done right, you'd never know it had happened,' Vin pointed out.

Branch nodded. 'Well, keep pushing. Someone must know something about the man. What else do we have?'

Jaz waved nervously from the back of the room. Branch beckoned her forward.

'The second photograph you got from Bernie Franks,' she said. 'I got a hit on the woman.'

She pinned an enlargement to the board, then looked meaningfully at Branch. 'It's not from police resources,' she said. 'I did . . . um . . . a kind of lateral search.'

Branch frowned and then nodded as he got her meaning. 'Go on,' he said.

'Well, she has half a dozen aliases. I've printed a list and some background. I'm just getting copies made. Her birth name was probably Maria Dubrovna, but we can't be sure even of that. She grew up in the old Yugoslavia, when it was still a communist state, moved to East Germany when she was in her late teens, then she disappeared altogether for a while. She surfaced in the early eighties, when she had an affair with a French diplomat – this was in Moscow. She's suspected of acting as a courier for both UK intelligence and for East Germany. She speaks a dozen languages, and she was a definite associate of this Gustav Clay's. I'll get more information soon and put it in the files.'

Branch called Jaz over at the end of the briefing. 'You faxed the photo over to our friend Charles Duncan?'

She nodded. 'The result came back fast.'

'A bit too fast.'

'I thought so too. He sent a note saying there was more, but he had to clear it first. Sir, what do you think is going on?'

Branch shook his head. 'I think we've got to focus,' he said. 'Kat Marsh and her little girl are all we should be concerned about now. The rest can fall into line.'

'And what about Anthony Palmer – whoever he was?'

'Jaz, I think that's the problem. The "whoever he was". I have a feeling we're not the only ones looking into that. And we've got to be cold about this. We know he's dead. So far we don't even have relatives needing closure. We have to hope the woman and child are still alive, so they get our attention.'

Jaz nodded. 'Anyone spoken to Ian Marsh today?' she asked.

'I don't know. Tess hasn't been here. I made a routine call this morning, but after that . . . Why?'

'I just think it's strange,' Jaz said. 'If someone I loved had been taken, I'd be making a right nuisance of myself, hassling anyone that could tell me anything.'

FORTY-EIGHT

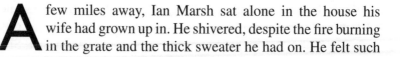

few miles away, Ian Marsh sat alone in the house his wife had grown up in. He shivered, despite the fire burning in the grate and the thick sweater he had on. He felt such a chill inside of him that it seemed never to be truly warm. Ian Marsh, frozen to the core, frozen to the tips of his fingers. Frozen into inaction.

'My fault,' he whispered to his absent wife and missing child. 'All my fault.'

Tess wasn't sure why she had driven home via Ian Marsh's road, but it was something she had done many times in the past week. Sometimes she had driven straight down the road. Sometimes she had slowed and looked at the house, mostly hidden behind the high hedge. Sometimes she had stopped her car a little way down the road and just sat there, watching, waiting, though for what she couldn't have said. The same impulse had taken her to and past the house in Church Lane. Tess could make no sense of any of this. How did it all tie together? The respectable professor. The supposedly respectable estate agent, Anthony Palmer – though a man who seemed to have no friends, no family, no past. Abductors who took a woman and child and then . . . then what?

She turned the car around and parked on the opposite side of the road a few doors from Ian Marsh's house. The rain had cleared but the sky was still leaden and the fireworks from local gardens merely served to highlight the dense cloud. Tess hated fireworks, always had, even as a kid. Her family had all gathered together for a regular bonfire – siblings and cousins and even her gran. Tess had liked the bonfire and the food and the family gathering, but the fireworks had always left her cold, unable to understand how people could get excited over a few brightly coloured explosions.

Through gaps in the hedge she could just make out that a light was on in Ian Marsh's house. In the living room she and Vin had sat in so many times. She visualized it now. Old-fashioned and cosy in a haphazard, overstuffed kind of way. She had never been able to gauge much about Ian Marsh or his wife from that room. It had been created by an earlier generation, put together according to the taste and habits of another couple. Ian and Katherine Marsh had simply inherited it, moved into that space, but made no impact upon it.

Tess realized that she was hungry. She should go home, eat

something. Instead, she drove to a Chinese takeaway she knew and ordered chicken and cashew nuts with egg-fried rice. Then she drove on a little further down the coast and sat in her car to eat her meal, listening to the radio, finding solace in a country music programme that played songs of love and loss and broken hearts. Briefly, she thought of Alec. He'd mentioned he was going to the fireworks in Pinsent, with his wife and some friends. He even seemed to be looking forward to it. Tess wondered if she'd ever be one to enjoy domesticity.

So, she asked herself, what exactly was she doing here? She told herself that she'd driven out towards Halsingham because the takeaway she liked was out in that direction, but she knew that was a lie. This had always been her plan. Why else would she be parked up at the side of Ian Marsh's cottage on Church Lane?

Quietly, Tess got out of the car and slipped around to the back door. The keys she had taken from the evidence box had now been copied and replaced and this wasn't the first time she had let herself into the property on Church Lane or even into Ian Marsh's other house – though that was something she had to be more cautious about. Church Lane, on the other hand, was easy. Not overlooked and far enough from the neighbour's house that she never noticed Tess's incursions.

Tess stood in the kitchen, cleaned now by a professional company Tess herself had recommended, though she knew even they would never get rid of every trace. Blood would remain, hidden in the cracks of the flagstone floor, the tiny gaps in the cabinet fixings, absorbed into the new paint on the kitchen walls. Traces would remain.

Tess stood and inhaled the scene. She closed her eyes and remembered the hanging man, the CSI moving purposefully and quietly around him. The click of the camera shutter . . .

Eyes still closed, she erased them from the scene, took away the officers and their quiet intensity. Left only the hanging man and her own presence. She could hear her own breath now, was conscious of her heartbeat, the pulse of blood in her ears. She lifted her head as though looking up, but kept her eyes closed, remembering every detail of the body, the look, the presence, the smell, the pain.

In her mind's eye she saw his assailants. Faceless, sexless, even, but she assumed both male. She visualized where they must have stood. The one behind, manipulating the rope, the chokehold they had on their victim. One standing where she stood now, or maybe a pace further back, looking up at the victim. Winding that tight fibre about his body, twisting it tight so it bit into the flesh, twisting it tighter still. The knife wound in the side – Tess mimed the upward thrust. Most of the blood on the floor would have come from that knife wound. Arterial blood, spurting out, hitting the ceiling at one point, trailing down the body and on to the floor.

That was an oddity, Tess thought. The rest of it had been relatively clean. There would be blood on the knife, blood on the assailant. Blood that spurted out and covered the man driving the knife upward into the wound.

Tess mimed the movement again. No, the angle was wrong. It was all wrong.

One man would have held the rope, pulling it tight around Anthony Palmer's neck. It hadn't been a sliding noose, merely a way of applying a choke hold across the windpipe.

The other stood in front of him . . . and there was evidence that Anthony Palmer's feet had been bound and tied down to prevent him from kicking out at his assailant. His ankles had been ripped and torn by the same monofilament. It had taken a while before they understood what he'd been tied to, but marks on the heavy oak table suggested it might have been that. The noose man maybe sitting on the table to add extra weight and provide him with the ideal position from which to increase the tension.

So what about the knife wound?

Tess moved round slightly, thinking again about the angle of thrust. From the side, she thought, and the assailant wasn't worried about getting Palmer's blood all over him. Somehow that seemed at odds with the rest of the scene – and they knew the blood had spurted all over this man because there was a void in the spatter pattern on the floor and wall.

'A third man,' Tess said softly. 'There was a third man. I'm bloody certain of it.'

*   *   *

Tess didn't look back as she got into her car. If she had she might have caught the hint of a movement in the shadow beside the garden hedge. After she had driven away the shadow detached itself fractionally, stood silent and still until the tail lights of her car had disappeared.

He then retreated to his own vehicle and made a call. His companion fired up the ignition and eased out from between the trees, following Tess's car up the hill.

FORTY-NINE

O n 3 November, Professor Ian Marsh failed to turn up for work. In itself, that wasn't to be wondered at; he'd officially been absent, on compassionate grounds, since his family had disappeared, but in the past week he'd come into his office twice, at least trying to keep up with his admin, see a few of his students and help spread the workload created by his absence.

His colleagues were of the quiet opinion that he didn't actually do a lot when he did come in and they were also awkward around him. What do you say to a man going through what he was going through? But they rallied and supported and tried to include him in any way they could, hoping it would at least help attach him to the land of the living. In the view of several of them, Ian Marsh was now a man living in the shadows, not a part of this world, even if not quite consigning himself to the next.

The third day of the month was important though, if only to the PhD student Professor Marsh was supervising and who he'd promised he would still see. For half an hour, his appointment waited for the professor in the corridor outside his locked office. After another half-hour, he left a note for Ian Marsh and went to get a coffee, hoping the professor would have rolled up by the time he got back. Returning, he ran into the professor's neighbour, who sympathized and called Ian Marsh at home and then on his mobile. Then phoned round within the department to see if anyone else knew where he might be.

By mid afternoon, Tess had been made aware of the problem, Marsh's worried colleagues having called and suggested someone go round. Just in case . . .

Tess and Vinod duly went. 'You think he might have topped himself?' Vin asked as they sat in the car outside the Marsh house.

'Bloody hope not,' Tess said. 'I can do without another fricking body.' She sighed. 'If he has, then I just hope he's left a bloody note, preferably one that confesses to what he's done with his wife and kid and ends with him being sorry.'

Vin got out and waited for her to join him. 'You really think he might have done it?' he said. 'I know you don't like him, but . . . I don't know. It doesn't smell right, somehow, you know? I mean, if he did kill them, does that mean he did for Anthony Palmer as well?'

'I don't know,' Tess said. 'I suppose that would depend on how he did it, if he did, and I'm not sure I even want to think about that.'

No one answered the doorbell. Vin went round the back while Tess knocked on the neighbours' doors. Ian Marsh's car wasn't there, she'd noticed, so that suggested neither was the professor. One neighbour thought she had seen him drive off that morning, but she couldn't be sure of the time.

'Was he carrying any luggage?' Tess asked.

The woman frowned, considering. 'Only that shoulder bag of his. That old leather satchel type of thing he takes everywhere.' She frowned, doubtfully. 'It might have been yesterday. You should ask those journalists down the road. They'd know, wouldn't they?'

Tess thanked her and returned to where Vin now stood beside the car. 'No sign of him, alive or dead,' he said.

'The neighbour saw him go off this morning or maybe yesterday. I suppose it's possible he intended to drive to the university and something happened. Best check for RTAs and call the local hospital. We'll drive his route and then check with his colleagues again.'

Vin nodded and they pulled away. 'How come you know what route he takes?' Vin asked.

Tess hesitated, not sure she wanted him to know, but also sure that he'd guessed by now. 'Because I've been watching him,' she said. 'Because even if he didn't kill his wife and child I'm sure he played us. And, Vin, I don't like being played.'

She paused at the road end to speak to the constable on duty. The press pack had diminished; days of nothing happening were hard to report and just the dregs and shreds remained. Professor Marsh had been logged leaving yesterday morning. He'd not been logged as returning.

'And no one thought to report this?'

The young officer flushed. 'I wasn't on duty,' he protested.

Tess drove off, too annoyed to respond. She should have checked in more often. She should have put word out to keep a close eye on the professor. But he wasn't officially a suspect; he hadn't been told to stay put; he hadn't permitted a liaison officer to come and assist him. And he'd spooked her. That was the truth of it. Tess still felt edgy from the last time she'd visited the Marsh house. She hadn't wanted to admit to that, but it was the truth and it had led her to be careless. To keep out of Ian Marsh's way and hope someone else did that part of her job for her. It appeared no one had.

Vin was talking on the phone, checking for possible road accidents and hospital admissions. But there was nothing. By the time they arrived at the professor's office it was dawning on Tess that the man had deliberately disappeared. They spoke to the PhD student and to the professor's colleagues. He had spoken to no one, left no messages, informed none of them of possible plans.

'What now?' Vin said.

'Back to the house. We take the place apart.'

'There's still a possibility he's there. He might have topped himself. We should have gone in before.'

'The neighbour and our log said he left. No one saw him come back. He's not there.'

And she was right. They entered through the kitchen door, Vin breaking the small window and then reaching through to turn the key. Inside it was emptily quiet. The sort of quiet, Tess thought, that settles on a house when it's been uninhabited for a while.

Vin followed her upstairs. Everything was tidy, precise and clean. She paused at the entrance to Desiree's room. It was eerily neat and empty. Pink and white and lilac and filled with toys and books and teddy bears. She turned away quickly.

'Anything missing from the bedroom?' she asked.

'I can't tell if he's packed anything. But there's something I didn't expect to be there.'

He pointed at the bed. Lying on the pillow was a mobile phone. In a bright pink case. With gloved hands, Tess picked it up and flipped the cover open. A flashing light announced a text, unread. 'This has got to be Kat's phone. How the hell did it get here?'

'There's a message.' Vin's voice was tense and hoarse.

Tess opened the message screen. She turned it towards her partner.

'Time's up, Professor,' the message said.

'He's been in contact with them,' Tess breathed. 'And he didn't say a bloody word.'

FIFTY

The start of November had brought storms and heavy rain. By the Friday of Bonfire Night the rain had eased a little, but the firework display on the bit of land between the recreation ground and the beach happened against a fractal background of raindrops and rising tide. The crowd had wrapped up against the cold and damp in wellingtons and thick coats and the bonfire had somehow been lit and then kept alight. The blaze, red and gold against a grey world, lit the faces of the crowd and while Patrick tilted his face skyward to watch the rockets fly, Harry found that mostly he just watched his son.

They had been coming to the display ever since they moved back to Pinsent and tonight Naomi and Alec had joined them, leaving Napoleon safely in the care of Marie, Harry's mother. They'd be going back there to eat later, sharing Bonfire Night food and good company.

Patrick's face was as pale as ever, the untidy dark hair blown into tangles as his hood fell back. The firelight danced on the pale skin, touching it with colour, the way Patrick so often touched his otherwise monochrome art. He's beautiful, Harry thought. Not handsome; that was too harsh, too masculine a word. Patrick was beautiful and Harry felt as though someone had taken his heart in their hands and crushed it to pulp. His chest was too tight, his breath held as he worshipped his child and recognized, fearfully, that he was becoming a man.

Naomi too had her face tilted towards the sky. She could still perceive a little in the way of light and shade and fireworks still possessed some of their magic as a result. She clasped Alec's arm tightly and Harry, glancing at them for a moment, saw his friend smile. Alec had been more settled of late, more of his old self, though Harry knew that the recovery was still fragile.

The fireworks ended, the last of the redness falling into the sea and the music fading out to nothing. Spontaneous applause broke through the crowd and Harry clapped because his son was clapping. He could recall nothing of the display. Now, as the firelight illuminated only the grey of the breakers crashing on the beach, Patrick turned to Harry, a grin on his face. 'Awesome,' he said. 'But I'm freezing now.'

People had begun to drift away, some towards the stage where live music would play for the next hour or so and families would dance and eat the hog roast. Steam roast, Harry thought, with all the rain. Others moved back towards the town and home, and the four of them joined the slow exodus from the recreation ground and back on to the promenade. There was something else to celebrate tonight. Against all expectation, Patrick had passed his driving test the day before. Harry, Patrick's mother and his stepfather had all contributed towards getting him a little car – or more likely, Harry thought, towards getting him his insurance, as the quotes he'd found were, frankly, unbelievable. The car would be the cheapest, easiest part of it. He planned on handing the money over to Patrick tonight when they got to Marie's.

'Any more news on that poor woman who went missing? The one with the little girl,' Harry asked as they stepped on to the promenade.

'Nothing,' Alec said. 'Everything seems to lead to a dead end. There's been talk, of course. A shift of focus.'

'What kind of shift?'

'Well, it's a peculiar sort of kidnap when no demands are made, the abductors don't even make contact. Confidentially, I think the team are probably looking at Marsh. And now he's disappeared.'

'Disappeared? That isn't in the papers.'

'No. Officially, he's gone to stay with friends. But he took off, they think on Monday morning. Not a hide nor hair has been seen of him since. That's confidential, of course.'

'Goes without saying,' Harry said.

'Do the police think he might have staged it?' Patrick asked.

'You mean he's a suspect?' Harry was horrified. 'But why kidnap your own . . . Oh, you mean they suspect he might have killed them?'

'He has an alibi for when they were supposedly taken, but . . . well, there are no new leads. There's no one else involved so far as the police can tell.'

'And this Nathan Crow?'

Alec shrugged. 'Still in the wind, as they say.'

Harry saw Patrick look suddenly uncomfortable. Had Gregory told him something, Harry wondered. He dismissed the idea. Patrick hadn't mentioned seeing Gregory recently and Harry felt reasonably sure his son would have let him know if he'd shown up again.

'How come you know so much about it?' Harry asked.

'We don't, not really, but an old colleague is on the investigation. She's come round to let off steam a couple of times.'

'I can understand the need,' Harry said.

Conversation turned to Patrick's driving and other, more random subjects. Tess had definitely felt the need to let off steam, Naomi thought. She'd come round the night they'd discovered Katherine Marsh's mobile phone, furious and distressed and not seeming to understand why she felt that way. She had told them about the phone, told them about the day she'd visited Ian Marsh and he had so disturbed her. Reiterated that some man from the Home Office seemed to be calling the shots and then she'd gone and Naomi had understood that she had come and ranted at them in full knowledge and probably hope that they'd pass what she told them on to

Nathan Crow and Gregory – though she still doubted that Tess would have admitted as much.

Naomi had duly passed everything along.

'Figures,' was all Gregory had said.

Patrick slid an arm through hers and Naomi dropped back so she could walk side by side with the young man.

'What's on your mind?' she asked.

'Oh, nothing major.' Patrick said. 'I was just thinking. Everyone is out here enjoying themselves tonight; it's all so ordinary and so . . . well, you know. And probably in the next street or the next town, there's someone getting beaten up, somebody breaking into a house, someone ill treating their kid. Someone like Gregory doing whatever. It's like we just float on the surface most of the time and all around us, people are drowning.'

'And that's nothing major?' Naomi joked. 'Are you really OK?'

He squeezed her arm. 'I am,' he said. 'I realized something the other day. I realized that as an artist I probably thrive on thinking and knowing that kind of stuff. It was a shocking kind of thought for a while, but then I thought about it and I realized there were far worse things to be. I see what's really going on and I create art that maybe makes people think. I don't think that's such a dreadful thing.'

Naomi squeezed his arm in return. 'I think you're doing OK,' she told him.

At ten p.m. on 5 November, a woman was seen staggering down the centre of Great Wentworth High Street. That in itself might have attracted little notice. There were three pubs on that road and one small nightclub in a side street off it. But what did attract attention was the fact that she was barefoot, had no coat and was dressed only in what looked like a tattered nightdress.

That and the fact that she was obviously distraught.

The police and an ambulance arrived on the scene, by which time she was sitting in the lounge bar of one of the local pubs and the landlady had wrapped her in a blanket.

'We can't get any sense out of her,' the landlady told the paramedic. 'I think she's looking for a cat. We asked her name but she keeps talking about the cat.'

It wasn't long before the landlady finally put two and two

together and got the right answer. By the time Katherine Marsh had been admitted to hospital, the local press were ensconced in the Blue Monkey, drinking beer and listening to the account of how the missing woman turned up, half frozen and 'in a right state' and the locals had rallied round to help.

'But where's the kiddie? That's what we all want to know,' the landlady demanded. 'And that husband of hers. Gone missing too, I heard.'

The story grew in the telling. By midnight, Katherine Marsh had turned up, starving and naked and calling for her child and screaming to the world that her husband tried to kill them both.

'How is she?' Tess asked as she rushed into the waiting room. Vin had made it fifteen minutes ahead of her and had had a chance to speak to one of the paramedics. For both of them it had been a ninety-minute drive from Pinsent to Peterborough.

'Dehydrated and totally off her head.'

'He used those words, did he?'

'Actually,' Vin said. 'Pretty close. I spoke to one of the doctors. He said – and this is just a preliminary assessment – that she may have had a psychotic break. He doesn't know if she'll be able to tell us anything.'

'She's said nothing?'

'Just her name, over and over again.'

Tess called Katherine Marsh's uncle and aunt. The local police had been notified as soon as Kat's identity had been confirmed and had visited just a few minutes ahead of Tess's phone call.

'Shall we drive up? Should we be there? What can we do?'

'Hold fire for a bit,' Tess said. 'I don't think she's in a fit state to see anyone just yet. I'll ring just as soon as I know anything. I promise.'

'And what about the baby?'

Tess closed her eyes. The question was inevitable, but she'd still dreaded it. 'We don't know, yet. I'm sorry, we just don't know.'

Katherine Marsh lay on her side, a drip in her arm. Her hands were bandaged. She was crying.

'Katherine? I'm DI Tess Fuller . . . Tess. Can you tell me what happened to you?'

Kat Marsh didn't move. The tears fell but she didn't even look at Tess.

'Katherine?'

Tess looked up at the doctor. She shook her head and motioned Tess back into the ante room.

'What happened to her hands?'

'We took photographs. They're on the laptop.' She turned the computer so that Tess and Vin could see. 'Her feet were cut to ribbons. She's walked barefoot for a fair way. She'd still got one sock, but seems to have lost the other. Her hands were bruised and blooded. She'd ripped one nail right off.'

'She had?'

The doctor shrugged. 'Perhaps I should have said that one nail was ripped, right down to the quick. The palms of her hands, you can see, it's like she's gripped rough wood, full of splinters, and there are splinters of glass. It took a while to get them all out.'

'What was she wearing?'

The doctor pointed to a nearby table. 'A nightdress, a t-shirt, one sock. I'm guessing the t-shirt and sock were hers; the night-dress is a size eighteen. Katherine Marsh can't be more than a size twelve.'

Tess looked at the clothing. Muddy and torn, what was left of the sock was more hole than fabric. The t-shirt matched what she was known to have been wearing the day she was abducted.

'And she's said nothing?'

'Just her name.'

'She's not spoken about the child?'

A shake of the head. 'Inspector, right now she's not going to respond. She's shocked and exhausted and dehydrated. Try again in a few hours, when she's slept and we've got some fluids into her. That could make all the difference.'

'You think she might be more inclined to talk to family?'

'I really couldn't say. Sometimes it's easier to accept family support. Some people . . . sometimes when there's been a massive emotional trauma, it's easier to talk to a stranger. But I've never had to deal with a patient who's been through anything like this.'

'No sign of sexual assault?'

'No. Nothing like that. Come back in the morning. She might be able to talk to you by then.'

'Well, what do we make of this?' Vin asked.

'We try and work out where she came from. Surely she can't have come far, not dressed like that. It's bloody freezing out there.'

'Out buildings, barns. We need to set up a search radius. What do you reckon. Five miles?'

'We need to talk to the people who know the area,' Tess said practically. 'And go back to the pub, see if anyone noticed which direction she came from.'

Vin nodded. 'What about the baby?' he said. 'I can't see her leaving the kid behind.'

'Not if she was still alive,' Tess said.

FIFTY-ONE

Naomi's phone rang. It was two in the morning and she immediately thought the worst. Something bad had happened, some crisis in the family.

Instead, it was Gregory. 'Kat Marsh turned up,' he said.

'Dead or alive?'

'Alive and alone. You heard anything?'

'Gregory, why would I have heard anything?'

'I suppose you've got a point. Naomi, anything you do hear . . .'

'And the little girl?'

'Apparently not.'

'Shit. Do you think the television news will have more?'

'You stick the telly on; I'll check on the Internet,' Alec said. But half an hour later and despite the television news from the Blue Monkey; updates (there were nothing of the kind) from outside of the Marsh home and a bulletin from the hospital that said she was being treated for shock and police were waiting to interview her, there was nothing useful to be had.

'We've got a lead. Naomi, we need to be able to speak to Katherine. Can you help?'

'God's sake, Gregory, what do you think I can do?'

There was silence as he thought about it. 'Like I said, we've got a possible lead, maybe something we can trade with Tess Fuller. Can you fix up a meeting with her?'

'I'll try,' Naomi said. 'But I don't know if she'll go for it.'

'Of course she will,' Gregory said. 'It's her chance to break the case. Make a name for herself. Just ask her, Naomi. She'll bite.'

He was probably right, she thought.

'The other thing you've got to tell her is that Katherine Marsh isn't safe in that hospital.'

'She'll be under guard,' Naomi reassured him.

'Yeah, right,' he said. 'Just tell her. Hopefully she'll take notice.'

'In danger from whom?'

'From whoever took her; whoever still has her child. Naomi, if we can find out how she got away—'

'I don't see how. Look, I'll do what I can. You know what gets to me though? I can't believe she'd leave her child behind.'

'She wouldn't,' Gregory said flatly. 'Which means either Daisy is dead or Daisy was taken from her.'

Neither option was one Naomi wanted to consider.

'I know. I'll be in touch.'

Neither she nor Alec could sleep then. They got up and found a rolling news programme on the television, supplemented that with reports on the Internet. It might still be the middle of the night, but the media loved a human interest story, Naomi thought.

'Alive and alone, Gregory said.'

'That can't be good.' Alec shook his head. 'And nothing on Ian Marsh yet, presumably. You think he's still alive?'

'I think I don't like his odds, whoever gets to him first.'

Vin and Tess haunted the ward. They had spent time at the Blue Monkey, walked the streets where Kat had been found wandering. CSI were tracking the bloody footprints as far as they could, but it was slow work. They'd talked to their colleagues and a search would be begun at first light. Local farmers had been alerted and would help out by searching barns and outbuildings, but even setting a five-mile radius, the search area was massive and difficult. Fields and copses and fens. Scattered communities and abandoned farm buildings. There were also Second World War bunkers, they were told. Locked up tight now, but with passageways that were unsafe, partly closed and largely unmapped.

'She's got to talk to us,' Tess said. 'Anything she can tell us would help.'

And so they had retreated to the hospital again and paced the corridor, drunk foul coffee, and waited.

Just after seven o'clock the doctor approached and told Tess she could have another try.

'I'm still not getting much sense out of her, but the fluids have helped and she's more lucid.'

Tess drew up a chair beside Kat's bed. 'Remember me?' she asked. 'I was here earlier. I'm with the police, Kat. Can you tell me what happened to you?'

Katherine Marsh stared at the ceiling, examining the tiles with a focus and concentration that seemed utterly strange, then abruptly she turned her face towards Tess. 'They took my baby,' she said. 'They took my little girl. Someone came and grabbed her and I tried to fight them, but they were much too strong. And she was crying and reaching out for me and I couldn't reach her. I heard her screaming. I heard her crying for me. They came and they took my child.'

Tess was taken aback. Finally, she asked, 'Katherine, did you see anyone? See their faces? Anything you can tell me?'

Kat had turned away again. She was staring at the ceiling once again, her bandaged hands clutching at the sheets, and Tess knew she replayed that moment in her mind when they, whoever they were, had torn her child away from her. She knew instinctively that Kat was incapable of getting beyond that. She was caught in a loop and could not break out.

But she had to try. 'Katherine, how did you get away? How did you escape?'

Nothing, just the hands moving, clutching, grasping, releasing.

'Katherine, can you tell me anything about where you were held?'

But it was useless. Katherine Marsh no longer even heard her. She was lost in some other place, unable to escape that dreadful moment. That utter, all-encompassing loss.

She was aware that Vin and the doctor were no longer alone in the side room. Vin knocked at the glass and summoned her forth. A man in a smart suit stood just inside the room. A big man, whose presence seemed to dominate, to fill the space.

Tess frowned at him.

'You don't know me,' the man said. 'But your boss does. You can check with him.'

'And you've got a name?'

'Charles Duncan.' He must have seen the flicker of recognition in her eyes. 'I'm guessing I've been talked about,' he said.

'In passing. So, what are you doing here?'

'Going back with you to Pinsent. We've got work to do.'

'We're not ready to go back yet,' Tess said frostily. 'And I don't take orders from you.'

'Your sergeant can handle whatever there is to do here, so grab your stuff and we'll be off.'

'Tess,' Vin said. 'Branch texted me while you were in with Mrs Marsh. He says you should go.'

Tess took out her own phone, and checked her messages. She scowled at Charles Duncan. 'To do what?'

'First off, to go and speak with your friends the Friedmans. It's time to work together, don't you think? The woman's back, safe. Now we've just got to find her little girl.'

FIFTY-TWO

Annie recognized the woman standing in her garden. She wondered how long she had been there; decided it could not have been more than a few minutes as the dogs had not barked before. They stood now, one each side of Annie, poised for action or welcome, whatever Annie should decide.

She opened the French doors and stood aside. Mae crossed the lawn slowly and waited to be invited in. Like a vampire, Annie thought. Needing permission to cross into Annie's world.

'Why are you here?' she asked.

'Because you're the only one of us that's stopped running. The only one I could find in a hurry – and I am in a hurry, Annie. Otherwise I'd never have come here.'

Annie studied the older woman for a moment before acknowledging that. Mae was showing her age, she thought. The face was tired and lined; she wore no make-up and the roots showed at her parting. That shocked Annie, brought home to her that Mae really was desperate. Annie had known Mae since she was thirteen or fourteen and the woman had never been anything less than immaculate.

'What do you need?'

Mae relaxed, just slightly. 'I need you to set up a meeting. I know he's been looking for me and that,' she smiled wryly, 'is part of the problem. That brother of yours will get me killed yet, Annie.'

Brother Nathan. Mae had always called him that, referred to them as siblings, and Annie couldn't really disagree.

'When and where?'

'Nathan can choose, but make it fast, Annie. I don't have much time and I need to talk.'

Annie could see the fear in the woman's eyes. 'Who's after you, Mae?'

'Who isn't, sweetheart? But one of them will get me and it'll be soon.'

'Tell me. I can pass a message on.'

Mae shook her head. 'I want protection, Annie. I've got something Nathan wants. I know what happened to Ian Marsh's wife and child. I know where the baby might still be. And I know why Ian did it. That's got to be worth something, hasn't it?'

Nathan can't protect you, Annie thought. No one can. Not now. You're already dead, I can see it in your face. 'Why Ian did it? What do you mean, Mae?'

'He thought he could buy his way out of his mess. He'd got himself on the wrong side of Rico Steadmann, made promises he couldn't keep. He persuaded Bernie Franks to make it look like his wife and child had been taken. I think he did it to protect them – and himself – but it didn't work out that way, did it? Poor fucker didn't understand that Bernie was always one of Rico's boys.'

'What does he have that Rico wants?' Annie asked, but Mae just shook her head.

'Account numbers, details of Clay's old accounts, I think. I don't know for sure.'

'Why would Ian Marsh have access to those? If they exist any more. Mae . . .'

'I don't know. I only know what he told Steadmann. That he could get access. Maybe from Nathan?'

Annie didn't push further. It seemed that Mae had half a story – either that or she was playing more games.

'I need a number,' she said.

Mae handed her a slip of paper and then turned to go. Behind her, Annie heard a sound that told her Bob was in the hall. Mae heard it too.

'You're fooling yourself, you know,' she said as the door opened and Annie's husband stepped through. He halted on the threshold as he saw Annie was not alone. 'You can't hide forever. Our life finds us.'

Annie shook her head. 'It's not my life any more,' she said. 'I stopped running, Mae. I'm not hiding. If something wants to come for me, it'll have to come here. This place is my fortress, my last stand if need be, but I'm done with running.'

'You always were a fool,' Mae said softly. 'But I loved you and Nathan, you know that.'

She turned and walked away, across the lawn and through the gap in the hedge that led up on to the bank and then to the footpath over the hill. Annie watched her go, the slip of paper clasped in her hand.

'Who was that?' Bob asked. He came over to her and laid his hands on Annie's shoulders. Together they watched Mae disappear among the trees, and then Bob reached around her and closed the door. 'It's getting cold,' he said. 'Winter will be unforgiving this year, I think.'

Annie nodded, mourning for another small fragment of her past she knew would soon be shattered and gone.

FIFTY-THREE

Charles Duncan had a better car than she had, Tess thought. And he drove faster than she would have done on the winding roads. Miffed and irritated, she didn't speak much for the first half hour or so – she was also a little unnerved by the speed at which he took the bends and was of a mind to let him concentrate on the driving. She occupied herself by checking through the news feeds on her phone.

'What are they saying?' Charles Duncan asked at last.

'That Katherine Marsh reappeared at ten-fifteen last evening. Barefoot and almost naked. The landlady of the Blue Monkey took charge and called the police and wrapped her in a blanket. That she was alone and evidently in shock. Most of the reports have Desiree Marsh dead and buried. A couple are speculating about child trafficking.' She looked across at Charles Duncan but he didn't react.

'There's a lot of speculation about Professor Marsh. Most are rehashing the official line, that he's off staying with friends, but there's a lot of people starting to wonder why he's not been brought to the hospital. Then there's a whole load of stuff about search teams and asking for volunteers.'

Charles Duncan nodded.

'Why did he run? Is he dead?'

'Professor Marsh? He ran because he was being threatened. Alive or dead? I really couldn't say.'

'That text message on Katherine Marsh's phone. *Time's up.* What did that mean? Time's up for what?'

'Any ideas?'

'There's no sign of them asking for money. Whoever they are.'

'And your best guess is . . .?'

Tess let out an exasperated huff. 'How the hell should I know? Was he selling secrets – he seems to have had the connections. Was this Nathan Crow involved? Bernie Franks? That Mae Tourino woman?'

Charles Duncan shook his head. 'Nothing as complicated or as esoteric as that,' he said. 'When it comes down to it, Tess, it's all about the money. Money and power, nice old-fashioned motives. Unfortunately, the players are anything but nice or old-fashioned. They all want to be ahead of the game, your Professor Marsh included. They all want more than they have – with the possible exception of Nathan Crow and his friends. Annie Raven I think genuinely wants a quiet life now. Gregory Hess—'

'Who?'

'Oh, an associate of ours and of Nathan's. I think he just wants to get back to that boat of his and sail off into the sunset. I'm not sure even Nathan Crow knows what Nathan Crow wants. Ian Marsh baited the hook and Nathan bit. I suspect he probably realizes that now and I expect him to be pretty annoyed, shall we say. I don't give much for Ian Marsh's chances if Nathan gets to him, or Bernie Franks, or Rico Steadmann – you recognize that name, I see.'

'The name, yes. I've had no dealings.'

'Lucky you. But you probably have, without knowing it. Steadmann has fingers in all the pies. Controls great chunks of the heroin coming in from Afghanistan. He's involved in people smuggling, the sex trade. He's a good all-rounder is Rico Steadmann.'

'So what's the link to Ian Marsh?'

'Complicated,' Charles Duncan said. 'If you don't mind, I'll wait until we get to the Freidmans; then I only have to explain myself once.'

'Alec's retired,' Tess said. 'He keeps reminding me of that.'

Charles Duncan laughed. 'But he has a direct link to Nathan Crow and Gregory Hess,' he said. 'Something I and my associates no longer have. So he's going to have to un-resign for a while, I think. I need his help, Tess, and so do you, and I think Nathan Crow and Gregory could do with mine. This is all about the ends, not the means.'

FIFTY-FOUR

N aomi and Alec had the television on when Tess arrived. Tess watched as the rows of officers and volunteers paced slowly across the flat fenland landscape she had so recently driven through.

'This is Charles Duncan,' she told them. 'I'm sure he has a job title, but he's not shared that information.'

'Home Office,' Charles Duncan said.

Naomi laughed and Tess felt a strange desire to join her. 'Really,' Naomi said. 'That's a pretty broad set of possibilities.'

'You'd best sit down,' Alec said. 'I'll put the kettle on.'

'So what's the news on Katherine Marsh?' Naomi asked.

'She's in shock; probably won't be able to tell us much for a while. She's cut and bruised and we don't know how far she'd walked but was half frozen when she was found.'

'And nothing on the child? No news from the kidnappers?'

'No,' Tess said. 'Anything you might know that we don't?'

Alec placed the tray he was carrying down on the table. 'No,' he said. 'I don't think there is; just a message that Katherine Marsh isn't safe in the hospital. That her abductors may still try to get to her.'

Tess stared at him. She hadn't really expected a straight answer to her question but it seemed that Alec had decided the time for secrets was over.

'Nathan contacted you?' Charles Duncan asked. 'Or was it Gregory Hess?'

'Funny,' Naomi said. 'I never thought of him as having a last name. I suppose he has several to choose from.' She smiled sweetly in Charles Duncan's direction. 'So, what's all this about?'

Briefly, Charles Duncan told them what he had told Tess on the way there and then elaborated.

'About eighteen months ago we got a tip-off that an associate of Rico Steadmann's was looking for a deal. He'd been running from Rico for about five years by then, was broke and scared and I think just tired of running. We took a bit of convincing that he'd still got anything to offer us – after all, he'd crossed Steadmann five years before and so far as we knew had been out of the picture. But it seems he'd kept some of his associations and one of them persuaded us that he still had something to trade. So we fixed him with a cover story, a new job and a new address and he talked.'

'Anthony Palmer,' Alec guessed.

'The same. And the man who persuaded us to listen to him

was Ian Marsh. Then eight or nine months ago the job up here came available and Marsh offered to rent him the cottage. No one thought anything of it. Until Anthony Palmer was killed.'

'How did this Palmer cross Rico Steadmann?' Naomi asked.

'You know anything about Steadmann?'

Naomi nodded. 'Just before my accident I'd been working down in London. Serious Organized Crime Unit. Alec and I weren't together then and I seriously thought of relocating. I'd applied, and I'd got a good chance . . . Anyway, everything changed and that was that. But Steadmann is an interesting man. From an interesting family – if you like that sort of thing.

'The family were refugees, came over here from Germany in 1941, escaped by the skin of their teeth. But after the war, Steadmann senior went back and tried to reclaim some of the property they'd had. There were rumours that he'd stashed bullion in the basement of one of the properties they owned. Anyway, whatever the truth, post war, their fortunes looked up. They'd got legitimate business in property, a chain of pubs, couple of hotels if I remember right. And illegitimate interests in just about everything else. But it was always very low key and the Steadmann family did a lot of good work – kids' charities and that sort of thing – and that kept their public persona sweet.'

'By the nineteen sixties and seventies,' Charles Duncan took up the story, 'the Steadmanns had been eclipsed by the likes of the Krays. The Steadmanns were never part of the criminal gangs that dominated back then. Rico Steadmann's father relocated the whole family. They settled in Leeds, became respected members of local society, and because of the links they maintained in Germany, both sides of the wall, were even of use to Her Majesty's government on odd occasions. By the late eighties, Rico had taken over, the Berlin wall was down, and they set about legitimizing their trade links and taking advantage of new markets that suddenly opened up with the fall of communism. We think that's when the likes of Gustav Clay started to take an interest. Steadmann knew people that Clay had to be careful not to know and a woman we know as Mae Tourino, among other aliases, acted as courier between Clay and Rico Steadmann.'

'The way he was killed,' Tess said. 'What's your take on that?'

'How was Palmer murdered?' Alec asked.

'Um, I've got some of the pictures on my laptop,' Tess said. She looked at Charles Duncan, wondering exactly how far this sharing thing was going. 'OK if I . . .?'

He nodded.

Alec took his time looking at the crime-scene photographs. He described them to Naomi.

'It sounds sort of ritualized,' she said. 'It's very specific.'

'You'd be right about that,' Charles Duncan confirmed. 'We think whoever did this was emulating another murder, or should I say other murders. I'd like to suggest that it was sending a message, but frankly, most of those capable of reading such a message are dead and gone.'

'What then?' Naomi asked. 'Is someone trying to prove a point? Send a warning?'

'I suspect that Rico Steadmann himself was involved in the killing,' Charles Duncan said. 'I suspect it was done this way by him or under his supervision simply because he was curious. I think he wanted to see it done. For Steadmann, this was the way traitors had been dealt with. He once had an associate, name of Mason, who specialized in that kind of torture and assassination.'

'And we still don't know what Palmer took from him. Or how he found him. Did Ian Marsh betray him?'

'We think the answer to that last question is yes. To the first, Palmer stole money. A lot of it. He also tried to muscle in on Rico's connections, take a cut of the action for himself.'

'And what did Ian Marsh have to gain?'

'Ian Marsh had used his own connections to . . . OK, we have to take a step back here. You are aware of Gustav Clay. You're aware, I think, that one of the things he did was run a sort of underground railway. New identities, new lives for those he chose to save?'

Naomi nodded. 'Molly Chambers told us something about that,' she said. 'There was no protection for those who acted as interpreters or worked for British troops or government officials. A great many people died because they found themselves wrong footed when our people pulled out. Clay helped Molly and her husband to change that when they could.'

'And set up a very complex network to facilitate it. Yes. Nathan

Crow and Annie Raven were rescued by Clay, you know that. He saved them; he them controlled them. Eventually they had to break free of him.'

'And Ian Marsh?'

'Was a party to much of the action. Sometimes he even selected those who could and should be protected. I believe that in part our professor is a man of conscience. I think he's also a greedy man.

'What we understand is that Marsh, even after he'd taken up academia, remained a part of Clay's wider network. From time to time, Rico Steadmann made use of it. From time to time Clay made use of Rico Steadmann.'

'And once Clay had gone, the likes of Steadmann moved in to make use of his networks,' Alec guessed.

'They did. And Ian Marsh found, or thought he found, ways of increasing his cut. The trouble was, Palmer threatened him. He threatened to blow the whole scheme. We didn't know just how deep in Steadmann's pocket Ian Marsh was until Palmer told us. Ian Marsh then betrayed Palmer to Rico Steadmann. Palmer was then killed. We think Ian Marsh escaped Rico's censure only because he still had something to trade.'

'And Ian Marsh was there, wasn't he?' Tess said.

She'd surprised Charles Duncan, she realized. That pleased her.

'How do you know that? Did you work that out when you went back to Church Lane?'

It was Tess's turn to be surprised. 'You've been watching me?'

'No, I had someone watching the house. I thought Marsh might just turn up there.'

'I think he finished the job,' Tess said. 'The knife in the side. It doesn't fit with the rest of it. There's nothing slick or patient about the stab wound. It was angry. Impulsive, almost.'

'And how does the kidnapping fit?' Naomi asked. 'Gregory is of the opinion that Ian Marsh staged it.'

'And I think he's right. I think he got Steadmann to carry it out. I think the plan was then for Marsh to disappear and the family to be reunited. Professor Marsh knew, or suspected, that after Palmer spilled what he knew, we'd get around to arresting him. He was trapped between trusting Steadmann and hoping

Palmer hadn't told him too much or waiting for us to act. Presumably he made an agreement with Steadmann that they'd use their smuggling routes and their protection, to get Ian Marsh and his family out of the way. How he thought he'd be able to square that with Katherine is another matter. But he's an arrogant man. I don't suppose it occurred to him that she'd cause problems.'

'Any more than it occurred to him that Rico Steadmann wasn't trustworthy,' Alec said.

'I think he knew that, but was left with too few options. I also suspect that he wanted to be at Palmer's death, so he'd find out what Palmer knew or had already told.'

'Or maybe he wanted to prove he was still loyal to Steadmann,' Naomi said.

'That's also a possibility and until we catch up with him, or we are in a position to start making arrests, we're not going to find out.'

'But that doesn't explain the text messages,' Tess put in. 'Did they come from Steadmann?'

'Text messages?'

'Katherine's phone turned up at the Marsh house. Whoever left the photograph that caused Nathan Crow to take off into the wild blue yonder also left the phone. They were in touch with Marsh. The last message told him that he was out of time.'

'For what?'

'For whatever he'd promised to deliver, I suppose,' Charles Duncan said. 'He handed over his wife and child, promised something in return for a new life for all of them, and then failed to deliver. At least that's the way I read it. Exactly what he was trading is more difficult. It could be information, it could be money.'

Naomi thought about it, decided it sounded plausible. 'So,' she said. 'Exactly why are you here?'

'Because you have a means of contacting the . . . shall we call them the other half of the investigative team,' Charles Duncan said. 'We know Gregory and Nathan Crow went to see Bernie Franks, a known associate of Rico Steadmann. We know they have ties to Mae Tourino and that there are pieces of this we don't have.'

'And why would they help you?'

'Because of the child. Because for once we all have the same aim in mind. Because Nathan understands enough to realize he can't make any move, live any kind of independent life, unless and until he squares Clay's empire away once and for all.'

Naomi thought about it. Charles Duncan was being disingenuous, she thought, putting a positive, Nathan-friendly spin on this. She had a reasonable grasp of the kind of black hole Gustav Clay's death had left and that it was a toss up which element of the criminal classes – government sponsored or old-school thieves – plugged the gap and how effectively. Clay had straddled both camps and Naomi had come to view them, anyway, as elements and pointers on the same continuum. What had happened, she wondered, to the idealistic young copper she'd once been?

'We'll pass your message on,' she said. 'But I can't promise a response. You can understand that Gregory in particular is a little wary of representations from his old employers.'

'Different department,' Charles Duncan said.

'I'm sure he'll feel reassured.'

'What was Palmer's real name?' Alec asked.

'Sorry, can't tell you that. It probably isn't relevant anyway.'

Naomi heard the sofa creak as Charles Duncan got to his feet. 'Thank you for your time,' he said. 'Be sure to pass my message on, won't you? Soon as I get your call I'll set up a meeting.'

'I wouldn't hold your breath,' Alec said. 'We're standing on the sidelines, Naomi and I. Not players.'

'You're not that naive, Alec,' Charles Duncan said.

He and Tess left after that, leaving Naomi and Alec feeling heavy with unease.

FIFTY-FIVE

Mae's eyes narrowed as she slid into the booth opposite Gregory. The café was trying for fifties American retro, but it was trying a little too hard; the result was more a Disneyfication of the original than a replica. 'I asked to speak with Nathan.'

'And Nathan sent me.'

'He doesn't trust me?' Mae smiled.

'Any reason he should? The way I see it, and Nathan is inclined to agree, is that you and Marsh set him up to take the fall for this. All he wants now is the information you might have.'

'And I want something in exchange.'

'Annie said you wanted protection. Not going to happen, Mae. Even if he could I doubt very much he would.'

'Then you get nothing from me.'

'Mae, you want to give us what you know; if you didn't you'd be halfway across Europe by now, selling yourself to the highest bidder, just like you've always done.'

'Maybe I've nowhere left to run to.'

'Happens to all of us in the end,' Gregory said. The waitress came over and he ordered another coffee and one for Mae. 'You want anything to eat?'

Mae looked at him as though he'd gone mad.

'Look,' he said. 'When Gustav Clay departed this life, it was inevitable that the world, our world, would change. We could try and keep a lid on things, but when someone like Clay dies, secrets he kept, rules he broke, those who want revenge for wrongs committed so long ago that there's barely anyone left alive to remember them – they all come out of the woodwork looking for their cut. Mae, we're the lost generation now. There are bullets with our names on for the whole damned lot of us and with Clay and his ilk passing, some of those bullets are going to be fired and some of them are going to catch more than one of us when they ricochet.'

She laughed. 'You're getting poetic in your old age, Gregory.'

'No, I'm just getting real. I had a dream a while ago, Mae. Four men dead in a room I didn't know, but could have been a hundred rooms I've passed through or been in or killed in over my lifetime. Four men, one shot fired. Mae, just tell me what you came to tell and I'll act on it and we'll do our best to deflect the fire, but that's all we can do. All any of us can do.'

The smile was gone now. Annie was right, Gregory thought. Mae was looking old. Tired and worn down and worn out.

'What was Ian trying to sell?'

She shook her head. 'Not if you won't help me.'

'No one's going to help you. No one can. You figured that out for yourself. Whatever decision you have made you must have known no one else could rescue you.'

Mae said nothing, but bright spots of colour touched her cheeks and Gregory had the strangest feeling that she was ready to cry.

'Ian said he knew how to access Clay's crisis fund. Millions, he reckoned.'

Gregory tried not to laugh out loud. 'Mae, that's all bollocks. Clay was government funded and when he wasn't he drew down favours from all over the place, Rico included on occasion. Clay didn't have a fund; Clay had his house and a few personal accounts.'

'You don't know that.'

'Nathan knows it. Nathan knows exactly what Clay's resources were. He spent enough time managing them.'

'Nathan didn't know everything. Ian told me. An offshore account. He reckoned he could get the numbers. He—'

'From who, Mae?'

'I don't know. From Nathan, maybe. Look, all I know is that Rico's been making a lot of moves since Clay died. He's bought a load of property. Warehouses and development stuff, mostly. And he's been liquidating a lot of his other assets, piling everything he can offshore. I don't know what he's planning, Gregory, but I don't think he plans to stick around. With Clay gone, it's all changing. It's like his death started the dominoes falling and now they've started they aren't going to stop. Getting access to Clay's little fund would be the icing on the cake.'

Gregory gave up. For all he knew there had been a crisis fund, but he doubted it. Ian Marsh had most likely been spinning Rico a line. Most likely too Rico Steadmann knew that, had just played him, getting what he could. People like Bernie Franks and Rico Steadmann didn't always have a reason for doing things, at least not the kind of reason anyone else would understand. He let it go. He and Nathan could argue the ins and outs of that later.

'The child, Mae. Where is she?'

'One child, Gregory. Why the hell should I care about one child?'

'Truthfully? I have no idea. Maybe you're growing soft or maybe you didn't set as hard as you like to think. Frankly, I don't give a shit. I just want to know what you know.'

There was a long silence. The coffee arrived and was ignored.

Gregory watched the door, wondering, not for the first time, if she was simply playing for time.

'I know where they were held,' she said eventually. 'The baby was moved. They've got a customer for her, but the sale can't be made for a day or two.' Mae shrugged. 'Maybe I should just let it happen. It's a rich family, loads of money and all they need is a blonde-haired toddler to make their life complete. There could have been worse fates for little Desiree. But I persuaded him, Gregory. *I* persuaded him that he should just sell her on, to a family. To someone who could look after her. Who *would* look after her. That's got to count for something, doesn't it?'

'So, go to the police, tell them. Let them decide what it counts for.'

He thought he'd blown it. The look of hatred that crossed Mae's face, she would have turned him to stone in a heartbeat. Instead, she looked away. 'Wish I could smoke,' she said. 'What is it with the world? I can't even light up in a public place any more.'

'The child, Mae.'

He watched her face, certain that she'd finished with him. That he'd failed, or that she didn't know as much as she made out after all.

He took a copy of the photograph Nathan had received from his pocket and laid it on the table. 'Someone sent Nathan this. Any ideas?'

To his surprise, he saw her blanch; even her lips seemed to grow pale.

'Ian took the picture,' she whispered. 'He and I, we'd meet up from time to time. We'd . . . Oh my God.'

Gregory watched as she began to put things together. 'Ian took the picture,' she said again, her voice flat and despairing.

'And sent a copy to Nathan? Why would he do that? Mae, did you leave a note with your name on it at Ian Marsh's house?'

She shook her head. 'I was never there,' she said. 'I was responsible for keeping check on the woman and kid.'

'Seems someone wanted to implicate you, Mae. Right from the start.' And make certain that Nathan was well and truly hooked, Gregory thought.

She was looking past him now and something flickered in her

eyes, some recognition or realization. It made Gregory uneasy. He could see the door but the arrangement of the booth meant that the back of the diner was invisible to him.

Mae seemed suddenly to make up her mind. 'I don't know where she is now. But I know someone who does.' She felt in her coat pocket and withdrew a folded piece of paper, slid it across the table to Gregory. Then she was gone, hurrying from the diner as though the Devil himself was on her tail.

Gregory pocketed the paper and signalled to the waitress for the bill, waiting, even though every nerve, every muscle yelled at him to get the hell out.

The waitress came across. Behind her, Gregory glimpsed a man leaving and then a couple. Neither looked his way. Gregory stood, glancing towards the back of the diner, seeking whatever it was Mae had seen. He dug in his pocket for his wallet and paid his bill, adding a tip, then sidled out past the waitress as she collected his money.

Outside, Gregory glanced up and down the road. Mae was nowhere to be seen. The couple were across the road, standing at a bus stop. The man he had noted had also disappeared.

Walking back to where he left his car, Gregory felt like a marked man. Mae's bullet was in the air; he could feel that, seeking out its target. He had no wish to be caught by its ricochet.

FIFTY-SIX

K at had fallen into an uneasy dream. She lay in a dark place, walls rising high all around her and painted a dull and light-denying black. Desiree was asleep beside her and then some great hand crashed through the wall, grabbed the child and tore her away. Kat woke, bathed in sweat, her heart beating its way out of her chest and reality crashed over her, crushing her down. Worse than her dream.

'Do you want some water?'

She turned her head towards the concerned voice and for a moment couldn't place who he was. Then she remembered: the

Asian policeman who'd been there before, with the small, pretty woman who'd said her name was Tess.

He poured her some water and she struggled to sit up. Kat could see he was torn between offering to help her and fear that it would be an inappropriate thing to do. She took the water, her hands trembling.

'I dreamed I was with her,' she said. 'Then she was taken away.'

Vin sat back down beside the bed. 'Can you talk about it? Anything you can tell us about where you were held would help.'

She nodded. 'I'll try.'

'Good.' He smiled. 'Tess had to go,' Vin said. 'Are you OK talking to me?'

'I'll try,' Kat said again. 'I just don't know where to start.'

'Anywhere you can. How about if I ask questions? Would that help? Can you describe the place where you were held?'

Kat closed her eyes, but even though the lights were on, darkness lurked. She opened them again. 'An old building,' she said. 'Inside, there was like this big box. Desiree and I, we were locked in there. Someone gave us food and water and nappies for Desi, but I knew there wasn't enough. I had to make it last in case they didn't come back.' Tears flowed and her voice failed. Vin waited patiently for her to regain control.

He felt in his pocket and produced a chocolate bar. 'Want to share?'

She nodded and he unwrapped the chocolate, broke off some squares and offered them to her. Kat forced the tension from her shoulders and took a piece. This was just what she needed, she realized. Something really ordinary. Something normal.

'A stone building,' she said. 'With wooden floors. And so quiet. I couldn't bear the quiet. Where's Ian?' she asked suddenly as though the idea of her husband had suddenly occurred.

Vin hesitated. 'We don't know,' he said. 'He left home a few days ago and we don't know where he went.'

She stared at him as though trying to make sense of the words, but she didn't seem capable of formulating the questions.

'A stone building with wooden floors,' Vin prompted. He offered more chocolate and she took another square. She seemed so fragile, Vin thought. Ready to fall back into that hiding place inside her own head. 'With a big wooden box inside. How did you get out, Katherine?'

'Kat,' she said, her attention seeming to wander for a moment.

'Kat. Have some chocolate. Take a sip of water. You're doing fine.' It was like questioning a child, he thought. Like he needed an appropriate adult. Through the window into the ante room he could see a uniformed officer, chatting to a nurse as she sorted paperwork. The nurse kept looking Vin's way, checking everything was all right. As all right as it could be.

'How did you get out?'

She took a deep breath. 'I heard footsteps,' she said. 'Two people. A woman and a man. The door opened and they came inside. The man hit me and I fell and then he picked up Desiree and he left. I could hear her screaming, crying, calling for me, but I couldn't get up. My head . . .'

'You're doing well,' he told her again. 'Just take it slow.'

'I can remember the woman bending down to look at me and I tried to reach her, but it was like nothing was working. I think I must have passed out and when I came round it was all so quiet again. Desi wasn't there.'

Vin broke the rest of the chocolate and laid the pack on the bed. This was currency now. She told him something, he gave her sweets. He didn't question it. Whatever worked, whatever bridged the gap and kept her talking. She took another square and stared at it.

'In the bag,' she said. 'Someone left food and water and chocolate in the bag. Desi ate most of it. They left batteries too. I've never been so thankful for anything. They left me a light.'

She sipped more water. The door opened softly and the nurse from the ante room slipped in. She laid another bar of chocolate on the side table and then left again.

'I'll be sick if I eat all that,' Katherine said.

Vin smiled at her. 'We'll share,' he said. He broke off a square and ate it, taking time to let it dissolve on his tongue. 'When you came round?' he prompted. 'It was quiet and you were alone.'

She nodded. 'And I was cold. I'd kept a blanket wrapped round me but it had fallen on the floor when he knocked me down. Then I realized there was a draft. Just a little one. That the cold was coming from somewhere. Then I saw the gap in the door. It was just a crack, but when they left, they hadn't locked the door. The woman hadn't locked the door.'

'So you opened the door. And then . . .'

'I felt so sick. My head hurt. I wanted to drink but there was no water left. I'd given it to Desi. I pushed on the door and it opened wide. I thought they were playing with me. That I'd get out and they'd be waiting, but there was no one. The place was empty and it was cold and I could see the window high up in the wall. It wasn't quite dark.'

'And then what?' Vin asked gently.

'I managed to get down the stairs, but when I got to the door it was locked up tight. That was when I knew she'd tried to help me. She'd waited until the man was out of sight and then she'd only pretended to lock me in. But she couldn't do anything about the big door.

'I got back up the stairs and then I knew the only way out was the window. There were more stairs up to this kind of platform and I could reach the window from there. The stairs were all rotting away, so I tried not to walk in the centre of them. I wanted to get out, to find Desi. I just kept thinking that. I had to find Desi.'

She paused and looked fully at Vin. 'Why did Ian run away?'

'We don't know,' Vin said cautiously. He knew instinctively that he mustn't lie to her. That she'd sense it and shut him out. But what was safe to say?

'Maybe he went looking for us,' she said.

'Maybe he did.'

She held his gaze, considering his words, and he saw something die as she found them wanting. Kat looked away, her fingers taking another piece of chocolate, her brain barely noticing what she did.

'You made it to the window,' Vin said.

'The glass was cracked. I picked up a bit of broken stair and I shoved at it. It broke. I cut my hands, but I managed to make a hole big enough to get through. I could see there was a creeper of some sort and I just hoped it would hold me. I didn't really think about it; I just wanted to get out. If I'd had to jump, I think I would have.'

She finally looked at the square of chocolate between her fingers, melting now, the corners rounding with the heat of her hand. She ate it slowly, her eyes seeing something not in the little room.

'I could see lights,' she said. 'So I guessed there must be a road or some houses and so I headed for them. I don't know how far it was, but it got dark and then very dark. And then it was light and there were buildings and people and . . . and that was it.'

'Can you remember the people in the pub?'

'I think so,' she said. 'It's all mixed up. Voices and bright lights and being cold.'

'You must have been very frightened.'

She nodded. 'Is she dead?' Kat asked.

Again he had to balance his answer. Truth, lies, somewhere between? Worse, he didn't know which was which.

'We don't know,' he said. 'We have to go on hoping.'

She nodded. Tears streaming down her face now. She hadn't asked about Ian again, Vin noted. Perhaps she sensed that something was badly wrong. Vin hoped he would not have to be the one to confirm that for her.

FIFTY-SEVEN

'What was this place, do you reckon?' Gregory said. 'I'm guessing a mill of some kind. It's by the river; there's the remains of a water wheel. It's got to be a couple of hundred years old.'

He considered for a moment, looking at the fenland landscape that surrounded them. 'Of course, it could have been something to do with drainage,' he said.

Gregory shrugged. They had parked the car a quarter of a mile back down the track, pulling on to the verge and tucking in close to the hedge. They had seen no one, heard no one. A couple of miles before making the final turn, they had crossed a railway line with an unmanned crossing. In the distance now they could hear a train, slow and rumbling. Freight, Gregory guessed, rather than passengers.

It was late afternoon, twilight fast approaching, but they'd heard about the search on the radio news and didn't want to risk leaving their own until the following day. Sooner rather than later, someone would recall this ancient structure and come looking.

The main door had been padlocked. The chain and lock were new. Nathan left it alone and they circled the building looking for the way Kat Marsh might have escaped. The dyke alongside the mill house was overgrown and stagnant. Looking across the fields, Gregory could just make out another stretch of water. He guessed this one must once have been linked to that, but now it was little more than an elongated, silted pond.

'She couldn't have got out this way. She'd have fallen in.'

Nathan nodded and then circled back the way they'd come. 'There.'

There was a window halfway up the wall, the glass broken. Glass on the ground glinted as Nathan shone a torch on it. 'Blood,' he said.

'Looks that way.'

Ivy and a stunted ash tree clambered up the old brick. Nathan could see scrapes and breaks where she'd half climbed, half slithered down.

'Stay here,' Nathan said. 'I doubt it will take your weight.'

Gregory nodded and Nathan began to climb. Soon he was at the window. Gregory watched as he slid through.

It was getting dark now. Gregory stood and listened, watching the last of the sun fade from a leaden sky. It would rain, he thought. Wash Kat's blood from the glass and into the rich, black soil.

He leaned back against the wall and settled in for the wait.

Inside, Nathan lowered himself down carefully. The window was placed above a rusted platform; a gantry overhead indicated that it had been used for loading something. Steps, half rotten and with many missing, led down on to the upper floor. Nathan descended slowly and carefully, then paused and played his torch around the walls and empty space. He listened to the silence, the stillness. A dead place, he thought, jealous of its privacy and isolation.

It took him a moment to realize what he was seeing. That what he was seeing was out of place. A structure had been built on the upper floor. From his position on the steps he was effectively looking down on to it – but not quite into it, built as it was somewhere close to the middle of the wooden floor, rising solidly amid the age and decay. Slowly, Nathan descended the rest of the steps and went for a closer look.

Pacing it out, he estimated it was something like ten feet by ten wide and about the same high. He was immediately in no doubt that this was where Katherine Marsh had been held prisoner.

His feet disturbed dust and grime and, shining his torch down, he could see clearly where other feet had done the same. Nathan crouched, but there was no detail he could make out. Just the sign that someone or several someones had walked here recently. There were signs that the floor had been reinforced to take the weight of the large wooden crate. In other places, he could see holes in the timber floor and through those holes could see the beams holding the floor in place. Even now they looked strong and heavy, Nathan thought. This place had been built to last. On the third side of the cube, Nathan found the door. It stood open now, but had been secured by two massive bolts. Nathan stepped inside. The mattress, the chemical toilet – soiled nappies piled beside it. A plastic bag, a pathetic little lantern, coarse blankets. Kat and Daisy had been kept here.

Nathan felt the anger surge and fought it down. This was time to be calm, to think, not to feel rage. Pulling on a pair of latex gloves, Nathan inspected the black plastic bag lying on the floor. The remains of sandwich wrappers, apple cores and chocolate bars. Bottled water. Sustenance for maybe a few days, certainly not enough for the week or more she had been kept here. Had Daisy been here all that time as well?

Nathan backed out and flashed the torch around again, looking for any sign of others being here, leaving anything behind. He doubted there would be anything but went down anyway to inspect the lower floors. Apart from evidence of footprints in the dust, nothing remained.

So, someone had unlocked the door, Nathan thought. Someone had come here and left the door of the crate unbolted, but then locked and padlocked the outer door.

Mae, Nathan guessed. Mae, but she'd not been alone. Someone had put the padlock and chain back on the entrance to the mill. Was that when they had taken Daisy from her mother? How long had it been before Kat had realized she had a way out? Had she made her way down to the main door first and found it barred? Had she thought this was just a sick joke – released from her first prison just to find herself still confined? Or had she headed straight for that high window?

Mae – and Nathan just knew it had been Mae – would have considered she'd given Kat a fighting chance. Nathan found he was surprised that Ian Marsh's wife had actually taken it. Reluctantly, he revised his opinion of Katherine, just a little.

He'd been here long enough and, in truth, learnt little. He guessed that Mae had wanted him to see this place in part so he understood the risk she herself had run, crossing whoever had abducted Kat and the child.

Always theatrical, Nathan thought. Always wanting to emphasize the point. Mae never seemed to grasp that there were times to be subtle. He made his way back up to the window and examined it carefully before going back through. Looking at it, he guessed that the glass had been cracked before and that Kat must have broken it, cutting herself in the process. How badly had she hurt herself? The distance across the fields to where she had been found was, he calculated, a rough eight miles. It wasn't the closest settlement; there was a village four miles or so back down the track and then down the little B road. But she wouldn't have known that and, looking out of the window, Nathan understood what had brokered her decision. There were lights on the horizon. Lights that looked like a road or a group of houses. She'd have seen them from up here and taken the most direct route she could to find help.

'Good for you, Katherine,' Nathan said.

FIFTY-EIGHT

I'm tired, Naomi thought, then remembered that she'd been up since two in the morning. It was now just after six in the evening.

Once Tess and Charles Duncan had gone they had decided to go out, unable to settle in the little flat. Naomi joked that Duncan had probably bugged the place. Then it hadn't felt like a joke. Finally, they'd made their way to the local pub and ordered a meal.

'You think Gregory will cooperate with him?' Naomi asked.

'I doubt it. Would you?'

Naomi shrugged. 'I don't know. But I don't think Charles Duncan is as committed to finding Desiree as he is to caulking the sinking ship Clay left behind. I smell damage limitation here.'

They were silent for a few minutes, while both tucked into their meals. 'You think the big Tesco will still be open?' Naomi asked.

'Should be. I think it closes at ten. Why?'

'Because I think Patrick needs a new phone. Or at least a new sim card.'

'We shouldn't involve him, Nomi.'

'I want him to send a text, that's all. Let Gregory know they have company. I think when he asked to speak to Tess, he didn't have the likes of Charles Duncan in mind. If they have the facts, they can decide what to do.'

'OK,' Alec said. 'If Harry agrees, of course.'

'Patrick is an adult now,' she reminded him.

Nathan and Gregory had headed south again, tracking the man Mae had named. Gregory felt momentarily guilty about the woman – but only momentarily. Mae had made her choices. She'd had opportunities to get out. Clay had ensured she had a pension and an escape route, but she'd not taken it. You should know when to quit.

Beside him, Nathan shifted uncomfortably. 'Pull in and I'll take over,' Gregory said. They'd both spent more hours behind the wheel lately than was good for them. Back and knees complained and Gregory was increasingly aware that he was no longer a young man. Old breaks ached; old scars grew sore.

'You think this is a wild goose chase?' Nathan asked, drawing into the next lay-by.

'I think it could be. But I think she'd already committed herself. She'd got nothing to gain by lying and Phelps is one of Steadmann's men. So . . .'

Nathan got out of the car and stretched. Gregory took his place in the driver's seat.

'She reckoned we'd got a couple of days,' he said. 'Before the sale goes through.'

He was talking about a child, he thought suddenly. But it felt easier, using neutral language, not dwelling too much on the realities.

'So, we'd better get moving then,' Nathan said.

Kat Marsh stared up at the ceiling. The nice policeman had gone off for a well-earned break when they thought she'd fallen asleep. She may well have dropped off for a few minutes, Kat thought, but she couldn't be sure. The line between waking and sleeping and some other limbo state was no longer very well defined. She floated – no, floated sounded too peaceful and this state wasn't peaceful. She *existed* in some strange, lost, amorphous place. Nothing felt real, including Kat herself. It was as though someone had invented her . . . and got bored halfway through, so that she was still thinly sketched and almost transparent.

She thought about her little girl. Where was she? Was she all right? Was she even still alive?

And she thought about her husband. Where had he gone and why? The policeman, Vin, had been so cautious when he talked about Ian, as though he hadn't wanted to hurt her – as if she could be hurt more. The only thing that could stab her deeper in the heart was if bad news came about her baby.

Desi couldn't be dead. Kat couldn't countenance that. She'd die too. She'd be unable to go on.

FIFTY-NINE

'You can still redeem yourself, Ian,' Rico Steadmann said. 'You can still make this right.'

'I just want them back. I made a mistake. I thought—'

'You thought you could cheat me,' Steadmann said quietly. 'But you've seen how I deal with cheats and liars, Ian. You helped me get rid of the last cheat and liar.'

He watched the disgust and discomfort cross Ian Marsh's face. 'Don't lie to yourself, Ian. You enjoyed it. The feel of the knife going in. The smell of the blood.'

'You're wrong,' Ian Marsh said. 'I've seen enough blood. I don't – can't – take pleasure in it. You forced my hand, Rico. That's the only reason—'

'The only reason was greed, Ian. You're no better than the rest of us. You have enough and you want more and you fool yourself that you can deal with the consequences.'

The breeze from across the river was cold and damp. Across the field, Ian could see the lights of a nearby town, but all around was deathly quiet, twilight still.

He was aware that two more people walked across the field to join them. A woman and a man. A woman he knew; the man obviously just one of Steadmann's.

Mae.

'The account numbers, Ian?'

'I told you. I don't know them. I thought I could get what you wanted, but Nathan—'

'Kept you too much at arms' length. He knows. He knew all of Clay's secrets.'

Ian Marsh shook his head, sure of his ground on that at least. 'Not all,' he said.

Rico Steadmann sighed. Mae and the man stood close to them now. Mae looked scared, Ian thought, but also oddly resigned. She knew what was coming, just not precisely how it would arrive.

'There's a way of making recompense,' Rico said.

'How?'

'You shoot Mae for me.'

'What?'

He stared from Rico to the woman and back again. 'Oh, I know the two of you have a past,' Rico said. 'So, you trade the past for the present. Your lover for your wife and child.'

He looked back at Mae. Her eyes bulged and her mouth shaped in a tight little 'no'.

'I can't,' he said.

Steadmann handed him a gun. It was small and neat and sat easily in Ian's hand. It felt like a toy.

'A Colt .25,' Rico said. 'It's a vintage piece, Ian. From 1910. Over a century of efficient kills.'

Mae whimpered. She struggled against the two men who now gripped her arms.

'And I get my life back if I do this?'

Rico inclined his head.

Slowly, Ian raised the gun. He fired a shot and then another, his range so close it was impossible to miss. She was dead after the first shot. He was surprised at how little recoil there was; somehow that added to the feel of it being a toy gun.

Someone took it from his hand.

'I can go now,' he said. 'You told me.'

'And I lied,' Rico said. He took the gun from his associate's hand and shot Ian Marsh through the temple.

'Get rid of them,' Rico said. 'The river will do. I want them both to be found.'

Stake-outs were never much fun, Gregory thought. And they were desperately unprepared. He knew that Nathan was suddenly very aware of how isolated the two of them were. Gregory had been a lone wolf for most of his professional life, but the younger man had been a part of a major organization, backed by his guardian, supported by funds, weapons, resources. He'd had little time since Gustav Clay's death to adapt himself to the change in circumstances.

Right now, it was just the two of them with a couple of hand-guns and limited ammunition. And it was raining. Hard. A mixed blessing in that it kept people inside but also cut their visibility dramatically.

Earlier that evening he had received a text. The number was unknown but he'd opened it anyway. Patrick, helpfully, had signed his name at the end. And added a smiley face. Gregory didn't know whether to be amused or insulted. Did he look like a smiley-face kind of guy?

He'd called Patrick back and they'd talked, Patrick passing on what Naomi and Alec had told him.

'They got me some new sim cards,' he said. 'Naomi thought I should be careful.'

'Where are you now?'

'Amusement arcade on the promenade. It's bloody freezing. Dad reckoned it would be a good place. Public and noisy,' he laughed. 'This is the last week before it shuts for winter.'

'Glad I got my timing right,' Gregory said.

Naomi and Alec must be really concerned, he thought. To involve the boy like that. But then Gregory had involved him anyway, hadn't he? By going to see him. By making that contact. He was suddenly angry with himself. Harry was right; he was a storm-bringer.

Nathan was restless. He kept checking his watch. Gregory was relieved when a car finally turned the corner and pulled into the drive of the house they were watching. One man got out and went inside. A light came on. A bit of luck and he'd be alone.

Gregory got out and closed the door quietly. Nathan followed and they made their way to the house. It was in a suburban street; too many houses too close for Gregory's liking. They'd already checked the place out. It was heavily alarmed and Gregory hadn't ruled out the possibility of a panic button. Their man was part of Rico Steadmann's legal team, high up in his organization but with enough clout in the legitimate world that any attack on him would create outrage.

We, Gregory thought, are about to make a lot of noise.

They had decided to take a direct approach. Nathan went up to the front door and rang the bell. Gregory stood in the deep shadow off to the side, out of sight of the CCTV cameras that showed the residents who was at their door. Nathan's hood was up against the foul weather, a pizza carrier in his hands.

The front door opened. 'You order a pepperoni with extra onion?' Nathan asked. Not waiting for a reply, he pushed forward, urging the man inside. Gregory followed close behind.

SIXTY

'How badly is he hurt?' Annie's voice was tense.

'It's bad, Annie. He's lost a lot of blood. One bullet was a through and through; the other's still in there. He needs help, Annie.'

'Bring him here.'

Gregory calculated time and distance – and the risk that Steadmann's people would guess what he might do.

'No,' he said. 'I know a place. It belongs to a friend.' He gave Annie Molly Chambers' address. It wasn't as isolated as he'd have liked but was secluded enough and he knew he could get in easily. It was the best he could do.

He glanced back at Nathan. He lay on the back seat, barely breathing and deathly pale. Gregory swore. Stupid, he thought. They'd been so bloody stupid and now Nathan might well die.

Phelps had not been cooperating. Gregory hadn't expected an easy run but it was starting to occur to him that the man was simply playing for time. Nathan had been going through his office, checking paperwork and computer files. They both knew they'd have to make it fast, get what they could and run.

Phelps had been almost laughing at him. He'd screamed in pain as the third of his fingers were satisfied to Gregory's impatience. The crack satisfying, the scream very real. And he'd given a name. Just the one name.

And then all hell had broken loose.

Nathan had shouted. Gregory had run. He'd heard the shots and dashed to the office where Nathan lay on the floor. The shots had come through the window at the back of the house. Gregory lifted the younger man, hauling him on to his shoulder and then dashing back down the stairs.

They had made it to the front door, wrenched it wide. Gregory prayed the car was still there and no one had made the connection that it was theirs. He had left it unlocked.

As they came out of the house someone fired another shot and Gregory turned and fired back, using the moment when they dived for cover to exit through the gate. He reached the car, shoved Nathan on to the back seat and leaped into the front.

The shooter had broken cover now and fired towards their car. Gregory heard the bullet hit, but nothing shattered, nothing stopped; he floored the accelerator and sped away, praying that he could lose his pursuers in the side roads and then make it back on to the motorway.

Only after ten minutes of frantic driving did he risk a stop and examine Nathan.

He was barely conscious, his chest and back bloodied. It was hard to see how badly he was really hurt, but Gregory feared the worst.

And so he had called the one person he knew Nathan would trust. He just hoped he could reach her in time and that she'd know what to do when he did.

SIXTY-ONE

Mae Tourino's body was fished from the River Pen on the Monday morning. She'd been in the water for a couple of days and there had been no attempt to hide the fact that she'd been shot in the head.

'The body count is rising,' Vin observed. 'I suppose she should be grateful it was quick.'

Tess said nothing. She looked at the woman's face, bloated and bruised, flesh nibbled by something – she tried not to think of what. Skin already starting to slip. Another day or so and it would have begun to slough from the under layers; as it was, she was still recognizable – just – as the woman in red in Nathan's photograph.

'We're close to town,' said the local officer, acting as their liaison. 'A half-mile across that field and you're almost on the high street.'

Tess nodded. 'Maybe she'd come from there. No car or anything?'

'Nothing we've found as yet. You want to take a walk?'

She told Vin to stay put. They were still dragging the river and it was possible something useful would turn up. She walked with PC Dale across what he called the field and she'd have called waste ground. 'This is the wakes,' he told her. 'Where the fair used to be held. Still is, twice a year; the fun fair comes back and the council cleans up the land for them. Rest of the time, it's just the field.'

Tess scanned the area. Scrubby bushes separated it from the river; a couple of horses, tethered on long ropes, grazed the rough grass. 'What about the owners of the horses?'

'We talked to them. Didn't see a thing; wouldn't tell if they had. We keep an eye on the nags, make sure they've got water and they don't get stranded when the floods come. This is a flood plain,' he explained. 'That's all that's kept it from being snapped up by some developer.'

Tess glanced sideways at him, wondering if he was serious. Why the hell would anyone want to build here? Mosham was a little market town. It had, she figured, once been a slightly bigger market town, maybe even had aspirations, but what was there here?

He was right about the proximity of the high street to the field, though. Dale let her through a narrow alleyway and they were there, standing in a surprisingly lively street of shops and pubs and little cafes. It looked prosperous, Tess thought, surprised, and some of that surprise must have shown on her face. Dale's lips twitched in a swiftly hidden smile. 'We've survived the worst of the recession,' he told her. 'Most of the shops are still occupied and not by pound stores and charity shops either.'

'And how did you manage that, then?' She was genuinely curious.

Dale frowned, thinking. 'The way I figure it, this is a rural economy, but it's mostly still tenant farmers and the same land-owners who've owned the land since the year dot. It's still a mixed economy, a bit of arable, some cattle, some market gardens, cottages to let and so on. It's never been a rich economy and it's always been kind of locally based, you know, selling to local people, trading with other little towns. Me mam reckons we could go back to the Domesday Book and you'd find the same names doing the same things. It's stable.' He shrugged. 'Maybe we didn't have that far to fall. Whatever it is, I'm not going to complain. You got that picture?'

She nodded. 'Where do you suggest we start?'

He pointed up to his right. 'Top of the road and work down this side, back up the other?'

'Sounds like a plan. I don't suppose there's much in the way of CCTV?'

Dale laughed. 'The pub over there, The Lamb. He's got a camera. The George Hotel, just down that a way. I think they've got a couple. This is hardly crime central. I've already put the word out for everyone to make copies of anything they've got for the last week; we might get lucky.'

'Thanks,' she said. 'Let's hope.'

It was a slow process, going shop to shop, pub, café, asking if anyone had seen a woman who might well have changed her appearance several times since the photo had been taken. Dale was a great help, Tess thought. A familiar face that the locals seemed ready to respond to. He spent a few extra minutes at each place, chatting and introducing Tess, making it easy for her to ask her questions, but she still felt impatient, wanting to press on more quickly, even while she reminded herself that his method was getting her further than she'd have managed alone.

Then they struck lucky.

'I remember her,' the waitress said. 'She was drinking coffee with a man. At least, he drank coffee, she didn't touch hers. She didn't stop long.'

'Who paid?' Tess asked.

'Oh, he did.'

'In cash?'

'Yes. Left me a nice tip too.'

Tess showed her Nathan's picture. 'Was it this man?'

'No.' The waitress shook her head. 'I'd have remembered him. The man was older. Short grey hair, tallish, but . . . I don't know, ordinary?'

'Would you recognize him if you saw him again?'

'I might. I'm pretty good with faces.'

It might be worth getting a sketch artist, Tess thought. 'Did they leave together?'

'Uh, no. She left in a hurry, like she had to be somewhere.

He sat for a minute or two more, then asked for the bill, paid me and then he left.'

'Did you notice which way he went? And you've no CCTV here, I guess.'

'No, but he turned that way.' She pointed back the way they'd come. 'He passed The Lamb, so they might have caught him, I suppose.' She looked from one to the other, eyes bright with interest, obviously hoping to be enlightened.

'Thank you,' Tess said. 'You've been very helpful. You didn't see which way the woman went?'

'Oh, the other way, I think. I'm almost sure. I was serving someone, so . . . Is this to do with the body in the water? My boyfriend said his mate Ken said they'd found a body. The fishermen this morning?'

Tess thanked her again and Dale paused to exchange a few more words as Tess waited outside. 'You'll not keep a thing like this quiet,' he told her as he joined her on the pavement. 'It's the most excitement they've had since . . .'

He tried to think of something comparable and then gave up. Shrugged. 'To The Lamb, then,' he said. 'Hope we get another lucky break.'

They were walking back up the high street when Tess's phone rang. It was Vin.

'I think we've just found Professor Marsh,' he said.

SIXTY-TWO

Gregory was heading north again. He'd left Nathan with Annie and, unexpectedly, with Bob Taylor.

'If she needs anything, she can't leave him,' Bob said. 'If the neighbours want to know . . .'

'I'll think of something. Go, we'll cope.'

He had been forced to stop briefly at a motorway services. He took the opportunity to grab some coffee and food and check the newspapers and the Internet for news. He called Patrick and told him Nathan was hurt and where he'd left him.

'Can you let Alec know? He'll probably be mad as hell, but—'

'No, he won't. If Molly was home, she'd help out. Alec knows that.'

True, Gregory conceded. But Alec was still an ex-policeman. Gregory was asking him to hide a crime.

'You could do with some help,' Patrick said. 'Maybe you should talk to this Charles Duncan bloke.'

'I doubt he'd like our methods,' Gregory said.

'Gregory, no one is going to like your methods. But there's just you now. I'm guessing there's an awful lot more of them.'

Quite a lot more, Gregory thought. He knew the boy was right. 'Patrick, tell him I'm headed north. That we've got a lead on a place Desi might be. Rico's been investing heavily in property. Mostly old warehouses. I've got some intel, but that Charles Duncan bloke will have more resources he can throw at it. All I've managed to find out is that she's in one of them. Some are going to be demolished, but one or two are being renovated, turned into expensive flats. You need to tell Charles Duncan that we believe Rico's using them for storage. No, I don't know what. But it's the best we've got. Desi has to be in one of them. I'm off to try and narrow the search. Tell him that.'

'OK,' Patrick said. Gregory could hear him scribbling. 'Be careful. Please.'

The papers Gregory had scanned had been full of speculation. Where was the Marsh child? Where was her father? Then, a little later, the news came on the car radio that Ian Marsh's body had been found, along with that of an unknown woman . . .

'Well, at least we know where he got to,' Gregory said. 'Rico got the pair of them. I'm sorry.' He apologized to the absent Nathan. 'I know they were friends of yours.'

An hour later and the news reported a shooting at the house of international lawyer Gordon Phelps.

'I didn't shoot him,' Gregory commented, 'and I'm pretty sure Nathan didn't.' Rico's cleaning house, then. It was all happening too fast. We're not going to be in time, are we? Gregory thought.

What do you want me to do, Nathan?

He knew what the answer would be. Gregory nodded. 'We do what we said we'd do. We keep going. Keep looking. Hugh

Ryder, Phelps said. He's the one handling the deal. He's got to know where she is.'

And they'll guess that's where I'm headed, he thought. I've always been the man when there's long odds, but even I don't think much to these.

The bullet was in flight and Gregory knew he had been named.

Vin sat beside Kat's bed. Tess stood in the ante room with the doctor and the armed officer who'd been guarding her, but he had the job of telling her the news.

Logical, he supposed. She'd been talking to him. They'd formed a relationship, but even so he'd rather be anywhere else.

'Is it Desi?' she asked as he entered the room. His face must have given him away. Vin sat down and shook his head.

'We've no news of Desiree,' he said. 'It's Ian. I'm sorry, Kat, but Ian's dead.'

She stared at him, shaking her head, disbelieving. He thought she'd break down. He got ready to summon help. Instead she seemed to gather her resources. 'How?' she said.

'He was pulled from a river this morning.'

'He drowned?'

'No. He was shot. I'm so sorry, Kat.'

'Shot?'

He watched as she absorbed that. 'The people who took Desi. Did they shoot him? And please don't tell me you don't know.'

'It's likely,' he said. 'We're still trying to piece it all together. Kat, did you ever hear the name Mae Tourino?'

She frowned, began to shake her head. 'It sounds sort of familiar,' she said. 'But I can't place where from. She sounds like an actress. Maybe that's what I'm thinking of.'

An actress, Vin thought. Truer than she knew. 'I have to go,' he said. 'But I thought you should hear it from . . . from someone familiar.'

She smiled at him. A watery, despairing smile, but still a smile. 'Thank you,' she said. 'You've been kind.'

Patrick caught a bus to Naomi's flat, hoping she'd be back from the advice bureau. Alec wasn't home either and he wasn't

answering his phone, which meant he was probably at the hospital
having physio. The only times they didn't answer their phones
were when they'd gone to the hospital or Naomi was working
at the advice bureau.

Naomi, at least, should be back soon. He hoped. Patrick
perched impatiently on the cold, damp steps outside the house,
waiting for someone to return and wishing he'd insisted on them
giving him Charles Duncan's number. Naomi arrived half an hour
later, by which time he was wet and cold and feeling pretty
resentful. Alec was with her.

'Patrick? What's wrong? You're frozen. Come inside.'

By the time they'd got up the stairs, Patrick was practically
dancing with impatience. He told them about Gregory's phone
call and, to his relief, they took over. Naomi was on the phone
to Charles Duncan within minutes. Patrick got the impression that
someone had tried to pass her around or fob her off, but she'd
yelled down the phone and Duncan was miraculously produced.

Alec called Harry – much to Patrick's surprise – and the two
of them went off to Molly's place.

'Why call my dad?' Patrick asked when Naomi was off the
phone.

'Because Alec still can't drive very far,' Naomi said. 'His arm
can cope with the local stuff, but Molly's place is a good fifty
miles away. Anyway, can you imagine anyone more reliable than
Harry for the practical stuff?'

Patrick couldn't. 'So what do *we* do?'

'We sit tight and act as control,' she said. 'If Gregory calls,
we pass the message on. If Charles Duncan calls we do the same.'

Patrick felt oddly let down. 'He said Nathan was badly hurt,'
Patrick said.

'Well, Alec and Harry can both do first aid and I'd imagine
Annie Raven knows a hell of a lot more than that. Patrick, I'm
sure Gregory will be all right.'

Napoleon went over to him and put his muzzle on Patrick's
lap, waiting to be stroked.

'You really like him, don't you?'

'I suppose I do. I mean, I know what he is, Naomi. I'm not
stupid and I know what he's done. Well, I can guess some of it.
But yeah, I like him a lot.'

So do I, Naomi thought, though that really did go against the grain. Her old, official self screamed in protest. I used to think the world was black and white when I could still see it, Naomi thought. Now I can't see it any more, I know for sure it's all just many shades of grey.

SIXTY-THREE

J az was in her element. Charles Duncan had given her access to information she'd never have been able to get at in a million years via the police system and hooked her up with experts from his team. They'd set up a Skype link and were cross-referencing locations and land searches.

Rico Steadmann had a series of shell companies through which he bought and sold property, vintage cars, commodities – Jaz knew she would never have tracked them back to him. But that work had been done. Their intelligence said that they should concentrate on 'North'. That was such a typically southern attitude, Jaz thought. North was a pretty big description. They focused on those properties where Rico had known associates. But it still left a big chunk of data.

'Warehouses, old commercial properties,' Jaz said. 'There's something here very close to where Katherine Marsh was found. There's a group of three, due for redevelopment, close to Bernie Franks' pub.'

They matched information to location, to local knowledge. Teams were dispatched. It was impossible to cover everything. Jaz found herself called upon to make decisions. She knew what was at stake, and that the chances of getting it wrong were so high as to be unthinkable.

'Just do what you can,' Branch told her, when he saw her hesitation.

News of the Phelps shooting reached them. Blood at the scene indicated that someone had been injured and had fled.

'Phelps was in no position to do the shooting,' Charles Duncan said.

'You think it was Nathan Crow, or his friend?'

'That finished the job? No. I think when they left him, Phelps was probably still alive, and probably wishing he wasn't. The best guess is that his boss didn't want loose ends.'

'Which suggests that we're on to something,' Branch said.

Katherine Marsh had been allowed out of bed. Her feet, badly cut and bruised and still healing, hurt even in the soft slippers one of the nurses had brought in for her. She had walked to the window and stood looking out. The view on to the car park was uninspiring, but pleasingly ordinary. She watched as visitors came and went, taxis dropped off, ambulances passed by on their way to somewhere. She wondered about her husband. Ian was dead. Why was he dead? Had he been shot trying to find Desiree?

Or had something else been happening, something she didn't know about? Kat had trusted her husband, but she'd known he had a strange and mysterious past. That there were many things about him she didn't know – and didn't choose to know. Had that been her fault? Should she have asked more questions?

Her feet hurt and she was sure her left one had started to bleed again. She welcomed the pain. It was real and external and could be fixed with bandages and painkillers or by taking the weight off and sitting down.

Inside, she felt as though something had ripped her apart. She was empty and hollowed out and the space that was left had been filled with something that was both leaden and amorphous. It spread through her, weighing her down, pressing her organs and her thoughts and her emotions into some tiny, intense, painful space.

Where was her child? Was she scared? Was she alive? Did anyone know that she didn't like carrots but would eat her weight in chocolate and cheese if they let her? That she liked her apple sliced and not puréed. That she liked to be sung to and cuddled and . . .

It was as if Kat's body could no longer hold her upright. She crumpled in on herself, the sudden pain in her abdomen, in her chest, in her head more than she could bear. She bent over, knees collapsing, folded in half and then in half again by the suddenness of the pain.

Hands lifted her; someone helped her back into her bed.

'Make it go away,' Kat begged, but she knew that nothing could.

SIXTY-FOUR

Fourteen hours since Nathan had been shot. It was now mid afternoon. Gregory spoke to Annie. He was improving, she said, and Alec and Harry had arrived.

'They've been great,' she said. 'Alec told the neighbour he and Harry were doing some decorating before Molly got back. They even borrowed another pair of steps.'

Gregory laughed. It was a relief to be able to laugh over something.

'Tell Alec we didn't shoot Phelps,' he said.

'Gregory, you don't have to do this. Come here, let someone else take over.'

It was tempting, he thought. Far too tempting. 'I can't,' he said. 'You know I can't. Not yet.'

'Take care, then. They'll be waiting for you.'

Pale sun had broken through the thick cloud and the rain had finally stopped. Gregory moved slowly up the fire escape at the back of the building. He'd noticed a window, just slightly ajar on the third floor. Two below the one he wanted. The fire escape was hidden from street view by the angle of the building. The office block, sixties ugly, wedged into a space between much older red bricks housed a couple of law firms, an estate agency on the ground floor and an employment bureau specializing, so the sign said, in Industrial and Warehouse. Gregory just hoped that whoever had their window cracked open would not be in the office when he arrived.

He paused on the fire escape and peered cautiously through. The office was empty, the door open, and he could see two young women chatting in the room beyond. As he watched, one left and he glimpsed the corridor. Slowly, Gregory opened the window and climbed through. He could hear a voice in the office. The woman he had seen was speaking on the phone. Gregory moved towards the door and waited.

'Just a moment and I'll find that for you,' she said. Gregory hoped that whatever 'it' was didn't bring her into the back office. He shifted position so he could see her through the half-open door. The woman, humming to herself now, was searching through a filing cabinet. Gregory took a chance; he moved through into the outer office and hurried for the door.

'Can I help you?'

She had turned as he reached the door. He stood now, door slightly open, his hand on the knob.

'I think I'm on the wrong floor,' he said. 'The employment agency?'

She smiled. 'Oh, you've come up one too far. People do it all the time.'

Gregory thanked her and left. He listened for a moment, heard her resume the phone call. It all seemed kosher, he thought, but alarm bells were ringing. What if she worked for Rico? What if . . .?

Gregory consciously pushed his fears aside. Annie had been right. He should have given it his best and backed away. But he hadn't and it was too late now.

He ran up the next two flights of stairs, opened the door to Hugh Ryder's office. A secretary looked up, smiling. Then her smile faded as she saw the weapon in Gregory's hand. He gestured for her to go through to the inner office. Her face was white; for a moment he thought she might faint. She opened the door and he held the gun to her back as they went through.

'He's not here,' she whispered. 'He went out an hour ago.'

'Went where?'

'I don't know. Really, I don't know.'

He sat her down in the office chair, took long cable ties from his pocket and fastened her hands behind her back, arms wrapped around the back of the chair. He used another to lock her wrists to the chair. Then went for her feet. 'Kick me and I'll break your knees.'

She didn't kick.

'His appointments for this afternoon.'

'In the book.' She was belligerent now. Still scared, but also mad as hell.

Gregory flicked through the diary on the desk, aware that he didn't really know what he was looking for. That the man might already have gone. That Desi might already have been handed over.

'The kid,' he said. 'Where is she?'

'How the hell should I know? I don't know anything about a kid.'

He heard a sound in the front office and turned, just enough to keep the door in view. Other paperwork lay scattered across the desk. He eyed it thoughtfully. Listening. The woman was listening too, he realized. She knew.

In the diary was a notation that clearly wasn't a time. Three fifty-two. No one made an appointment for three fifty-two.

On the desk lay a rental contract. A set of car keys. A couple of other legal documents that to Gregory's eyes could have been anything. They reminded him of the guff he had signed when he'd bought his house – his one, benighted attempt at being a regular citizen. Then he spotted something.

Three fifty-two. The number was the same as on the building contract sitting on the desk. Two things occurred to Gregory at that moment. The first was that this had been deliberately left for him to see. That it was just another one of Rico Steadmann's games. The second thought was that this is where he was keeping Kat's child. He was certain of it. The bill of sale wasn't for the warehouse, it was for the little girl. Rico wanted him to see that and to understand and to know there wasn't a thing he could do.

He was aware of the secretary, looking at him. She was laughing.

He was ready when the door crashed back. He came out shooting, hitting one man in the arm and another in the stomach. The second man fell, screaming. The first came on. Gregory shot him again. He fell and this time stayed down. But there were footsteps, running on the stairs. Shouts. Automatic gunfire that ripped through the stud walls. Gregory felt the bullet hit. The sudden fire in his shoulder. He hit the ground and began to crawl.

SIXTY-FIVE

Gregory knew he had no chance of making it out through the offices; his only option was the fire escape. The likelihood was they'd have that covered too, but what choice did he have?

He'd walked, eyes wide open, into a trap. Now he'd just have to do the best he could.

He felt in his pocket for the second clip. His left arm hung useless at his side, blood dripping from his fingers and on to the floor. He was close to the window now, and above his head the automatic fire ripped the walls apart. He figured he had until it stopped, then they'd be through the door and his chance would be gone.

Desperate, he hauled himself to his feet and staggered to the window, wrestling with the catch. A bullet hit the wall, fractions of an inch from his head. Plaster and glass shrapnel clawed down his face. He opened the window and fell through. Glancing back he saw the secretary slumped in the chair, her face half ripped away by the automatic fire. Then he looked down. Below him the fire escape turned back on itself, blocking his view of anyone coming up from the ground. He knew they'd be there. Of course they'd be there. Fighting nausea and shock, struggling to keep on his feet, Gregory began the descent.

'Sir, we've got reports coming in of fires at several of the addresses we have. Steadmann's properties. And one report of an explosion.'

Branch turned to the officer. 'Show me,' he said.

She brought up the computer screen and pointed to the feeds she was tracking.

'Jaz?'

She nodded confirmation. 'Two fire officers injured. Three major fires, near as damn it simultaneous.'

As they continued to monitor, another was reported, sixty miles away.

'He's cutting his losses,' Branch said. 'Getting rid of whatever he was storing there before we close in.'

'Reports of a body at one of the buildings. Near the entrance.' Jaz told him. 'Sir, this does not look good.'

How many shots did he have left? Probably four in this clip, Gregory calculated. True, he'd got the second clip, but with his damaged arm, reloading would be a trial. He'd be slow. It wasn't something he could contemplate without at least minimal cover and there was nothing on the fire escape.

He'd moved as fast as he could, knowing it was only a matter of time before they came after him from above. He fired a warning shot back towards the window. It ricocheted off the metal steps and hit the wall. He stumbled on. Below him were sounds of feet, thundering upward. Gregory knew he was trapped. He looked for another way. He was approaching that window now, the one through which he'd entered the building. Praying that it was still open, Gregory quickened his pace. He reached it just as another burst of gunfire clattered down.

Bit of luck, Gregory thought, those coming down would shoot those coming up and save him some bother. Someone must have recognized the dilemma; he heard shouting, swearing from those below.

Gregory pushed through the window and practically fell inside.

Through the back office and back out into the reception where he'd spoken to the woman. She was still there. She froze when she saw him with the gun and then began to scream. 'Shut the fuck up and get the hell out,' Gregory snapped at her. She fled and Gregory followed her through the door.

He'd gained himself moments, he thought, before they realized what he had done. Leaving the office, he made it to the stairs. He could hear the woman, still screaming, and other voices now, raised in terror. If they had any sense, Gregory thought, they'd shut up and get out of the way. Someone surely would have called the police by now. He'd almost welcome the chance to get himself arrested. His shoulder was bleeding profusely. He knew he was losing too much blood. His vision was becoming blurred and his ears filled with fog. He made it to the front door and crashed out into the empty street. In the distance he could hear sirens. Behind him gunfire and shouts. He turned away from the sounds and looked for a place to regroup, stumbled into a narrow alleyway between two more buildings and then into a yard. A gate stood open, leading on to a cycle path. The path was narrow and Gregory thought he'd made the wrong call. That he'd trapped himself again. Then he saw another opening, leading off the path and into another yard. More offices, he thought. And industrial bins.

Gratefully, he collapsed behind them. His clip was nearly empty now and with great difficulty he managed to change it for the new one. Then he took out his phone.

Who could he call? Annie was too far away. And everyone else . . . There was no one else. Gregory felt suddenly, shockingly alone.

So he called Patrick, knowing he probably wasn't going to make any sense but wanting to pass on what he knew. Someone else could do the rest, couldn't they?

'I'm hurt,' he said. 'Patrick, tell that Duncan bloke, tell him I know where she is, but they've got something planned. I don't know what.'

'Gregory, listen to me. Where the hell are you?' Naomi had seized the phone and was yelling at him. He took a deep, steadying breath and looked around, trying to describe where he was. He could hear the police sirens a couple of streets away. He heard her conferring with Patrick.

'OK, I know where that is. We're coming to get you. You just sit tight. Understand?'

She was gone before he could argue. Gregory leaned back against the fence, listening to the strange silence. The sirens had ceased to wail; the gunfire had stopped; no one shouted. He could just hear the clatter from the kitchen. He was behind a restaurant, he realized. Offices and a restaurant shared a yard. Had he told Naomi that? He thought he must have done. He closed his eyes, desperate for sleep, then forced them open again, knowing that if he slept he might not wake up again. Instead, he breathed slowly, steadily, using his pain to keep himself conscious, gathering what was left of his strength. The bullet was still in flight, Gregory thought. It had not yet found its mark.

*   *   *

'You're sure you can do this?'

'I can do it. You talk to that Home Office man and I'll drive. I think I know the way. I had my lessons near there.'

Patrick took a deep breath, tried not to think that he wasn't even insured yet, never mind insured for driving Alec's car. What mattered was that Gregory was hurt and that he'd reached out to them.

He guessed it would take about ten minutes to get there; it was not far from the university and in an area of town that was largely occupied by students, rundown offices and cheap places to eat. It was the first time he'd had to plan a route on his own and he knew he was lousy at anything like that. He got things back to front and all mixed up. Panic set in.

'I don't know which way to go. I thought I did, but . . .'

'It's all right, Patrick, just tell me where we are now,' Naomi said. 'And just hope they've not made anything one-way since the last time I drove a car.'

He glanced anxiously at her, something close to laughter threatening to break to the surface. He managed to tell her what road they were on and where.

'You need to take the next left,' she said. 'And then right almost immediately. Don't worry, Patrick, between us we can do it.'

He did laugh then, unable to help himself. Then, as though someone had drenched him in cold water, the laughter faded and the panic returned. 'I can do this,' he told himself, then realized he had spoken out loud.

'You can do it,' Naomi confirmed.

Gregory heard the car pull into the yard. He peered out from behind the bins and saw Alec's car hove into view. For one surreal moment, he only saw Naomi. Then he spotted Patrick. The boy left the engine running and hurried over.

'Can you stand?'

'Yes.' Relief flooded him. 'I know where she is,' he said.

'Fat lot of good that's going to do you.'

Gregory whirled around, pushing Patrick aside. The man stood in the gateway leading back on to the cycle path. His weapon pointed directly at Gregory's head.

'He'll blow the lot before you or anyone else has the chance to get to her. The kid's dead. Rico doesn't like loose ends.

He'd stepped closer, smiling, assured. Gregory guessed how he must look. He didn't blame the man for feeling cocky. If he looked the way he felt, he must look like shit. He summoned himself for one last stupid act and threw himself towards the man with the gun. He was dimly aware that beside him Patrick moved too, following his lead. Gregory smashed into the man, knocking him off balance and then bringing him down. Patrick had aimed for the gunman's arm, knocking it aside. They all hit the ground together, Gregory falling into a burst of pain that almost finished him. The world was red and then black. He fought to stay conscious. He heard the explosion of a gun fired at close quarters. He struggled to stand, to open his eyes, saw the gunman on the ground, a hole in his chest, his pistol on the ground. He must have fired, Gregory realized, as he launched himself on to the man. He had no recollection of there being any conscious thought.

Patrick stared at him, then grabbed Gregory's sleeve and started to pull him towards the car. Somehow Gregory found himself on the back seat, Naomi shouting at him again. 'Are you all right? What the hell just happened?'

Patrick shoved the car into reverse, shot back and then forward again.

'Tell me where to go!' He was shouting too. Maybe it was catching, Gregory thought. He was bleeding really heavily now; it was seeping into the seat covers and dripping on to the floor mats. He could hear it, hitting the rubber, unnaturally loud.

'Tell me where to go!'

He heard the words properly this time. Struggled to recall the address.

'That's close to the university,' Naomi said. 'Patrick, it's left at the lights, OK. Gregory, are you sure?'

'Sure as I can be.'

He heard her on the phone again. Alternating a sharp conversation with commands to Patrick.

'They won't get there in time,' he said. He wasn't sure how he knew; maybe the gunman's words, maybe his obvious confidence, but he just knew they were nearly out of time.

'How bad are you hurt?' Naomi asked him.

'I'll survive. You did well back there.'

Patrick laughed nervously. 'My dad's going to kill me,' he said.

Gregory studied the boy. His hands were trembling from the adrenalin rush, but his face was calm, his eyes focused and intent as he scanned ahead.

'I look too young to be driving something as expensive as this,' he said.

'So you drive carefully, but not too carefully. Keep up with the flow of traffic and don't make eye contact with anyone,' Gregory told him.

Patrick nodded. 'OK,' he said. He slowed for the lights, then turned, following Naomi's instructions.

Gregory closed his eyes and leaned back in his seat. They'd be too late. He knew they'd be too late. All this effort, all this risk, but he was sure they wouldn't be in time.

SIXTY-SIX

'You know where that is?' Branch asked Tess as Naomi's message was relayed to his team.

She nodded. 'Get going, then. I'll get you some back-up.'

She nodded again and then ran from the briefing room, Vin at her heels. They'd only got back an hour before, arrived to news of fires and explosions and dead lawyers and a shooting at an office block. Someone had declared war, she thought, but no one knew where the front lines were.

Beside her she heard Vin murmuring something that sounded suspiciously like a prayer. At that moment, she'd have joined in, if she could remember any, but the only thing she could recall was something from Sunday school when she'd been about five years old.

'Gentle Jesus, meek and mild' probably wouldn't cut it just now.

Please God, Tess thought, just let this turn out right. Too many people have died. Don't add Kat's little girl to the list.

* * *

Patrick brought the car to a halt. 'There's a fire,' he said.

Gregory cursed.

'Then we wait for help,' Naomi instructed. 'There's nothing we can do.'

They all got out of the car, Gregory leaning against the door, not trusting his legs to support his weight. They had pulled on to a strip of waste ground beside an old factory by the canal. The building next door had been demolished and this one was heavily boarded, ready for the same. Flames and smoke billowed from the roof.

'What if she's in there?'

'Patrick, there's nothing we can do.'

The boy moved away from the car. He was scanning the building, his hands clasping and unclasping, horrified that he might have to stand and wait, knowing that the child might be inside, that the flames might get to her, that she might burn.

'Patrick! No!'

Gregory had seen the intent in the boy's eyes, but still not quite believed it and then when he'd reached out, he'd been too slow to stop him as Patrick took off. He stumbled forward a step or two, but the ground came up to meet him, red and black and painful.

He could hear Naomi yelling at him, demanding to know what was going on. Knowing but not wanting to know. Painfully, Gregory made it on to his knees.

'He's gone in,' he said. 'Naomi, I can't follow him. I can't even bloody stand.'

Patrick dragged the door open and ran up the stairs. He could hear the flames roaring, but they'd not yet reached this part of the building. The smoke had, though, drifting towards him down the stairs.

What the hell was he doing? This was just mad. His dad really would kill him – if the fire didn't get to him first.

And then he heard her. A small sound at first, until he rounded the next flight of stairs. A child, crying, scared and angry in equal measure.

Patrick ran, climbing higher, taking the steps two at a time. The sound of flames was louder now, the smoke thicker. He could hear her, on the other side of a closed door. Not even stopping to think that anyone but Desiree might be inside, Patrick hurled himself at the door. Half rotten, it gave against his weight. She was there, sitting alone in the middle of the floor. Desiree saw him, wailed louder and lifted her arms.

Naomi was shouting at the phone, her words only partly intelligible, control all but gone. Gregory thought about taking it from her, but he didn't seem to have the strength. From what he could gather, help was on its way.

He struggled back on to his feet, resting against the car for support. Small explosions from inside the factory pushed blasts of heat and flame through the roof. As Gregory watched, two of the windows blasted outward, glass showering down into the canal.

'Get out of there, Patrick, please get out. Now!'

Gregory could see nothing beyond the smoke that billowed outward from the building. His ears rang, some sounds obliterated by the effects of the blast, others seeming oddly amplified, though he couldn't tell if he really heard the sounds or if his eyes supplied the cues and his brain filled in the gaps. The groaning of falling timbers filled the air, the shattering of glass as it fell from the upper windows. Christ Almighty, Gregory thought.

He stumbled forward. Patrick was in there. He had to try and get him out. A louder, larger blast knocked him from his feet, knocking the air from his lungs as effectively as a left hook to the stomach and his feet didn't seem to belong to him any more. He'd forgotten how to walk, never mind how to stand upright.

Patrick, Gregory thought. Desi. Oh God, this would kill Harry.

Behind him he could hear Naomi cry out in her own agony of fear and then, belatedly, sirens as help finally arrived.

Slowly the dust and smoke had begun to clear, the sound of crashing glass now more real – definitely sound and not memory. Gregory peered through the fog, a movement catching his attention and then a sound. The unmistakable crying of a young child. The cry was angry and scared and utterly indignant and Gregory felt his heart leap. His logic and the rest of his senses told him what he was hearing was impossible, but it was there; he could hear the child crying. It was real.

He stumbled forward again, his feet still ready to fail him, legs as weak and unsteady as if he'd been recovering from a fever. And then he saw them. The boy standing in the dust, blood pouring from a cut above his eye, but standing. And he held the little girl tightly in his arms. Both were soaking wet, shivering, water pouring from their bodies and on to the ground.

'She's cold,' Patrick said. 'We had to dive into the water. I was scared she'd drown.'

The baby had begun to wail, clinging to Patrick as though searching for any residual warmth. Gregory could see how hard the pair of them were shivering. I thought you were dead, he thought. I thought I'd killed you both.

'You're crying,' Patrick observed.

'Fuck,' Gregory said softly. He wiped his eyes, but the tears kept falling. 'Fuck.'

EPILOGUE

It seemed as though everyone had been holding their breath. Finally Bob looked up from the portfolio he had been inspecting and gestured to Patrick to sit down. The young man did so, trying not to show the desperation he felt; trying not to jinx things.

'I can't offer you much in the way of pay,' Bob said. 'But I do need an assistant. You could work here on the days you're not at uni and . . . I'd do all I could to help you develop . . .'

'Yes,' Patrick said. 'Please. That's what I want to do.'

Annie gently drew Harry aside, leaving the artists to talk.

'He will get over this,' she said. 'And he can drive over every day, stay when he wants to. We'll take good care of him.'

'No,' Harry said. 'He won't get over it.' He seemed to be ignoring the rest of her statement and so Annie waited, understanding that he had something important that he needed to say.

'He won't get over it. What's happened will just become a part of him. We don't deny our pain or our fears or our memories; they shapes us, but if we're wise enough we just learn to use them. Not let them use us. You understand me?'

He looked directly at Annie and she nodded. 'You know I do,' she said.

'Have you heard from Gregory?'

'He's away on his boat. Nathan is with him. I think they've both got a lot of thinking to do. Gregory's found some land up in Scotland. He's talking some nonsense about keeping sheep.'

Harry had to laugh. 'I want to see that,' he said.

He looked over at his son. Bob and Patrick were both talking, hands animated, a slight flush on his son's face. 'It's all going to be all right,' Harry said.

His son had survived; the future was still possible. The child had been rescued and although he could only imagine what the mother must still be going through, she'd be all right too. She had a second chance.

'They'll talk forever,' Annie said. 'How about you and I take the dogs for a walk? The woods are glorious this time of year.'

Harry nodded and the two of them slowly crossed the lawn, dogs scampering at Annie's side.